Truth in the Name

A Christian Thriller

F. D. Adkins

To my husband, Steve,
who has shown me that with God's strength and hard work,
one person can accomplish anything.
You are the love of my life and my best friend.
Thank you for encouraging me to chase my dreams.

To my amazing children, Landon and Layna,
who never stopped believing in your mom.
I love you both with all my heart.

Truth in the Name

Prologue

Dark shadows conceal every thought as exhaustion consumes me. Like a loose light bulb flickering from short surges of electricity, every beat of my heart sends pulses of pain shooting through my head. Why are some things so hard to remember? I sit hunched over my computer, massaging my temples as my phone rings. I have an exam in Anatomy and Physiology in the morning, and for some reason, I can't find a way to memorize all these bones. *Temporal bone, Ethmoid bone, Lacrimal bone, Zygomatic bone...*I try to focus and ignore the ringing...again. This makes the fifth time in the last ten minutes. The ringing stops, and I try to break the skeleton into sections and make up a funny song in my head that will help trigger my memory. I almost have a start, but then there goes that blasted phone again.

"Alright! Alright!" I spout through gritted teeth as I make my way across to my bag and pull out my phone. "It's Mom. I should have known when it wouldn't stop ringing," I mumble. My mother is always so persistent.

"Hel..." I start to say. Mom's terrified screams echo so loudly that the phone jumps from my hand, and I almost drop it. "MOM! What's wrong?"

Through my mother's sobbing wails I manage to catch, "Your sister... Gone."

I look at the clock. *Oh no. I was supposed to meet Eileen for lunch.*

"Mom, I can't understand you. I forgot I was supposed to meet Eileen for lunch. She's probably upset with me."

Mom's desperate words finally pour out. "Ellie Hatcher, you aren't listening. Eileen never came home from school today. We have tried and tried to reach her, but she won't answer. I called the police. Finally, after badgering them because I knew something wasn't right, they tracked her phone. You know mothers always know when something's wrong. They found her phone in her car abandoned on the side of the road."

I take a deep breath. Eileen has to be okay. My sister has always been a little dramatic, and now that she is sixteen, she is a lot dramatic. "Mom, you know how Eileen can be. She probably just pulled over and got in the car with a friend."

Mom's sobs turn into gasps for air. She is so hysterical that she is almost hyperventilating. "WHY...huuuuuuh...doesn't... huuuuuh...anyone...huuuuh...get it?...huuuuh... She ...huuuh...wouldn't...leave...huuuuh...the car...huuuh...door...huuuuuh open...huuuuh...   huuuuh...leave...huuh...her keys...huuuh...her   phone...huuuuh...her   purse... huuuh...behind!"

For a moment it feels as if I am hovering outside my own body. My heart drops, and I fall to the floor with it. I know my mom is right. This sounds very wrong. My little sister has to be alright. She just has to.

How could I have forgotten about lunch today? Now I may never see her again. God, please help her. Please...help my sister!

Chapter One

Two Years Later...

I run...hard. All the stress releasing from my body as my feet pound on the trail. At five a.m., the running trail that surrounds my apartment complex is deserted except for a few security guards on patrol. As I jog back up the steps to my studio apartment, the sweat drips from my forehead, and my heart thumps. My body is fatigued, but my mind is renewed. For these thirty minutes a day, the weight that crushes my body and soul into the ground lifts and I feel free.

I always do my best thinking during my run. I thought of a good solid thesis for my English paper. As soon as I finish with the rest of my morning routine, I might even have a chance to get started before I log on for class.

I swipe wisps of hair from my eyes and unlock the deadbolt. First thing in the door, after removing my shoes, of course, because I would never track germs onto the floor of my home, I get on my knees in the living room to read my Bible and pray. God empowers me to get up every day and tackle all the obstacles to come, so I refuse to miss giving thanks for the gift of the day. Today could be a hill, or it could be a valley. Either way, I know I need God's guidance to get through it.

I shower, make the bed, and pretty much clean my whole apartment. As I make my way to the kitchen, I do a quick check to be sure the living room tables are perfectly aligned with the lines on the hardwood floors. I power on my laptop, pour coffee in the largest cup I have, and settle at the bar in the kitchen to start my paper. I tap the space bar seven times and start typing.

Just as I type the last word of my first paragraph, the phone chimes. Like clockwork, every morning at seven o'clock, my mother texts. Then again at noon. And again, at three o'clock in the afternoon. And again, precisely at nine o'clock because I go to bed promptly at nine-thirty. Mom always sends the exact same text:

Please text back that you are okay and always know Mom loves you.

I quickly message back.

All good. I will always know. Love u 2.

As I lay the phone on the counter, I fight the tears that are pooling in my eyes. If only I could turn back the clock, maybe things would be different. I stare at the photo on the mantel. The girl in the picture has the same dark brown hair and green eyes as me. Even though I am older, she is taller. I got Mom's genes when it came to height. *How could I have forgotten to meet you for lunch that day? If...If...If...* Those words keep repeating in my mind, tormenting me. *If I had seen you that day, maybe you would have said something that would have helped us to find you.*

"BZZZZZZZZZ!"

My body jerks at the sound. *What? Oh.* It is only the intercom buzzer. *Who could possibly be here at eight o'clock in the morning?* I walk to the door and push the button. "Yes, can I help you?"

A black sedan with dark tinted windows shows on the video feed. It is a Crown Victoria, I think. The driver with dark glasses speaks into the intercom, and a deep voice reverberates, "I am looking for Ellie Hatcher."

"May I ask why you need to see Ellie?" A sense of alarm tingles up my spine, and my heart starts to race.

"My name is Frank Fentress. I work for the U.S. Government, Special Operations Division. I have a letter for Miss Hatcher from the president's office." His monotone words echo through the speaker as he places his thumb on the identification keypad.

The monitor feed displays his identification information on the screen.

Frank Fentress
United States Government
Office of the President of the United States
Special Operations Division

When President Denali took office in 2045, he implemented this new program to fix the identity theft issue. People no longer carry a driver's license or an ID, and plastic credit cards are nonexistent. There is a nationwide computer network, and everyone's fingerprints are stored in the database which serves two purposes. Before, criminals could only be identified if their fingerprints were in the system. Now, if you are a U.S. citizen fifteen years of age or older, your fingerprints must be entered in the system which makes matching the perpetrator with fingerprints found at a crime scene much easier. On top of that, your thumbprint is attached to your identity. You simply place your thumb on a small pad. If you are making a purchase, you can access which of your accounts you want to pay with, whether it be from your bank account or credit card. It has practically eliminated identity theft because your thumbprint is essential for any transaction. Because of this program, President Dennis Denali won the 2048 election by a landslide.

I stare at the screen like a zombie. *Is this for real? People don't just get special deliveries from the President of the United States.*

His voice shakes me from my trance. "Miss? Could you please direct me to Ellie Hatcher?"

"Yes, sorry." My words barely come out as a whisper as my mind processes the situation. "I am Ellie Hatcher."

"Miss Hatcher, this letter is urgent. I need to speak with you immediately."

I press the button opening the gate. "Okay, Mr. Fentress, I will meet you downstairs in the lobby."

I QUICKLY CHECK myself in the mirror to make sure I am somewhat presentable and hurry down to the lobby. The anticipation is eating me alive. What could this letter possibly be about? As I step into the lobby, a tall middle-aged man in a black suit with a black and gray paisley tie is leaning against the wall by a rack of brochures. Strangely, he is still wearing those dark sunglasses inside.

There is no one else in the lobby, but Mr. Fentress seems to be scanning his surroundings as if someone could be spying on him. "Miss Ellie Hatcher," he says in a hushed voice, "this letter is from President Denali. If you could just place your thumb on the pad to accept delivery."

"Of course." Trembling, I place my thumb on the pad, and my identification information pops up on his phone.

"Excellent." He pulls an envelope from his case as his eyes scan the room again. "Miss Hatcher, it is imperative that no one knows of this letter or the information it contains. Read the letter immediately, and you will understand. I will return tomorrow at the same time. Please be ready." He hands me the white envelope. There is no address. It just has my name typed in the center and a gold presidential seal where the return address would go. "Oh, and, Miss Hatcher," he whispers as he starts to walk away, "please read it immediately. The ink will disappear in about fifteen minutes."

With my heart beating so fast that my chest hurts, I turn and run all the way back to my apartment.

I RUSH IN and slam the door behind me. *How can the ink disappear in fifteen minutes?* My thoughts are running rampant as my shaking hands try to rip open the envelope. As my finger rips through the flap, the whole thing flings onto the floor. Grabbing it up, I pull the paper from the envelope. The letter crinkles in my fumbling hands as I struggle to quickly unfold it. My eyes fix on the words as I read:

Miss Ellie Hatcher:

As President of the United States, I am organizing a special crime division that will answer directly to me. This is a highly classified group that will need very specialized training. As crimes associated with identity theft have fallen, I must address the violent crimes in our nation. I have personally reviewed your background and credentials. Your work ethic in the criminal justice program at the University is astounding. Ellie Hatcher, I have chosen you to be a part of this group. Mr. Fentress will arrive at 0800 hours to pick you up tomorrow morning. You will take nothing with you. The training facility will provide you with everything you need. It is imperative that you understand the secrecy of this group. You must tell no one of this letter or of your departure. You should consider this a high honor as you are being called to serve your country. However, if you speak of this letter or tell anyone of your departure, this group will lose its anonymity, and your actions would be considered a federal offense. Thank you in advance for your service to your country. Be ready at 0800 hours for your transfer to the training facility. Congratulations.

Sincerely,
Dennis Denali
President of the United States of America

As I read the letter for the third time, the words start to fade. I place the letter on the kitchen counter and hurry to grab my phone to take a picture. There has to be something I am missing. I snap the picture, but the screen is blank. I look at the letter, and then back at the screen on my phone. How can the letter not show up in the picture? I stand there gripping the counter so hard my knuckles turn white.

I gawk at the page that now has gray wisps of smoke rising from it. Little spider webbing lines cover the paper like it is cracking into small pieces, and then the letter starts to disappear. With a faint fizzing and popping noise, the cracks in the paper get bigger and bigger until the letter is gone, completely gone. My thoughts are a jumbled-up mess. *What is happening? I am losing my mind! I just watched a piece of paper disintegrate into nothing.* I wipe my hand across the counter. There is no trace of the letter or the envelope. There isn't even a speck of dust. *Am I delusional? Has this whole thing been a hallucination?*

I try to replay everything in my mind. I run to the security monitor and tap on the history icon. I really opened the gate twenty minutes ago. That much was real. I am still wearing my shoes so I must have really gone to the lobby. *Oh no! Why am I wearing my shoes in the house? Now I have tracked germs and dirt all over the floor!*

Exasperated with myself, I kick off my shoes. I grab the mop and start scrubbing. The rest of this mess is beyond my control, but at least I can still manage to have a clean floor.

With the last swipe of the mop, I fall onto the couch and bury my face in my hands. I know this should be an honor, but how can I just up and leave without telling my family? My mother will be crushed if she can't reach me. She will think she has lost another child. How could I do that to her? But according to Mr. Fentress and this letter, I don't have a choice.

"Of course," I whisper to myself, "if this is not a choice, I have to stay positive. This is an honor. The president chose me. Of all people, he chose ME!"

Forgetting about my class, because what is the point in that right now, I grab my phone off the counter and slip on my shoes sitting on the rug by the coat closet. I have to go see my parents. Maybe a visit today will buy enough time until I get to the training facility. As I rush out the door, I pause, twist the doorknob seven times telling myself it is locked, and then let the adrenaline rush carry me to my car.

Chapter Two

As I walk in the back door of my parents' house, I try to push the mixture of anxiety and worry of causing them any more pain down deep inside. They have to think it is just an ordinary day. I keep reminding myself that I really should be overjoyed. I will be working directly for the president.

Looking so tired with her pale skin and creases on her forehead, Mom stands by the sink with a towel drying a stack of dishes. I don't know how she does it. My mom cooks for my dad, keeps the house spotless, and works nights as a nurse in the ER to pay the bills while my dad literally just exists. It is obvious that my mom is barely hanging on to her sanity, but she is doing what she has to do. Maybe her busy schedule helps to distract her from the gaping hole in her heart. My mom doesn't slow down long enough to fall apart.

Mom looks up from the dishes she is drying, and her eyes sparkle with excitement. "Ellie, what are you doing here? I thought you would be at home in front of that computer doing your studies."

I swallow hard and try not to let my voice crack. "Oh, I just needed a break. I thought I might drop by for a few minutes and maybe have a sandwich or something with you guys."

Mom's lips erupt into the biggest smile, and joy leaps from her mouth as she says, "You are in luck. I made chicken and dumplings this morning, and I have a lemon pound cake in the oven now. Your daddy is in the living room. Go say hi, and I will set the table." Mom opens the cabinet to get the plates as I walk into the other room.

Daddy is sitting in his reclining rocking chair staring at the television. I am not sure why because it isn't on. I ease over and put my arm around his shoulders. "Hi, Daddy!" Of course, he doesn't say anything. For that matter, he just keeps looking at the television, but he does lean his head against my arm. I know that means he is happy I am here. I just can't figure out why he won't speak. He hasn't spoken a word since February 10, 2047.

Daddy had gone down that day to where Eileen's car was found. Mom said that he stood there frozen staring at the car. The police finally escorted him home. Dad never cried. He showed absolutely no emotion at all. And he never spoke a word again. He hasn't even left the house since that day. My mother has dealt with this nightmare alone and taken care of my dad.

Mom yells that lunch is served, and I walk Daddy into the kitchen. Four mission style chairs surround a round red oak table. I sit between Mom and Dad, and we bow our heads as Mom thanks God for the food. When Mom finishes, I reach for the ladle to dip the chicken and dumplings onto my plate when the empty chair across from me causes my eyes to well up. I blink a few times and force the tears away.

Apparently, Mom has adapted to Dad's silence over the last couple of years. While we eat, Mom talks enough for them both, hitting on every subject from the weather to the latest news report to pretty much every patient she has come in contact with this past week. With Dad's lack of communication, I realize how desperate she must be for someone to talk to. We finish the meal, and Dad resumes his position in the living room with his eyes fixated on a black screen.

I work at clearing the table. As much as I love my parents, coming to this house rips at the wound of losing Eileen. Her music should be vibrating the ceiling, and Dad should be yelling for her to turn it down. She should be here telling me how angry she is that I forgot to meet her for lunch. *What if I had remembered…what if!* How does Mom deal with being in this house without Eileen?

Another ton of guilt presses down on my shoulders. I should have been here to help. But instead of reaching out to my parents, I have consumed myself with finding Eileen. I even changed my major to criminal justice. I want to explore and embrace every avenue to find her, and a career in law enforcement will give me access to those avenues.

I walk over and pull my mom into my arms. It is crazy how love always radiates from her. "Mom, I will do the dishes. Would you make us some coffee to go with that lemon pound cake before I go?"

Mom's face lights up. "Oh, baby, that is a wonderful idea. I would love some coffee. We could sit on the back porch and get some fresh air."

I CAN'T REMEMBER the last time my mom and I really talked for so long. I rinse the coffee mugs and place them in the cupboard. While Mom wraps up the leftover cake, I stroll into the living room. Two hours have passed, and Dad doesn't look like he has moved a muscle. I wonder how he doesn't get sores from sitting like that all day.

I lean down and kiss the top of his head. "Bye, Daddy. I love you."

He doesn't even flinch, so I make my way back to the kitchen. "Mom, I guess I had better head home now. Thanks for lunch and the coffee." I nudge her gray-streaked hair behind her ear and kiss her cheek. "I love you."

"I love you, too." Mom follows me to the door. "Thanks for

sitting with me a while. Maybe we can do it again soon. I have really missed long talks with you."

"Me too." I want to tell her about the letter, but I bite the tip of my tongue. As I turn to leave, I notice Dad standing in the archway to the living room. His glistening eyes meet mine, and a drip falls from his cheek.

Chapter Three

I trudge up the steps to my apartment. After our talk, I feel even worse for not being able to tell Mom about the letter and my special assignment. I amble into my apartment, put my shoes away, and sit back on the couch. My mind is going in a million different directions. *My parents...I'm leaving in the morning...what about my apartment...how long will I be gone...I haven't emptied the trash...*

I close my eyes. *God, please show me the way.* I sit there for a moment, and even though I still don't have the answers, an indescribable peace falls over me. The noisy static clears from my mind, and I get up and start with the trash.

As I tote the trash down the hall to the chute, it hits me. I just need to talk to Mr. Fentress when he arrives. If I explain my special situation, I am sure he will allow me to call my mother before I leave and let her know what is going on. President Denali would not want to cause my family any more undue hardship and pain. "Why didn't I think of that before?" I say aloud as I pull open the chute and drop in the trash bag. "I am such an idiot. I have been worrying for nothing!"

When I turn around, a lady and a little girl are right behind me. They are gazing at me with wide eyes and their mouths half open as if they are not sure whether to speak to me or not.

"Hello." I throw up my hand giving a little wave.

Apparently, they are choosing not to speak because their lips just hang there unmoving. I guess they never talk to themselves. I don't care. I have been given a job working for the President of the United States.

~

I WAKE UP. Actually, I get out of bed because I would have to have been asleep in order to wake up. I get in the shower and turn the water as hot as I can stand letting it penetrate my knotted muscles.

After I get dressed, I peer around my apartment. Anxiety fueling my OCD, I go through a few times making sure everything is off and unplugged. My fourth trip to check the stove, and I force myself to repeat the word "off" out loud so maybe it will stick in this frustrating brain of mine. I feel weird not packing a bag, but the directions clearly said not to bring anything.

The clock on the mantel shows that it is almost eight o'clock. I can't wait to talk to Mr. Fentress and get this resolved so I can call my mom. The intercom buzzer goes off, and the monitor displays Mr. Fentress's car at the gate. Trembling, I press the button to open it, and a couple of minutes later, he is standing in the hallway.

I fling open the door. "Mr. Fentress, I need to…"

"Good morning, Miss Hatcher. First things first." He extends the pad for me to place my thumb.

My eyebrows crinkle reflecting my confusion. He obviously knows it's me.

"I'm sorry, Miss Hatcher, but it is still standard procedure to get proper identification."

I extend my hand and place my thumb on the pad. "Mr. Fentress, I just need to ask you…

Suddenly I don't feel so well. A tingle flows down my arms and legs. The tingle changes to heat, and my skin starts to burn. As sweat beads on my forehead, the room starts to wobble and spin. My vision is distorted like I am looking through a kaleidoscope that keeps getting darker and darker.

"Miss Hatcher, what do you need to ask?" His words echo in my ears as if my head is stuck inside of a bucket.

His voice fades, my knees give, and darkness overtakes me.

Chapter Four

My eyes pop open in a panic. Someone is screaming. Wait. I am the one screaming. My head feels like needles are burying themselves in my skull. I pull to lift my arm, but I can't. Something is holding my arms. Something is holding my whole body down. Muffled conversation blends into the distance. My eyes strain to focus, but a light is blinding me. The voices are getting closer.

"Herb, she is waking up."

"Ok, Shelly, I am coming."

Something is weird about those voices. They have a computerized rhythm, yet at the same time, they sound human.

As the fuzziness starts to fade, I realize I am strapped to a table. Straight above me is a giant four-foot circular fluorescent light. And then something slides up right beside me. It appears to be a robot of some sort wearing medical scrubs. This one is fashioned to look like a woman. She is made of bronze colored metal, and her eyes are like deep blue crystals with red glowing dots in the centers. Her cheeks glow with a light spray of rosy-pink paint, and her ponytail of dark brown curls bounces as her hinged mouth opens and closes. "Well, hello there, dear. You woke up a little ahead of schedule on us!"

I have lost it...completely lost it. I think to myself as I gaze up at...well I don't even know what to call it. "Wh...wh...where...am...am...I?" I manage to utter from my heavy lips.

"You are at the president's special training academy, of course. Don't you remember?" She speaks softly with a southern twang.

"I...I...oh...my...head...hurts so bad," I grunt through gritted teeth trying to remember. "Mr. Fentress. He told me...to...put my thumb on the ID pad. Now..." I open my eyes rolling them side to side trying to take in my environment.

"Just a second, dear." The lady robot's head rotates backward, and her voice deepens taking on an angry tone. "Herb, where are you? This girl is in pain. Get. Over. Here. Now!" Her head spins back facing me, and her voice softens again. "We will take care of that pain in just a second, dear. You woke up a little bit earlier than anticipated."

"What did you do to me?" I wince, and my face scrunches as the needles dig deeper in my head.

"This is the first stop when a new recruit comes into the training facility. You will be working in the crime elimination division so, for your safety, we place a tracking device under the skin on the back of your head. It allows us to locate you immediately if you get in trouble. It is inserted under the skin on your head because your hair will always cover the scar and would not likely be located by someone intending you harm." Again, her head does a one-eighty, and her voice changes from this delicate soft nurturing tone as she screams, "Herb!"

"Sorry, sorry!" A masculine-looking robot rushes up. Herb has brown eyes with glowing red laser centers and appears to be wearing a black toupee on his head. He has on a white lab coat and a bright red bow tie. His voice is deep and raspy with a very proper, intelligent, pedantic edge. "Your pain will dissipate in three, two, one..." *And darkness overtakes me again.*

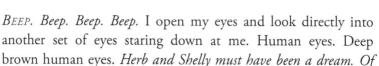

BEEP. Beep. Beep. Beep. I open my eyes and look directly into another set of eyes staring down at me. Human eyes. Deep brown human eyes. *Herb and Shelly must have been a dream. Of course, they were a dream. Robot doctors...with personalities. I think I am going crazy.*

"Finally...it's about time you come out of your stupor. Herb and Shelly must have given you too much sedative."

The human with the eyes is speaking to me. Why can't I speak? He has the most amazing eyes. Did he just say, Herb and Shelly? They are real. What is happening to me? I have lost my mind. COMPLETELY. I can't cry. I won't let myself cry. The tears just start streaming down my face. My body starts to shake with sobs.

"Hey, there. Please don't cry. I can't stand to see a girl cry. Please, it's ok." The man gazing down pleads with a sympathetic edge. He starts patting my head. *Weird. He is rubbing my head like he is petting a dog.*

I finally get my lips to form words. "Wh...wh...where am I?"

"Ok, now I know Herb and Shelly gave you too much sedative. Don't you remember anything?"

"I was supposed to go to a training center because the president had chosen me for a special assignment. Mr. Fentress came to pick me up. Being in my apartment is the last thing I remember until I woke up with some robot people that told me they put a tracking device in me for my safety...and I was pretty sure that was a dream, but now you keep talking about Herb and Shelly...and those were the names of the robots, so I don't know if it was a dream...and I ...am... so...scared. I don't get scared. But I am so scared. What is happening to me? Why can't I stop crying?" I look up and the brown-eyed man stands frozen with his stare fixated on me. I think I have scared him.

He reaches down and gently strokes my face with the tips of his fingers wiping away my tears. "Ok, so you are a little confused. That is to be expected. You did just wake up." He carefully sits down next to me as if I am a fragile china doll. He eases his hand over and places it on top of mine. "You are at the training center. They sedate the newbies before they bring them in because this is a top-secret facility, and they don't want to take any chances on its location being revealed. Herb and Shelly are real. Well, I mean, they are real robots. They are highly integrated prototypes with technology only available to the government at this time. The robots install the tracking devices because they don't make mistakes. They are accurate and precise in placing the device, and their hands never shimmy or shake. Herb and Shelly have been programmed to appear to have human personalities so that their patients feel more at ease. And right now, you are still in the medical unit. When you woke up in pain, Herb gave you a little extra sedative. However, I believe that he gave you a little too much because you have been sleeping for three days."

I squeeze my eyes shut and try to calm myself. *Please God help me. Please give me strength.* This strange man is still holding my hand, which I guess for most people should be a comforting gesture, but not for me. I like my space. And actually, I don't really know when this person washed his hands last. *Focus... I have to focus.* I open my eyes and look up into his getting lost there for a moment. Suddenly, I feel peace. *Who is he, and why is he being so kind to me?* "I – I'm sorry...but who are you...what do you do here?"

"That is really a very long story, but to summarize, I came here to train just like you are now. However, I just couldn't make it through training. I failed level three too many times. Usually, you are taken away if you fail a level three times, but for some reason, they gave me a permanent job back here in building one."

As he speaks, his voice grows quiet, and he almost chokes on the word 'fail.' I don't want to twist the knife deeper in what is obviously a sensitive subject, but I have to know. "So, what do you mean levels...how does this training work?"

"Well, I don't know a lot about it. I mean, I only got to level three. But supposedly there are fourteen levels of training. Level one is where you are now. It consists of getting your chip inserted and then settling in. The second level is where your hypnosis sessions begin. It is the first step of mental preparation in the training program. Also, at this level, you are expected to adapt to a new diet. No sugar or processed food is allowed. At each meal, you must eat a protein, a raw vegetable, a fruit, and a grain. It sounds simple, but the choices are very limited. For protein, the only choices are chicken and fish. It is the same for every meal. As for grains, you get the grand choice between brown rice or quinoa. I know it doesn't sound that bad...but, after a while, the same meal with no special treats gets really, really old. And the kicker is, no matter how sick you are of it, you are required to eat it...all of it...at every meal because your diet is specially formulated to support your training regimen. The third level steps up a bit. You move from hypnosis to having electrodes placed on your head for twenty-minute sessions. You have this treatment once a day. That process looks a little scary with wires attached to your head, and the wires do deliver small shocks to your brain. However, it is not bad at all. You don't even feel the shocks, and it gives you twenty minutes that you can actually rest. In addition to these treatment sessions, you start fight training. On the contrary, this is not that great as this is where yours truly continuously failed, so I can't give you any info beyond level three."

He stumbles again on the word 'fail,' so, I change the subject. "You know, you never told me your name."

"Oh, sorry. My name is Steve. I would be formal and shake your hand, but I am already holding your hand." Laughing he lets go and stands up. "I know I seem a little awkward and crazy. It's just that I have been here in this level one recovery room for so long, and you are the first newbie that I have really talked to. I guess my social skills need a little work."

He tries to run his fingers through his hair, but his hands are shaking for some reason. Instead, he pokes himself in the forehead.

Funny...I have been so self-absorbed that I hadn't even taken in his appearance other than his eyes. He is dressed like a scientist with his white lab coat and small round wire-framed glasses. The white coat makes his dark hair, dark skin, and deep brown eyes stand out even more. He is a little under six feet tall, and his muscular arms have the stitching on the sleeves of his lab coat stretched tight.

"Well..." he speaks like he is waiting for me to answer a question, "you haven't told me your name either."

"Oh! Sorry! I am..." Suddenly, Steve's expression grows strained, and his body starts to convulse. I jump from the gurney that I am lying on and wrap my arms around his body trying to calm his shaking. I strain to hold him up, but Steve's body becomes dead weight. As he slumps to the floor, he grabs my hand once more, and then his eyes close. Steve stops shaking. Steve stops moving. Horrified, my message to God starts repeating in my mind. *Please God let him be alive. Please God let Steve be ok.*

Frantically, I press two fingers to his wrist trying to check his pulse when two huge men in white lab coats rush in. It is then that I realize the alarm on my monitor is going berserk. "BEEP, BEEP, BEEP, BEEP." I must have jerked that heart rate monitor thing off my finger when I leaped off of the gurney. The two men grab Steve under the arms, and as they pull him away, Steve's hand slips from mine. In my hand is a small, folded piece of paper.

Chapter Five

That is why he grabbed my hand. Hurriedly, I fold my hand where no one can see the piece of paper and watch as they drag him from the room. A lady that I assume is a nurse comes in another door and immediately starts helping me back onto the gurney.

I pull away from the woman. "I am fine. You have to go help them. Why are they dragging Steve out of here? Shouldn't they be checking to see what is wrong with him? They did not even check his vitals."

"He is fine." Her voice is hoarse and raspy. "He has low blood sugar. It happens to him all of the time."

"That is dangerous. He could be in a coma. Go check on him please!"

Her tone becomes stern, almost angry as she hardens her grip on my arm. "I told you it happens to him all of the time. He refuses to eat what he is supposed to, and his blood sugar drops. He passes out. They drag him to the infirmary and give him glucose. As for you...I want you back on this gurney until you are checked out and cleared to move to the barracks."

I decide it's best to cooperate, so I get back on the gurney, slipping the piece of paper underneath me as I lay back. Miss Grumpy hooks my heart rate monitor back up and orders me not to move again.

"The doctor will be here in a bit to release you to go to orientation," she rattles off like a recording as she leaves the room.

Finally, after what seems like an eternity, an older man with white hair and a thin mustache enters the room. He is wearing a gray sport coat and a dark blue bow tie that looks like it came from the year 2010. "Hello, Sarah. I am Dr. Eckert." He reaches out to shake my hand. *Ugh. Why do people insist on shaking hands?* I extend my arm and shake his hand in spite of the nausea twisting in my stomach. I hate touching peoples' hands.

"I'm sorry," I correct him, "my name isn't Sarah. It is Ellie."

"No." His monotone voice asserts. "You are now Sarah. Once you enter the facility, you are given a new name. Yours is Sarah."

"I don't understand. Why do I need a new name?"

"Just the way it is." He sits and starts tapping on a small screen that he pulls from his pocket.

"That's all I get. No better explanation for changing my name."

Dr. Eckert stands and crosses to the door. Before he exits, he turns, and his unblinking eyes shoot a laser right through mine. "Sarah, you are fortunate to be here. You best learn to do what you are told and stop with the twenty questions. It will make your experience here much more pleasant."

A half hour passes, and finally, a woman barges in. She strides across the room toward me carrying herself with an air of authority. Maybe she ages well, but she doesn't look like she is much older than me. She is dressed in a dark blue business suit, and her hair is in a bun with every hair perfectly in its place. Brown eyes glare at me through the small silver rectangle frames of her glasses. "Hello, Sarah. I am Dr. Joanne Fleming. I will be the one to monitor your progress and keep an eye on your overall wellbeing while you are here at the training center. You have been released by Dr. Eckert, so let's get you moving." She motions toward the door.

I tuck my hand underneath my body to make it look like I am using it to help me get up. Carefully, I snag the paper between two fingers hoping she won't notice it. As I hop off the gurney and walk toward the door, I twist my hand behind my back making every effort to keep the note concealed. She leads me down a hallway with rooms filled with medical equipment, and then we make a right entering a dimly lit corridor. Instead of the wooden doors with the long, skinny rectangle windows in the hospital hallway, this corridor has metal doors evenly spaced down both sides. Each door has a small square window at the top and a giant number painted in the center of the door. We walk about two-thirds of the way down and stop in front of door number fourteen.

Dr. Fleming turns the knob and holds the door open gesturing for me to go in. "This will be your room for now." She points to a small closet in the corner. "In there you will find seven identical jumpsuits, one for each day of the week. Level one jumpsuits are light blue. You will learn more about the level process in your orientation, but for now, you need to get dressed. Move quickly as time is of the essence, and I will be waiting right outside."

As the door closes behind her, I stand and stare for a moment taking in this tiny room with a bed the size of a cot in the middle of the floor. A small door in the corner leads to the closet that Dr. Fleming had pointed out.

Dr. Fleming's voice almost shakes the door. "The clock is ticking."

I run into the little closet and start putting on this weird form-fitting jump suit. On the floor of the closet are these peculiar-looking silver shoes. The rubber soles are like sneakers, but the high tops go halfway up your calf like boots. It is like a fashion mixture of the Jetsons and the Beverly Hillbillies.' I assume I am supposed to put these on too. The hair on my neck stands up. I suddenly have this twisting in my gut telling me I am being watched. My eyes scan the room. Bare gray walls let me shake the feeling.

I still have the small, folded slip of paper so when I bend over to put on the shoe, I flip the paper open with my fingers, glance at it, and then drop it into my shoe before I slip my foot in. The paper reads,

NEVER FORGET.... Do not be afraid. For the Lord your God is with you wherever you go!

I step out of the tiny closet just as Dr. Fleming starts beating on the door yelling about the clock ticking. This lady definitely needs a vacation. Before I even get the door all the way open, she is rattling off about getting to the orientation room. I trudge along behind her down the hall, my mind pondering the note that Steve gave me. The "*NEVER FORGET*" all in capital letters seems odd...but I guess I am overthinking it. He knew I was upset and frightened, so I am sure he just meant to comfort me. I am thankful that God has sent another Christian to support me. Somehow, I have to find him and make sure he is okay.

We turn down another hallway and stop in front of a set of steel double doors. I come back from my thoughts as Dr. Fleming pulls open the door.

"Here we are. This is the orientation room. We are running late so please hurry and take a seat. President Denali's video will begin shortly." Dr. Fleming points to an open seat.

Ten small desks are positioned in a semicircle around a huge movie screen. Two women and a man are already seated at desks. I sit down and start to introduce myself to the woman at the next desk, but the lights start to dim. President Denali appears on the screen, seated behind his desk in the Oval Office. The American flag stands in the background. All of a sudden, music pounds from the speakers, and Denali's head starts to jive from side to side as he sings this song from a movie I remember watching with my dad. That was back when my dad turned on the television to watch it. *Bad Boys for Life* came out before I was born, but it was one of his favorites, so we watched it a lot.

Oh brother...what a day. Can things get any more peculiar? I press my lips together and gape at the screen in absolute disbelief that this is the President of the United States. Denali is bopping his head so hard that his combover has flipped the other way, and his bald head shines as the few strands of long hair almost reach his shoulder. Maybe he could borrow Herb's toupee.

Finally, he stops singing and starts speaking.

"Welcome, new recruits. If you are watching this, you have made it to level one of the training center, had your tracking device inserted, learned your new name, and discovered your trendy wardrobe. As you know, each of you has been specially selected by me personally so you should feel extremely honored. You are here to train to become a member of my special crime task force, Soldiers Against Crime. During my time as president, you are aware of the changes made that have practically elimi-nated identity theft. Now I plan to put a stop to all criminal activity. I select only elite individuals that possess unique skills to be a part of this crime unit. You have been given a new name in order to offer extra protection to your families. If you complete your training here, you will be dealing with the worst criminals in the country. Essentially, with your new name, your past exis-tence will be erased to ensure that your family will never be placed in danger. Now, as far as your training goes, there are fourteen levels. I am not going to explain each one because you are not going to remember it anyway. There is only one way to fail level one. This level is just for you to adapt to your new envi-ronment and your new name. Therefore, you are not to discuss anything from your past or speak of your previous identity. If you do, you will automatically be ejected from the program, and you will be reprimanded. Breaking the rules is considered a federal offense since this is training for a federal task force. You get one week here, and then you will move to the next building which is level two. Level two will be explained at that time. For now, enjoy your free week. But please utilize the workout facility because you will want to keep in prime condition. This training will be rather intense. I want to personally thank you in advance for your service to your country as we strive to create a perfect society for future generations. You will hear from me again in building two. Good luck to you all."

The screen goes black, and the lights slowly come back on. I don't know if it is fear, shock, or just plain not knowing how to react, but the four of us just sit here frozen to our seats. Miss personality aka Dr. Fleming bursts back into the room. "Okie Dokie. That's a wrap for level one orientation. Let's get you to the dining room for a quick dinner, and then to your rooms for a good night's rest. Follow me!"

We all creep along in silence except for the stomping noise of Dr. Fleming's high-heeled boots. She leads us down the hall through another set of double doors. Three round tables sit in the middle of the dining room with six chairs surrounding each one. The table in the center already has four trays placed on it with metal lids covering the plates. We take a seat, and Dr. Fleming leaves the room. I am starving so I take the plunge making myself the first one to remove the lid. *Hmmm. A burger and fries. Not so bad.* The others eye my burger and remove the lids from their trays. We all have the same. The man and one of the women grab up their burger and start chowing down. The other girl bows her head and appears to be blessing her food. I ask if anyone minds if I bless our food aloud. I would have suggested we hold hands as we pray, but we have already established that I don't like to touch peoples' hands. The first two put their burgers down, and we all bow our heads.

"Dear Lord. Thank you for our health and safety. Thank you for allowing us to be here together to share this meal you have given us, and for the opportunity that we have to help our country. Please bless this food to strengthen our bodies. Please be with each of us throughout this training and help each of us to do well. Most importantly let us honor you Lord in all that we do. In Jesus name we pray. Amen."

I open my eyes and take in the appearance of the other three at the table. The man has brown hair in a military style hair cut with a short, stocky build. One of the women has long black hair, deep charcoal eyes, and a tall, slender form. The other woman, the one that had bowed her head to pray, has shoulder-length blonde hair, bright blue eyes, and a helix piercing in each ear. Her body is petite but muscular.

"Well, I guess we should introduce ourselves. I mean our new selves." I let out a half giggle. "I am Sarah, and apparently I have absolutely nothing else to share about myself."

The man, who seems to have half of his burger stuffed into his mouth, manages to sputter out, "I'm Bob." A few seconds pass before he is finally able to swallow, and then he continues. "Just Bob. Funny they couldn't give me more of an original name. If I have to start with a new identity, I wish it were a little more unique."

"Well, I definitely got unique. I am Telisia." The woman with the long black hair waves to the group.

Laughing, the blonde lady gives her introduction. "Believe it or not, I am Delores. Honestly, do I look like a Delores?" She laughs a little harder. "Delores who...I do not know because apparently we don't get last names."

I hadn't thought about it, but she is right. "That is odd, isn't it. Maybe they just haven't told us our new last names."

Bob chimes in. "I vote we give ourselves new last names. I have to liven up this Bob thing a bit. From now on, I am Bob Balboa."

Telisia raises one eyebrow. "Like from that really old movie *Rocky?*"

"I happen to love that movie." His tone becomes a little defensive. "It is a classic."

Delores nods. "I agree. That is an awesome movie. They just don't make movies anymore like those twentieth century flicks. Anyway, it's nice to meet you, Bob Balboa. I am Delores Ducati. And yes, as in the motorcycle Ducati."

Bob grabs his side from chuckling so hard. "I love it," he chokes out when he finally gets a breath.

Telisia twirls her hair in her fingers. "Well, Telisia is different enough for me. I am going to keep it simple. Call me Telisia Smith."

"Alright, Bob Balboa, Delores Ducati, and Telisia Smith, I am going to be Sarah Sanguine because I am hopeful and optimistic that we are going to succeed. We are going to succeed together."

Chapter Six

I wake up early thinking about how the week flew by. The four of us didn't speak of our past, but we had a lot of fun with our new names and making new identities. The week we spent in level one was relaxed, and we pretty much just ate, worked out, and slept. However, we only had access to the hallway where our rooms were and the hallway with the gym and eating room. We weren't allowed back in the medical section, but I still tried to sneak peeks down that way to see if I could catch a glimpse of Steve. I need to know that he is okay. As hard as I try though, the doors are solid with no windows and are always closed. I tried asking Bob, Delores, and Telisia about him, but they had not met Steve. The only people they had encountered was Dr. Eckert and Dr. Fleming.

I roll off my cot onto my knees, clasp my hands together, and chat with God for a few minutes. The sound of footfalls in the hallway motivates me to hurry and get ready. Today is our graduation dubbing from level one...whatever that means. It is hard to believe we are graduating from anything. We haven't accomplished anything yet. I shower and slip on my day seven jumpsuit and space boot shoe things. Since I came with no belongings, I have nothing to pack before moving to building two except the little note from Steve that is hidden inside of my shoe.

I move down the hallway to the room where we had orientation. Dr. Fleming, Telisia, and Bob are already there. The desks around the giant screen have been moved, and now there are four light blue circles on the floor. As I walk in, Delores steps in behind me.

Dr. Fleming directs us to stand on the four circles. She takes her position in front of the podium that is situated off to the side of the screen and speaks into the microphone. "Ladies and gentlemen, we are here this morning to bid you farewell as you exit building one and begin climbing the ladder of your training in building two. Without further delay, President Denali is standing by to address you live via satellite."

The lights in the room start to dim as President Denali's face overtakes the screen. "Good morning and congratulations! The four of you have finished your week here in level one. You have successfully left your old self behind, embraced your new identity, and have already formed friendships with your new identity. This is not so much a graduation from level one, but more of an initiation as you begin your real training toward becoming a member of my special task force, SAC. Soldiers Against Crime is going to give Americans real freedom back, the freedom to go to bed at night with their doors unlocked, and the peace of mind that they are safe. As I work to pass new laws to heighten the punishment of violent crime in our country, SAC will work to solve crimes, new and cold cases, and capture the perpetrators. No case will be left unsolved or unpunished to the maximum. It is imperative that you pass your training because you cannot reenter society under your old identity. You have already gained too much knowledge as this operation is highly classified. You have been specifically chosen to serve your country, so ladies and gentlemen, serve it well. As I said, today is an initiation. As part of your initiation, the computer system that we now use throughout our country to identify each individual and prevent identity theft will be updated with your new identity. The old you will be gone and replaced with the new you. On the table at the front of the room is four tablets. One at a time you will walk forward, Dr. Eckert will prick your fourth finger, and you will place your entire hand on your screen. Hold it there for five seconds. When the red-light blinks on the screen, you can remove your hand and return to your circle where Dr. Fleming will hand you your briefcase."

The door opens, and Dr. Eckert enters the room. He marches up to the table carrying a metal tray of supplies.

Denali continues, "Okay, ladies first. Delores, step forward." Delores strides with no hesitation up to the front with a smile plastered on her face. She has been portraying this adventurous, no fear attitude, and I wonder if that is real or if she is just really good at hiding her anxiety. She thrusts her hand out to Dr. Eckert, and he gives her finger a quick stick with the needle. She places her hand on the first screen. *One, two, three, four, five...* the red-light flashes, and she slowly moves back to her spot. Dr. Fleming meets her there and hands her a small black briefcase.

"Next, Telisia, if you would step forward." Telisia's stiff legs seem to barely carry her over to Dr. Eckert. With an ashen face and trembling legs, she shoves out her hand like she just wants to get it over with. Dr. Eckert has to hold her wrist to keep her hand still while he pricks her finger. She places her hand on the screen, and then almost runs back to her spot. Fleming hands her a case, and I know I am next. I tap one foot seven times on the floor, and then I tap the other foot seven times on the floor. Yes, when I am nervous, everything is in increments of seven. "Now, Sarah, if you will step forward." My mother's tear-stained face keeps flashing like a neon sign in my head filling me with guilt, but I remind myself that I have no choice. I heard what he said. I know too much, and this is the government of the United States of America. I take a deep breath telling myself to be strong. A tear streams down my cheek as I approach Dr. Eckert. He acts like he doesn't notice. He just grabs my hand, sticks it with the needle, and points to the screen. I place my hand flat holding it there for five seconds, but with the acid rising and burning the back of my throat, it seems more like five hours. The light turns red, and I return to my spot in seven even-spaced steps. Dr. Fleming gives me a black case, and Bob is the only one left. "And now for Bob. If you will please step forward." Bob strolls over to Dr. Eckert like he hasn't a care in the world. In a blink, he is back and holding his case.

Denali clears his throat and then continues his speech. "Your initiation is complete. The black cases you hold contain all the documentation on your new identity. Of course, your prints are stored in the national database now under your new name. At this time, Dr. Fleming will escort you to building two where you will settle in a new room and view my recorded instructional video for that level. That is how each level will work. There are fourteen levels to pass before you are officially a soldier in SAC. Congratulations on being chosen, and good luck to you all."

The lights blink on, and Dr. Fleming begins her rat race. "Time is of the essence. Let's move." And she strides for the door clacking her heels on the floor as if the sound shouts her dominance.

We follow Dr. Fleming. As we hoof it down the hall, my thoughts are like dominoes crashing into each other. *Ellie Hatcher is gone. My mom has lost both of her children. How am I supposed to completely abandon my old life? Did Mr. Fentress lock the door to my apartment? How did I get myself into this?* I remind myself that I didn't have a choice. I was forced to accept this mission. However, that fact does not ease my guilt. Then, I realize that I should be thinking of my dad too, but I guess I am a little angry with him for shutting down on my mom. I mean he has taken 'not talking about his feelings' to a whole new level. Meanwhile, poor Mom is working herself to death while he gets waited on hand and foot. *He who is without sin among you, let him throw a stone at her first.*

I clench my jaw and purse my lips together as John 8:7 hits me upside the head. *Who am I to judge my dad?* I abandoned her too...long before I was made to come here. So, what right do I have to be angry with Dad? My insides just won't stop trembling. I can't shake the weight of the worry and shame.

Bob's voice breaks the silence. "You know I was just thinking how great this is. Now I won't have to make my car payment anymore."

Dr. Fleming wheels around. "Bob, heed my warning. Your words are dangerously close to being considered a discussion of your past identity." She swivels on her heels and clacks them on down the hall.

We continue behind her. I find it odd that we don't go outside as we pass from building one to building two, but through a small clear cutout in the wall of the passage, I notice a narrow opening of exposed granite rock covered in wire mesh.

Dr. Fleming marches us into the building and straight to the orientation room. Eight other people are already there. I wonder where they came from since we were the only ones in building one. Immediately the room darkens, and there is President Denali again. I have looked at his face way too much today.

Feedback wails through the speakers making my ears ring. Dr. Fleming adjusts the volume, and Denali's recorded speech begins.

"Welcome to level two of your training. Some of you are new here, and some of you are here for another go around. Either way, here is the lowdown on level two. Here you will begin a specialized diet regimen. Each meal will include a protein of either chicken or fish, a vegetable, a fruit, and either brown rice, quinoa, or whole oats for your whole grain. These meals are designed to give you the proper nutrition to fuel your training so you must consume all of it at every meal. You will also begin an intense fitness program at the workout facility. A trainer will be assigned to you. In addition, you will attend daily hypnosis appointments that will help you in coping with your identity change. Recently, a few changes have been made to our level two program as we realized that trainees were struggling with teamwork. So instead of private rooms, ladies will be in one room, and gentlemen will be in another. At the end of level two, as some of you may have already experienced, is an obstacle course designed to test your physical readiness for level three. You will be in teams of four. Although each person must complete the obstacle course, your advancement to level three depends on your entire team finishing. If one member does not complete it, your entire team must repeat level two. The reason for this requirement is to train you to work together and to unite with your fellow soldiers. So, help each other however you see fit to ensure your team's success. Good luck and so long for now!"

The lights come on, and Dr. Fleming stands at the front of the room. "Okay, we already have two groups that are here for the second time. You will remain with your group as you make your second attempt. The four recruits that just arrived at level two today will make a team. Might I remind you that you should make passing your top priority! You are only allowed three tries at each level. If you fail three times, you will be up for exile, as you cannot reenter society with your knowledge. At this time, I will show our newest four to the shared quarters to get into their level two wardrobe." As she finishes her speech, she has already sped halfway to the door. The four of us grab our cases and rush to follow her.

THE SHARED living quarters has ten cots lined up in two rows of five, and along one wall are ten oversized lockers. Three cots have clean linens folded and laid on top of them. I guess those are ours since we are the only three newbies here. Dr. Fleming shows us which lockers belong to us, and then she leaves us to get changed and put the bedding on our cots. As soon as the door closes behind Dr. Fleming, Telisia bounces on her cot and pops open her case. *Well, it didn't explode. So far so good.*

Anxiety has my body so tense that I can't move. I want to open my case, but I just stand there. I don't know if the reality of this situation just hasn't occurred to the others yet, or maybe they just aren't leaving anything behind in their old life. But the fact is that I will never see my mom or dad again. They have been erased from my life, and there is nothing I can do about it. I have the ultimate need to keep things within my control, and right now I feel like my life is a tornado twisting with no way to predict which way it will go next.

Telisia pulls a paper from her case, and her face turns white as a sheet. "You guys...uh...have to come take a look at this."

I force myself to move over to Telisia's cot. Delores and I look over her shoulder at a birth certificate. This birth certificate belongs to Telisia Smith born on July 7, 2029, in Sarasota, Florida.

"Don't you guys see?" Telisia glares up at us with wide eyes. "Smith is the name I gave myself."

I practically trip over my own feet getting to my cot. I sit on the side of the mattress, pop the latch, and jerk out the paper in less than three seconds. In a state of shock, I stare at a birth certificate for Sarah Sanguine born May 5, 2029, in Greenville, South Carolina. My face burns from my rising blood pressure. "How did they know? They must be listening to our every word."

Someone starts frantically pounding on the door. "Delores, Sarah, Telisia...are you guys in there? It's Bob. I got to talk to you."

Telisia opens the door, and Bob still has his fisted hand knocking in the air. "From the way you are knocking, I am guessing you saw your birth certificate."

Bob brushes past Telisia and trots right on into the room. His face is contorted, and veins are popping out on his neck. "As a matter of fact, Bob Balboa was born in Pittsburgh, Pennsylvania, on November 4, 2027. Anybody here got any words of wisdom because I am a little freaked out right now. I mean the speech about exile if we fail pretty much scared me senseless if I can just be honest."

"Look I have this really neat bag in my case with shampoo, soap, toothpaste, and all kinds of personal items." We all turn and look at Delores in disbelief that she could be happy about shampoo in this present situation. "Ooooh, and there is vanilla-scented lotion." She gestures to us with her rolling eyes.

Telisia and I get the message. We need to shut up. But, of course, Bob is so caught up in his fit of outrage that he pays no attention and just keeps ranting about how something isn't right. His voice grows louder and louder. I am trying to figure out how to calm him when he balls up his fist. Just as Bob is about to punch the door of one of the lockers, his face twists and his knees buckle dropping him to the floor with a thud. An alarm sounds, and two men rush in and drag Bob's limp body from the room.

Chapter Seven

My bottom lip quivers in terror as Bob disappears right before my eyes. Deja-vu. The exact same thing happened to Steve. I turn to see the blood-drained faces of Telisia and Delores.

With unsteady legs, I fall to my knees next to my cot and start pouring out to God. *God, please help. I don't know why this is happening, but I know you must have a reason. Even if I don't feel you, I know you are here. You have never left me. Please get me out of here.* Then suddenly my chest tightens, and a pang of guilt stabs through me. I wasn't there for my mom and dad when they needed me most. Why do I deserve for God to be with me now? How selfish am I? My mother is probably falling to pieces right now mourning the disappearance of another child, and I am praying for me. When did I become this self-centered? Sobbing I beg, *God, forgive me of my selfishness. I deserve whatever comes my way, but please ease my mom's pain. Please comfort her and help her to know that I am ok.* The stabs cuts deeper. *And, Lord, whatever is going on with my dad, for whatever reason it is that he won't speak, please help him through it. If it be your will Lord, allow me to see my family again. And please protect Steve and Bob wherever they have been taken. In Jesus name. AMEN!*

My body still heaving with sobs, I feel an elbow brushing mine. Delores is kneeling next to me whispering a prayer under her breath. Telisia's trembling body is curled up in a fetal position on her cot. Her face is smothered in her pillow muffling the sound of her whimpers. I creep over and sit next to her placing my hand on her back to try and calm her trembling. Delores slides up from the other side and does the same. We just sit like that. I don't even know how much time passes when Dr. Fleming bursts in making her presence known.

"Ladies, have you not checked your schedules? And why are you not dressed in your new uniforms? This is not acceptable. Delores, I came to find out why you have not arrived at your first hypnosis session."

"B-b-b-ut," I stammer, "Bob...wh...where did he go...and what schedule?"

Fleming's face reddens. "Bob was becoming violent. Violence is the very reason we are here. Our job is to eliminate violence. Bob is being reprimanded, and he will rejoin your group later. As for your schedule, Ms. Sanguine, it is in your case. Delores, you have approximately two minutes to change and be in the hallway. I will be waiting. Since you are already late, I will escort you. Remember, TIME IS OF THE ESSENCE."

The door closes, and Delores makes a beeline for her locker. She grabs a jumpsuit and the shoes. It is the same stupid-looking shoes that we had in level one. The jumpsuits look the same, but they are dark blue instead of light blue. I grab my case and finish looking through its contents. Besides the birth certificate, I find a bag of toiletries, a booklet with a map of the building on the front and a detailed schedule for the next two weeks printed on the inside, a weird pair of headphones with a tag that says, "wear while sleeping," and a diary with an ink pen. Crazy...with technology, how long has it been since someone actually used an ink pen to handwrite in a diary?

Delores flies past me and out the door. I check out my schedule. It is eleven o'clock now. I am supposed to meet with the fitness trainer in fifteen minutes for diet details and a workout regimen. I quickly toss the other things back in the case and hustle to my locker. One shelf contains seven dark blue jumpsuits. Another shelf has a stack of spandex workout apparel. A basket with undergarments sits on the third shelf, and in the bottom is a pair of actual cross-training sneakers and those crazy boot shoes. My actual workout isn't until two o'clock, so I grab a jumpsuit and the boots for the meeting and toss my case in the locker for now.

I notice Telisia at her locker. She goes back to her cot and starts putting her bedding on it. I can tell by her somber face and straight tight lips that she doesn't want to talk so I run to the bathroom to change.

Suddenly my heels dig in, and I come to an abrupt halt at the door. My thoughts start spinning out of control as a major detail in these living arrangements dawns on me. In reality, I am sharing a bathroom with other people. To me, that means this is a public restroom. My stomach knots, my heart races, and I feel the panic rising. I look around. The bathroom is divided into two parts. One section has sinks and toilet stalls, and the other section has showers and dressing rooms. I take seven deep breaths. *Don't panic. I can't let them see me have a panic attack.* I repeat to myself, "I can do all things through Christ who strengthens me. I can do all things through Christ who strengthens me. I can do all things through Christ who strengthens me. I can do all things through Christ who strengthens me. I can do all things through Christ who strengthens me. I can do all things through Christ who strengthens me. I can do all things through Christ who strengthens me. I can do all things through Christ who strengthens me." *Ok. Think it through. This is literally nothing compared to what you have already overcome. God is in control.*

I clinch my fists, pushing the panic down. I run to the wall and pull off a few paper towels. In one of the dressing rooms, I spread the paper towels on the bench and carefully lay my clothes in the center. Trying to block out the public restroom issue, I change my clothes as quick as I can. I discreetly move the note to my new set of boots and lace them up. In that moment, I picture Steve's writing on the note, and the verse plays through my mind. *For the Lord your God is with you wherever you go.* I am suddenly filled with peace.

I need the map of the building from my case, so I dash out to my locker. With the map in hand, I travel the hallways to the training room.

Chapter Eight

A small desk sits in the center of the fitness training office. As I enter, a massive lady stands up and steps around from behind the desk, and I do mean massive. She towers at least six feet tall and very few men have this much muscle bulk.

"Hello, I am Sarah. I am supposed to meet with the trainer at eleven fifteen."

"You are in the right place. My name is Ingrid, and I will be your trainer here in level two. Have a seat, and let's discuss your new diet and workout regimen for the next two weeks." She moves back behind the desk as I take a seat in front of it.

Ingrid hands me a chart and then opens her laptop. "Sarah, first of all, the ultimate goal is to get you past the obstacle course and into level three. You need the perfect number of calories from specific types of food to fuel your body and maintain your weight for the excessive amount of activity you will be engaging in. You are five feet four inches tall and one hundred twenty pounds. My calculations estimate you will need twenty-three hundred calories per day. For breakfast, you will be served two boiled eggs, a cup of oatmeal, a banana, eight ounces of milk, and sixteen ounces of water. Lunch will consist of a protein shake, a cup of quinoa, a grilled chicken and spinach salad, a cup of strawberries, and a bottle of water. And finally, for dinner, you will have ten ounces of grilled salmon, a cup of brown rice, a cup of broccoli, and a bottle of water. You must consume all the food served on your tray. Your schedule will specify the times, but each day you have a thirty-minute cardio session in order to improve your muscle, heart, and lung coordination. You will have a thirty-minute weight training session which will rotate daily between upper body, core, and legs. Then, one hour a day your team will go to the obstacle course to practice. Any questions?"

"So…what happens if I can't finish all of that food?" I clear my throat and try to speak a little louder. "I mean, it seems that it would be better to implement a couple of snacks throughout the day instead of three huge meals."

Ingrid grasps the sides of her head with her hands and rubs her temples with her fingertips. "Miss Sanguine, I understand your concerns, but I highly recommend you follow the rules and not question how things are done here. Now you are dismissed." Without making a sound, I stand and tread softly from the room.

DELORES IS CONVERSING with three other girls when I get back to our shared room.

"Hi. I am Sarah," I say as I walk over.

A girl with dark red hair and freckles tosses her hand up in a partial wave. "Hi, roomie. I am Rose, a second timer in level two along with Daisy here."

Daisy grins and pushes blonde curls from her eyes. "It is nice to meet you, Sarah. Rose and I are on the same team with Thorn and Ash." A small giggle escapes from her mouth. "Apparently they were into plants the day we came in."

I had not picked up on the connection of their names, but once she points it out, I can't help but laugh. "Well, it seems they had no rhyme or reason for our names. It is nice to meet you guys."

"It is time for lunch. We had better get ourselves to the dining room." Delores crosses the room and pulls open the door. "Telisia is at her hypnosis session now so I guess she will just come straight there."

As we amble down the hall, I touch Delores's elbow to get her attention. "So, Delores, how is this hypnosis thing?"

She leans toward me keeping her volume low. "It actually wasn't half bad. I found it to be pretty relaxing after the emotional seesaw of a day that we have had."

WE GO through a set of double glass doors to the dining room. Apparently, they plan for you to eat with your team because there are three round tables set up with four chairs at each one. Rose points to the table in the middle where two men are sitting. "That is Thorn and Ash. Come over, and I will introduce you." Delores and I follow Rose and Daisy tails behind us. "Thorn, Ash, I want you to meet Delores and Sarah. They are part of the new team."

"Nice to meet you," Thorn says as he stands and sticks out his hand.

Great. I get to shake hands again. No way out of it. I can't be rude. As I shake his hand, I return the introduction, "Nice to meet you as well."

Of course, Ash follows with his hand stuck out. *Why can't people just wave? Why do we have to share germs?* I shake his hand, and ewww, it is all sweaty. Ash lowers his head and forces a smile. "Hopefully, your team doesn't have to repeat level two like us."

"Is it that hard?"

"Well, the problem is everyone in your group has to get through it. All it takes to fail is one person not being able to do one thing in the course. Unfortunately, I am afraid of heights, so I made my contribution to this do over."

Not sure how to respond, I give him a little smile. "I am sure you guys will get it this time. Sometimes it's hard to overcome a fear. I try repeating a Bible verse like, 'I can do all things through Christ who strengthens me.' It takes my mind off the problem and reminds me that God is in control."

"Thanks. That is a really good idea. I will give it a try. I definitely don't want to be stuck at level two again, and I am sure the rest of my team would appreciate it if I would get over the height phobia. This whole thing is not what I expected or thought it..."

Telisia slides up next to me before he finishes and introduces herself. Another three men and a woman parade in. Instead of stopping for introductions, they just traipse right past us to their table with the exception of the woman. I am not sure if she is being sarcastic or giving us a warning.

"You guys better get to eating. You only have so much time to choke it all down." She plops down with her group. They immediately flip the lids off their trays and start eating.

"That is Darla, Jed, Liam, and Troy." Daisy leans in so they can't hear her. "You kind of have to overlook their friendliness. That group tried to buck the system their first go around. They thought they would take a stand. All of them wound up getting reprimanded. I don't know what that means or what happened to them, but whatever it was has made them even more resentful. She is right, though. We had better get to eating."

Reality hits as the three of us gather at our table. My stomach churns at the sight of Bob's empty chair. Why isn't he back? I have to find out what this reprimanding thing is. I open the lid to my tray and bow my head. I feel Delores take my hand. "Lord, thank you for being with us and for providing us with new friendships to help us get through this. Thank you for this meal. Amen." As she finishes the prayer, she gives my hand a squeeze before she lets go, which I am actually thankful for.

Normally, the anxiety would be boiling, but for some reason, the gesture calms me and makes me feel a little less alone.

In an effort to get this food down before I run out of time, I snatch up my fork and start stabbing away at the salad. I should ask if they have a special recipe to make the chicken so rubbery. I finally force myself to just swallow it because chewing it is not an option. I chug down the protein shake trying to wash down the pieces of chicken that feel stuck in my throat. The quinoa goes down easier, and thankfully, has no taste. I drink the water with the strawberries that I have saved for dessert. It turns out that there is nothing dessert-like about them. They are mushy, watery, and so sour that my face puckers with every bite. I am pretty sure they have been frozen and thawed. However, I have to see the cup as half full instead of half empty. I have food. I am not being starved so I will be thankful.

I watch as the repeats carry their trays to a counter in a window opening in the back of the room, so I follow suit. As I set my tray in the window and turn around, I bump right into Liam. He leans around me placing one hand on the back of my neck and places his tray on the counter with his other hand. After he sets his tray down, he reaches back and starts scratching the back of his head while he turns his face into my ear and whispers, "You might want to check on that guy in your group. He was curled up on his cot crying when we left for the dining room."

Liam steps back. "Pardon me." He shakes his head. "That was so rude of me to reach over you. I don't think I have introduced myself. I am Liam."

So, he knows they hear everything we say. He is covering. I play along. "I am Sarah. Nice to meet you, and no worries. I didn't take any offense."

He goes on his way, and I speed walk to catch up with Delores. I make eye contact and give her a wink. "I have twenty minutes before my hypnosis. What do you have next?"

She raises an eyebrow in a questioning look. "Umm, I have

that fitness trainer meeting. But I have twenty minutes before it starts too."

"Oh good. You want to walk with me to the guys' room and see if Bob is back?"

"Sure. I have my map. Let's see where it is." Delores pulls out her little booklet, and we find the men's dorm room.

I knock on the door, but there is no reply. I try again. Still nothing. I know I shouldn't, but I turn the knob and crack the door open just enough that I can peek in. Bob is curled up on a cot in the back corner of the room. No one else appears to be in there so I push it the rest of the way open and go on in. Delores follows me. I start to call out to him, but the words catch in my throat. Bob's whole body is jerking. While saying a silent prayer that he is okay, I cross the room to his cot. Bob is soaked in sweat, and his eyes are squeezed so tight that his eyelids aren't even visible. He has his teeth clamped around the corner of his pillow.

I kneel beside him and speak in a soft undertone. "Bob… Bob…it's Sarah. What happened?" Right now, I don't even care if they are listening. Bob looks pitiful. He sobs and his body shakes even harder. "What did they do to you?" With a jerk, he lets go of the pillow with one hand and places it on my arm. "Bob, please, you have to tell us what happened?"

With the other hand, quivering, he lowers the pillow from his mouth. "Ha-a-a-rd t-t-to ex-p-p-plain."

"Please try, Bob."

Bob pulls himself up and sits on the edge of the cot. His eyes are bulging and his lips tremble as he talks. "All I know is I woke up, and I couldn't move. My arms, legs, and forehead were strapped down to this metal table. I tried to pull at the straps, but that only made them tighter. This weird talking robot stood over me ordering me to relax. It said I had been brought there because of my dangerous outburst of anger, and I was strapped down to ensure that no one was at risk from my unstable frame of mind."

"So, they had you strapped down, and you were conversing with a robot?" Delores seems a little taken by the robot part.

"He is right about these robots. I met two of them during that special chip insertion procedure." I get up off the floor and sit next to Bob putting my arm around his back. "So, Bob, what else happened? I can tell there is more."

"I asked the robot what happened to the monsters, but he told me that I must have just had a bad dream while I was asleep. But...it was so real."

"What monsters, Bob?"

"I swear they were real, Sarah." Bob rocks back and forth.

"What did the monsters do? Tell us what happened."

"I was lying down just like I was when I woke up, and it was dark...pitch black dark. I was in a total abyss of darkness, and it felt like there was a shortage of air. I was sucking in so hard to get a breath, but I couldn't. A horrible rotting stench surrounded me. The smell was nauseating, and the acid from my stomach made me choke. These hands were grabbing at me...glowing red, wrinkled hands with long, skinny fingers and sharp, claw-like nails. The long fingers were holding me down. No...no, they were pulling me down. There were so many of these hands, and they were reaching up from below and yanking me down. And while all these fiery hands were grabbing and tugging at me, I heard these voices. They were whispering right in my ear. I could even feel their hot breath on my ear as they spoke. The voices mocked me. They said that I was a failure and would never be good at anything. They said that I was fat and ugly and that no one would ever love me. They kept on tearing away at me. The whispers told me I was an absolute nothing that wasn't worthy of living, and on and on. Then the last words I heard..." Bob lowers his voice until we could barely hear him. "The last words I heard before I woke up was 'only Denali can save you'." Bob wipes his face with his shaking hands. "When I came to, I was drenched in sweat. It had been so hot, so excruciatingly hot in my apparent nightmare, I thought for sure I must have burns.

The whispers kept repeating in my head, and all I could think was that I wanted to die.

I opened my eyes to a brightly lit room and a robot staring down at me. When the robot unstrapped me, it told me to return to my normal schedule, but my short fuse would be very closely monitored. Whatever that means."

"Bob, whatever this was that you experienced was not real. Whatever the voices said are not true. You are sitting right here, and you are not burned. This must somehow be related to their punishment for us. I know you have had a horrible experience, but you have to pull yourself together and focus on getting out of level two. We don't want to be here any longer than we have to, and we definitely do not want this to happen again. So, keep up with your schedule, finish your meals, and let's work hard to make sure we all get through the obstacle course. I have to hustle to get to hypnosis. Delores, get moving to your fitness meeting. Bob, do you know where you are supposed to be?"

Bob tries to look at his schedule with shaking hands. "I missed my fitness meeting when I was being detained. Now I am scheduled for cardio in the gym."

"Then get your gym clothes on in record time and get to the gym. I know it is hard. I can't imagine the trauma you have been through today, but if you want to get out of this mess, you have to bury it and get moving." I stand and grab his arm to help him up. Delores and I move like Dr. Fleming because, right now, time is of the essence.

Chapter Nine

I make it to the hypnosis lab literally just in time. I push through the door and, to my surprise, find Dr. Eckert waiting for me. I wonder why Delores didn't tell me that Dr. Eckert does the hypnosis.

"Good afternoon, Sarah. Talk about punctual. You arrived almost to the exact second of your appointment. Come on back, and we will get started." Dr. Eckert turns and leads me into a small dim room lit only by a couple of lamps. He directs me to take a seat in this plush chair with a footstool, and he seats himself in this smaller swivel chair in the corner.

"Ok, Sarah," Dr. Eckert speaks slowly enunciating every syllable of each word, "at your daily appointment during this level we will be administering hypnotherapy. The purpose of this is to help you leave your old identity behind and embrace your new life. Denali understands the emotional difficulty involved with this, so he has added these therapeutic sessions to help his trainees cope with the transition. Do you have any questions before we begin?"

"Yes, just one." I try to choose my words carefully so that I

don't appear to be questioning authority. "Why is it so imperative that we forget our old life? I mean can't we just use this new
name and identity just like an officer working undercover?"

"Miss Sanguine, obviously you are not going to let this rest
until I explain. So, let me paint a picture for you. Let's pretend
that you are investigating a violent gang known for mass murder.
They decide the best way to secure their freedom is to kidnap
your mother. Your mother is held hostage and possibly even
tortured. The gang will only release their hostage if the United
States government agrees to give them immunity, which I can
guarantee you will not happen. If you are tied to your old identity, your mother's address, job, and anything they want to know
is easily accessible. But if you have a new identity that has no
connection whatsoever to your past, your family will maintain
anonymity and safety. Therefore, it is essential that you truly
believe yourself to be Sarah Sanguine so you will not reveal
information that could lead someone to your family."

I guess that kind of makes sense. "Thank you for explaining.
I understand. I would never want to put my family in danger."

"To begin, I want you to focus on the wall in front of you.
There is a picture of President Denali in the center of that wall. I
want you to stare at that photo, focusing one hundred percent
on it, blocking out everything but my voice."

I do as he says, but it is kind of weird being hypnotized by
staring at a photo of President Denali. On top of that, it is a
really bad picture of him. He is smiling so big that his bottom
teeth are showing.

Dr. Eckert continues softening his voice and speaking even
more slowly. "Picture yourself in your happy place. Maybe you
are in a chair by the beach, all alone, listening to the crashing
of the waves or laying on a blanket in the middle of a flower-
filled meadow with the sounds of chirping birds and the breeze
swishing through the trees. There is no weight. You are like a
leaf floating on the water. Every muscle in your body is relaxed,
completely relaxed. Your heartrate is slowing. Your eyes are
heavy. You are Sarah Sanguine. You have always been Sarah

Sanguine. You, Sarah Sanguine, were born on May 5, 2029, in Greenville, South Carolina. You have no other identity. Sarah Sanguine is dedicated to President Denali's purpose to make the world a better place. Sarah Sanguine will follow Denali's direction. Sarah Sanguine will dedicate her life to achieving Denali's purpose to create a safe haven. Sarah, you will now come back to the training center. You feel yourself waking up. Sarah when I count to three you will be back in this room a new and refreshed person. One, two, three… Sarah, how do you feel?"

In all honesty, I couldn't focus on that picture, nor, after this day, do I feel relaxed, but I have to act like it. "I feel wonderful…like a brand-new person."

"Great. Then I will note that today's session was a success. So, let's get you on your way so you can keep the rest of your schedule."

I HAVE forty-five minutes before cardio, so I stroll leisurely back to my room to change. The fact that I have not seen one window to the outside puzzles me. I know this training facility is supposed to be in an undisclosed location, but it still seems strange that there are no windows. Hallways with closed doors are the extent of the landscape. I long for some sunshine or even to look out on a rainy day.

In our room, Telisia is curled back up on her cot, and Delores appears to be having a prayer time. I tiptoe in so I don't disturb them. I really need God's guidance right now, so I get on my knees for some quiet time too.

As I finish my prayer, I am disappointed that I don't have my Bible. Thankfully, I have memorized quite a bit of scripture, and I suddenly feel led to recite some verses each day, so I don't forget. *Never* Forget. Those were the words Steve wrote in his note. Immediately Isaiah 41:10 pops into my mind like God is speaking the words right to me. *So do not fear, for I am with you;*

do not be dismayed, for I am your God. I will strengthen you and help you; I will uphold you with my righteous right hand.

I still have a few minutes, and since I have yet to put the bedding on my cot, I get busy. I work to get the sheets perfectly smooth while letting Isaiah 41:10 repeat over and over in my head. I am so focused on the words of the verse that I don't even hear Darla approach.

"Wow! That is some serious care in making a bed. You know you are just going to mess up in a few hours."

Startled by her presence, I jump flinging my hand over my heart as it skips a beat. "Oh, hi. Well, I am a bit of a perfectionist about certain things, I guess. Character flaw, but it is how God created me." Giggling, I say, "My motto is if you are going to do something, you might as well do it right."

The corner of her mouth turns up in half smile. "I wouldn't call that a flaw. Sounds like a pretty good motto to me."

"Thanks!" I notice the time as she walks away and hurry to my locker to get my workout clothes and sneakers.

I try keeping my focus on the verse in my head instead of the germy bathroom as I change into my clothes. As I switch my shoes, I start to move the note but decide just to leave it. I will be putting my shoe boots back on soon. Shoving my jumpsuit and boots into my locker, I slam the door and make my way to the gym which is located right next to the fitness training office that I went to earlier. I am eager for this stress release.

Two double doors lead into a small vestibule with a door on the left into the cardio area and a door on the right into the weight room. I turn into the cardio room which has a stationary bike and a huge treadmill that are both facing a large screen on the wall. The treadmill does not have any handles or anything. It is just a huge conveyor belt probably five feet wide by seven feet long. Suddenly, an automated voice resonates through the room.

"Welcome, Sarah Sanguine! Please stand on the red circle in the middle of the room. We will begin with five minutes of stretching."

Well, this is different. I walk to the red circle, the enormous screen lights up, and a cartoon version of Denali appears. The animated Denali moves with the automated voice demonstrating each stretch.

After five minutes of stretching, the voice instructs me to move to the giant belt. "Today's run is on the Mesa Trail in Boulder, Colorado. Since this is your first day, you will set your own pace." A path appears on the screen with wildflowers all along the sides and big mountains in the background. "You may begin now."

I start to walk to get the feel of the belt. Music begins to play, and strangely, the tempo increases with my pace. I increase to a jog, and my mind starts to whir. *I have to figure out exactly how they listen to everything we say. Are there cameras everywhere? Surely there is some way that I can get information from the rebellious group. They have been through reprimanding, and I wonder if they had the same experience as Bob. I have to play the game, get through the levels, and gain their trust. My gut tells me something is not right about this whole thing.*

It seems like I have just started my run, but a checkered flag appears on the screen. The voice tells me to move back to the red dot for cool-down stretches, and cartoon Denali is back. After five more minutes of mostly holding some static stretches and taking some deep breaths, I move to the other room for the weight training session. This room has a smaller screen, but of course, the cartoon Denali appears on it demonstrating the correct posture and technique for each exercise. Today is thirty minutes of upper body strength training. I do push-ups, bicep curls, bench presses, tricep dips, and pull ups. As I finish up, cartoon Denali is dripping sweat and breathing hard. I guess he forgot to breathe properly during his workout.

Obstacle course practice doesn't start until five o'clock, so I have an hour to relax before I meet my team at the arena. I amble along down the hall after fitness training pondering on how to fish for information from the repeats that have experienced reprimanding. Bob seemed too shaken for that whole thing just to have been a nightmare. On the other hand, if I could just find Steve, I bet he could tell me what it is all about. *And I need to see that he is okay. Why do I keep thinking about him?*

All of a sudden, angry shouts thunder down the hall, and my heart starts to race.

Chapter Ten

I round the corner to find Rose, Ash, Thorn, and Daisy screaming at each other. Skittishly, I approach them. I know it is kind of risky getting involved, but I can't just stand by while people get dragged away.

"Hey, guys. Calm down." I glance up and down the hallway to see if anyone else is coming. "What are you all upset about?"

Ash's words almost jumble he speaks so fast. "It's my fault. They have changed the obstacle course. Now there is even more heights. I can't do it."

Thorn's nostrils flare as his panicked voice cuts in. "How can you be so selfish? Ash, if you don't do it, we all fail!"

Tears swim in his eyes, and his shoulders slump. "I don't mean to be selfish. I am horrified of heights." His voice cracks. "My dad was a construction worker. He was on a job setting beams for a big commercial skyscraper. The beam started swinging, and he...he lost his balance. He fell six stories. I was only four years old when he died. I have been terrif...ied..."

Ash's body becomes as limp as a spaghetti noodle. With no warning at all, it is like a switch on his body just gets turned off, and he drops. His head jerks from the impact of the fall barely missing the concrete wall. Like clockwork, here come the two men stomping toward us. They grab Ash under his arms and pull his body with his heels scraping along the floor down the hall. With my arms clutched around my body, my eyes follow his comatose form until he is out of sight.

The clacking of Dr. Fleming's heels breaks the silence. Staring at us with narrow eyes, she folds her arms across her chest and lets out a huff. Her stern controlled tone sends chills tingling down my back. "Were the instructions not clear? You were told that you cannot speak of your past. That means anything about your life before you came into this facility is off limits. So, unless you want to suffer the same fate as Ash and be reprimanded, I suggest you heed this warning." She turns and her clacking heels continue to scream at us all the way back down the hall.

Thorn's face appears totally devoid of blood. He drops to his knees in slow motion and mumbles under his breath, "What have I become?"

I kneel next to him with my mouth half open searching my mind desperately for something helpful to say, but before I find any words, Thorn's confusion sputters out. "I don't want to be angry, but I cannot stand the thought of failing and repeating this level a third time." Thorn buries his face in his hands. "Ash is probably being tortured or something right now, and I should feel bad. I mean I do feel bad, but not as bad as I should feel. I am still upset with him because I know he won't finish the course."

"Thorn, I want you to listen to me. What is happening to Ash is not your fault. You are not the one doing it to him. God made you, and he gave you emotions. He understands why you would feel anger under the circumstances. There is no way you could know what Ash had been through." I reach over and gently rub his back. "But God wants you to use this anger in a justifiable way like Jesus did in the temple when he overturned the tables. Jesus was standing for what was morally right, and he used his anger to stop those people from defiling the house of

God. You have to use this anger inside of you to help Ash. He cannot control his fear of heights, so somehow you have to help him get through this obstacle course."

Thorn lifts his head and wipes his eyes. "If I hadn't been pushing him, Ash wouldn't have spilled about his past. I should be the one being punished, not him. What if he doesn't come back?"

"Well, I know Bob came back. He was pretty shaken after, but he is okay. And I heard that all four of the people in the other group repeating this level went through reprimanding, and they appear to be fine. I am sure the experience isn't pleasant, but he will be alright. So instead of focusing on the guilt, pray for wisdom and guidance in helping Ash."

Rose walks over, and I push myself up. She gives Thorn her hand, and as he stands, she pulls him into a hug. "She is right. We have to help him. We are a team, and as a team, we will overcome this." Rose stretches her arm out to Daisy, and Daisy joins the hug.

As they embrace each other, I quietly disappear down the hallway to my room.

I ONLY HAVE thirty minutes left now before obstacle course practice. Telisia and Delores are both on their cots. Telisia has the diary from her case open on her bed, and I wonder if she is really writing in it. Darla is standing in front of her locker. I don't feel like talking, so I walk straight through to the bathroom. Tears feel like they could explode from my eyes any second, and I don't want to cause a spectacle or answer questions right now. Unfortunately, just the idea of having to go into that germ pit of a bathroom adds to my anxiety, but I need a tissue and a minute to myself. This place does not exactly offer a whole lot of options for being alone.

I grab a couple of Kleenex from the box by the sink. I don't recognize the person in the mirror looking back at me. Tears flow in little streams down my cheeks. My expression is blank. No smile. No frown. Just blank. My mind is like the white noise on those old television sets from the twentieth century. *Who am I?* Ellie Hatcher has been erased. I wonder what my mom and dad must be thinking. I don't even have the will to lift my hand and use the tissue to wipe my tears away.

Darla's reflection shows in the mirror as she walks up behind me. "You know, you can't let this place break you. That is what they want. It is like boot camp. They are weeding out the weaklings, and you don't appear to me to be a weakling, so just hang on."

"But, Darla, I am just so confused. I want that to be true. But every time I turn around, it seems like someone drops lifeless to the ground and gets dragged away for some reprimanding thing. Well, except the first time it happened, I was told the guy had low blood sugar." I blow the hair from my face. "We can't even see outside. For some reason, our secret location has absolutely no windows. And, to top it off, we are just supposed to forget everyone and everything we have ever known and become this new made-up person."

"Look," Darla steps closer and places her hand at the back of my neck, "I have been through reprimanding and so have the others in my group. That is why I followed you in here. You remind me of us during our first time through this level. We got to level two full of questions that we wanted answered. Heed my advice. You do not want to experience their punishment, so don't test them. Submit completely to the rules and work to get through the levels."

"What was your reprimanding like?" I am afraid of them hearing me asking too many questions, but I have to find out.

Darla squeezes the back of my neck a little tighter which I find a little strange, and her long nails are digging into my skin. Stiffening my muscles against the pain, I decide to endure it since I need answers. I notice she has her other hand on the back of her neck. *Maybe she likes to hold necks when she talks.* She stares me directly in the eyes as she speaks so low that I almost have to read her lips to follow along. "They want us to believe we are just given something to knock us out to stop us from whatever wrong act it is that we are supposedly committing at the time, but everyone in my group had the same experience. I remember lying there unable to move. The heat was suffocating. All these fiery red, wrinkled hands with long bony fingers were grabbing at me from below pulling me down. Faint voices muttered in my ear, and their words ripped my self-worth to shreds. The sulfur smell of their hot breath made the acid in my stomach boil, and I started to gag. With every word, hot breath smacked the side of my face, and the stench burned the lining of my nose. When I woke up, I was in such a state of deep depression that I did not want to live anymore. All I could do was curl up in a ball and cry. But then some stupid robot told me that it was just a nightmare, and I needed to get up and get back to my schedule."

We seem to be in a staring contest because neither of us blink. The lump is building in my throat as I try to talk. "That is the exact same story Bob told me."

"So, you know I am telling the truth. Just stop asking questions and pass the obstacle course." She moves her hands back to her sides as she turns to walk away. "You better hurry, or you are going to be late."

I nod forcing myself to get it together and wipe my face with the tissue. "I am actually looking forward to seeing the obstacle course. I'll see you at dinner."

Chapter Eleven

I meet up with Delores, Telisia, and Bob outside the arena. We go in, and Ingrid stands just inside holding four sets of virtual glasses. "Are you newbies ready to see what the obstacle course is all about?"

I try to pump myself up. "Well, I guess if we are going to get past level two on the first try, we better take advantage of the practice time."

"Work ethic. I like it." She hands a pair of virtual glasses to each of us. "Before you jump in yourself, I want you to be able to see the whole course. Put on these glasses, and you can watch me go through it. Then you will know what to expect. Once I get to the red flag, take off the glasses, and the four of you are free to start your practice. Just make sure you are finished and out of here in one hour. That is your maximum practice time per day. Alright, here we go."

We all get our glasses on. The glasses show Ingrid at the starting line. First, she runs through this giant spinning tube just like in a fun house at the carnival except this tube is turning at a warp speed. Once she gets through, immediately there is this black conveyor belt sloping upward at a forty-five-degree angle.

Ingrid digs her nails into tiny ridges in the belt and rides it up about ten feet. Then she walks across a beam suspended in the air that is about eight inches wide and thirty feet long. The problem is while she is balancing and walking across the beam, giant sandbags are swinging like pendulums that she has to dodge. At the end of the beam, Ingrid jumps ten feet down onto a trampoline mat and then runs through a corridor jumping five hurdles of flames that are three feet high. As she exits the corridor, Ingrid grabs a rope and starts climbing. She climbs about thirty feet to monkey bars hanging from the ceiling. Thankfully, a safety net is positioned below as she swings from bar to bar to the platform where she raises one of the flags. Ingrid waves to us returns the flag to its original position and leaves.

The four of us rip off the glasses. Telisia's face is as pale as a ghost, and Bob looks like he has just seen a ghost. Taking charge, Delores steps up between them. She grabs Telisia's hand in her right and Bob's hand in her left.

"Alright team," Delores's enthusiastic words echo, "let's start with a little talk with God."

Images of myself being scorched by those flames as I try to jump them is plastered in my mind, and I don't give a thought to my hand touching phobia. I step into the circle grabbing Telisia's and Bob's other hands as Delores begins.

"Dear Lord," she says, "thank you for our team and the bonds that we have already formed with each other. Please keep us safe and guide us through this course. Help us to have a productive practice, and if it be your will, that we would have success and pass the course in two weeks. In Jesus name we pray. Amen."

We drop hands, and Bob walks toward the start line. "I know it's usually ladies first," he says, "but in this situation, that doesn't seem appropriate. I'll be the crash test dummy." He sprints into the rotating tube with apparently no game plan because about a third of the way into it his feet fly out from under him, and the tube starts tossing Bob around like a cat in a clothes dryer. He isn't even fighting it. His body twists halfway

up the side and …plop…halfway up the side and…plop…
halfway up the side and…plop.

We obviously have no means to stop the tube so Delores
darts in and plunges into him like a fullback on a football team
knocking Bob out the other side. Then Delores grabs onto the
ridges in the conveyor belt and lets it pull her up. Bob follows
up right behind her. Telisia and I shove the glasses back on so we
can see the rest. Bob and Delores are on the tiny landing that
connects to the beam. Delores motions to him that she is going
first. She moves across the beam in small bursts as she waits for
the pendulums to swing before proceeding a few more steps.
Delores is almost there when the last pendulum crashes into her
body. Cleverly, she latches her arms around the sandbag and
swings with it. It swings back and forth over the beam a couple
of times before Delores finally lets go, barely catching the beam
with her arms. She pulls herself back onto it and rushes the few
steps she has left to the end where she leaps down to the trampoline mat. Bob appears to have his bearings back together after
the spinning tunnel catastrophe, and he eases out onto the
beam. He seems to be timing each step just right with the
swinging of the sandbags. As soon as the last one passes in front
of him, Bob leaps to the end of the beam and cascades onto the
trampoline mat beside Delores.

Delores and Bob stare at the hurdles of fire, and then they
just sit down on the trampoline. I take off my glasses. Nudging
Telisia I ask, "You want to see if we can catch up?"

"We have to give it a try sooner or later. I'm in."

I dart into the tunnel with Telisia right behind me. My little
sister and I used to love to go to the funhouse at the fair, so I am
a master at the twisting tunnel. In a second, I am out the other
side. When I turn around, Telisia is rolling out. We claw into the
conveyor belt and ride to the top where the sandbags are swaying
back and forth across the beam. Telisia steps out onto the beam
and completely misjudges the timing and the size of the sandbags. The first bag pounds into her with a thud, and I hear the
breath leave her body as the bag pummels her off the beam. She

sails through the air and then drops the ten feet down to the safety mat below. Telisia is moving around on the mat so she must be alright. She tries to say something, but she hasn't caught her breath yet. She finally just waves her hand signaling me to go on. I place one foot on the beam and wait for the first sandbag. Pushing off with the other foot, I make two quick steps to position myself on the beam between the paths of the swinging bags. I suck in a breath and hold it waiting for the second bag to pass by when the mechanical buzz of the equipment falls silent. The sandbags slow coming to a stop over the beam, and a computerized voice sounds, "Your time is up. Please exit."

I am dumbfounded. How can we be out of time already? I hadn't noticed, but there are metal escape ladders located around the course that lead back to the entry level. We migrate toward the door from where we are.

I am already on the same level as the exit, so I am the first one out. My feet plod down the hall to my room dragging my broken spirit behind me. I can't believe that we didn't accomplish more during our practice session. The possibility that we may not pass level two surrounds me in a cloud of darkness.

The punches keep coming as an instant alarm sets off through my whole body. I need a shower, and the only option is the shower everyone else in my room uses. If I am taking a shower that is covered in other people's germs, how am I supposed to get clean? I will leave the shower covered in more germs than when I went in. As silly as the rational part of my brain tells me it is, the obsessive-compulsive part senses impending doom. *God, please take control of my thoughts.*

Since I am covered in sweat, and it is almost dinner, I have no time to procrastinate. I grab a towel, my dark blue jumpsuit, and shoes and head to the shower. *Great.* I think. *There is no clean place to lay my towel and clothes, and why could they not give us shower shoes?* I take a deep breath. I go back out of the shower and grab paper towels to lay my towel and clothes on. I am ready now. Another deep breath. *Okay. Of all the things I am facing in this place, why is taking a shower the thing that is bringing me down. Just get it over with.*

For the Lord your God is with you wherever you go. I guess that means he is with me through this too. I force myself to not even think about where I am. Hurrying as quickly as I can, I get dressed and burst from the bathroom nearly plowing down Telisia and Delores.

I startle with a gasp, and my hand flies to my chest. "I am so sorry."

Delores's eyes bear into mine as she reaches out her hand and rests it on my shoulder. "Sarah, are you ok? Your face is so red. Why are you running from the bathroom?"

"It is hard to explain. I am feeling just a little stressed, that's all." Most people don't understand when you tell them that germs freak you out.

Telisia tries to put a positive edge in her tone. "Look, I know we had higher hopes for our practice today, but it was only the first day. Tomorrow we will get farther."

"I know. We make a great team. We will get it."

"You must have booked it back here after practice. We tried to find you." Delores utters as she walks into the bathroom.

"I feel so bad, you guys. I wasn't thinking. That was rude of me to leave. I needed a shower so I thought I would just see you guys here."

Delores laughs. "No big deal. We were just worried when you took off. We thought you were upset."

"Well, I really am sorry. Get ready, and I will wait for you. We can walk to the dining room together."

DELORES AND TELISIA emerge from the bathroom much calmer than I did. It is amazing that I have known them for such a short time because they feel like family. Again, God has provided for me. I believe they feel the same way because they did seem genuinely worried about me, and they didn't even think I was an idiot for my crazy behavior.

Everyone else is already in the dining room including Ash. He is sitting with Rose, Daisy, and Thorn talking like everything is normal, and I am pretty sure that he just cracked a little smile. Fighting the urge to rush over and ask him what happened, I sit down to eat first.

Bob must be starved because he rips the lid from his tray and already has his mouth full before he even reaches a sitting position. Delores is between me and Telisia again. She gently touches our hands and lowers her head. Bob doesn't let go of his fork, but somehow Telisia gets his hand anyway. Delores thanks God for providing for us.

I don't mean to stare, but my eyes keep flashing over to Ash. His relaxed demeanor has me confused. Anxious to hear Ash's story, I try to use Bob's eating tactics pushing in as much food as I can in record time. I start with the salmon which is surprisingly good. I prefer it with the skin on, but it is still good. Next, I try to scarf down the rice, but it has a pasty consistency, so I dump the broccoli on top of it and mix it together.

After I guzzle the water, I pile everything on my tray and watch for Ash to get up to take his to the counter. Finally, he slides his chair back and stands. I grab my tray so I can try to get to the counter at the same time he does.

"Hey, Ash! How are you doing?"

"I am okay. It has been a long day. Hard to believe it is only day one of level two."

"Tell me about it. This one day has felt more like a month." I step a little closer. "I have been really worried about you since they took you away earlier. I have heard that reprimanding is a bad experience."

"No. Actually, I left reprimanding feeling much better than I did before I went. The worst part was waking up tied down to that table."

"So, you didn't have any sort of nightmare?" I ask in a quiet voice.

"I did have something like a dream.... I guess it was a dream. It felt like it really happened though."

"I don't understand. You don't seem bothered or distressed by it."

"It wasn't bad. See, I was lying down. Below me, out of the darkness, were these weird, glowing, withered-looking hands with sharp nails stretching and grabbing at me, but their fingers never could make it high enough to get to me. And while the hands were clawing at me, there were these discreet, faint voices trying to reach and pull me down in ways the hands couldn't by telling me I was a failure, that I was letting my team down, and that my team would never pass because of me. But then above me was this glittery bright light. As I stared up at the light, I could feel this cool breeze passing over me. It was like I was sitting on the beach right next to the ocean. The rotten, rancid odor was replaced with the scent of fresh flowers. A voice boomed from above. The voice was so loud that it drowned out the vile whispers, and as the voice spoke, a strange peacefulness filled me. The voice said, 'Do not fear. They cannot touch you. They can never touch you. You belong to me. You have nothing to fear for I am right here with you.' After that, I woke up strapped to a table. A weird robot told me I was free to go, but they would be keeping an eye on me since I am now considered a rulebreaker."

How weird. I wonder why Ash's experience is different. It doesn't make sense.

"Sarah...everything ok?"

"Huh...oh sorry. I zoned out for a second. I was just wondering why your dream, or whatever it is they make you go through, is different. The other stories I have heard about reprimanding are terrible."

"Really?"

"Well, Bob was really shaken. And another person's story was exactly the same as Bob's."

Ash scratches his head. "Hmmm. That is strange. I guess I am just a weirdo."

"You are not. I am just thankful you are okay. I was so worried. And I know you are discouraged by this obstacle course, but we are all going to help you get through it. So, don't stress about it." With a smile, I lightly punch his shoulder and walk away.

Chapter Twelve

I wake up the next morning exhausted. Between the tiny cot with the super-thin mattress, Telisia sobbing half the night, and the million questions about this training gig spinning in my head, I might have gotten two hours of sleep. And since coffee is not on the menu, I foresee a very long day.

I get dressed and kneel by my cot to pray. As I pray, the fuzziness fades, and I sense God's hand motivating me. Normally, I would read my Bible at this time, but, even without my Bible in front of me, God shows me his word. Jeremiah 29:11 scrolls through my mind. "For I know the plans I have for you," declares the Lord, "plans to prosper you and not to harm you, plans to give you hope and a future." Suddenly I am reminded that I didn't have a choice in this. God already knew I would be in this place long before I was born, so this has to be part of his plan.

With God's reminder that he has a plan for me, I push myself to my feet ready to battle the day. I notice the other girls are heading to the door for breakfast, so I rush to catch up.

In the dining room, the repeats appear to have adapted to

the sleeping conditions. They are all lively and well groomed. On the contrary, our team couldn't look much worse. Bob has a bad case of bed head, Telisia's whole face is puffy from sobbing, and Delores and I need toothpicks to prop our eyelids open. I guess if the other teams look that good, there is hope it will get better. I lead our blessing, and then we just eat in silence. I think we are too beat to speak.

After breakfast, I go straight to hypnosis which I still have to fake. Apparently, hypnosis doesn't work so well on a stressed-out obsessive compulsive. However, pretending to be hypnotized since I am deprived of caffeine and collapsing from exhaustion isn't that hard. Dr. Eckert babbles something about my name being Sarah Sanguine. I somehow don't hear anything else that he says until the end. I am thinking about how soon this will be over so I can take a rest break. But in the midst of all his slow enunciated speech, he quickly murmurs, "Denali is your savior."

My head jerks at his words. *What was he talking about, and why would he say that?* I catch myself and freeze, hoping he didn't see me react. I am supposed to be hypnotized.

Pronouncing each syllable with clarity, he drags out, "Sarah Sanguine has no other family." Then he rattles off lightning quick, "You are a follower of Denali."

A knot forms in my stomach. Maybe it is all about this special crime unit, but this just doesn't feel right. Dr. Eckert tells me to wake up. At least, I still have him fooled. I have an hour to change and get to cardio so if I hurry, hopefully, I can squeeze in a thirty-minute power nap.

As I stagger from fatigue down the hallway a voice filters from somewhere ahead of me. I ease up my pace and step softly to see if I can figure out where it is coming from. The room where we did our orientation is in that direction, and there is a hall that leads to the left just past it. I peer around the corner and notice the first door in that hallway is slightly ajar. I tiptoe a little farther toward the door following the sound. When I am about ten feet from the door, I recognize Dr. Fleming's voice. Tucking myself up against the wall, I get my ear as close to the opening as I can. She must be talking to someone on the phone because I am only getting her side of the conversation.

"Yes, sir. We are aware that there are still some inconsistencies in the new reprimanding system."

"Yes. We know about the last subject's experience, and we are working around the clock trying to figure out why this is only occurring in some of the trainees."

"No, I am sorry, sir. At this time, we do not have any conclusive theories. However, we understand the importance and urgency of our mission, and we are giving every effort to obtain an answer so that we can be sure no more inconsistencies occur."

"I understand, sir. I will be in touch soon with an update."

My heart is racing, and I back away from the door quickly. I cannot let her find me listening. I turn and make each step as light and gentle as possible. I am almost to the end of the hall where I can escape around the corner out of sight when I hear the clack of her heels.

"Ms. Sanguine!" she yells.

I flip around. "Hello, Dr. Fleming."

She takes a few steps toward me. "What are you doing in this hallway? Nothing on your schedule requires your presence in this wing."

"I know. I accidentally took a wrong turn. I just came from hypnosis, and I was going back to my room for a quick rest before cardio. I guess I am somehow disoriented from the lack of sleep I received last night and the sudden absence of caffeine from my morning. I apologize. It won't happen again."

Her scowling tone makes me tremble. "I hope, for your sake, Ms. Sanguine, that it does not. As far as lack of sleep, did the headphones you received in your case not help?"

"The headphones? Oh, I forgot about those."

"Well, they were given to you for a reason. Be sure to wear them tonight. Now, do you know how to get back to your room?"

"Yes, Dr. Fleming. I turned, and I should have gone straight."

"Very well then. Be on your way." Her eyes are like lasers cutting straight through me. "Just be sure this quick rest of yours doesn't make you late for your cardio session."

"Yes, ma'am. I will definitely be on time." I quicken my pace down the hall. "Have a good day Dr. Fleming."

"You, too, Ms. Sanguine."

OVERCOME WITH CONFUSION, I fall onto my cot. Squeezing my eyes tight, I play Dr. Fleming's phone conversation over in my head trying to make sense out of her words. *Why did she refer to us as subjects? Subjects usually belong in an experiment. Ok, I am thinking too far into one little statement. Don't overreact. Maybe Denali is considering Soldiers Against Crime experimental until it succeeds in reducing the crime rate. Ok, that answers that. On to the next question. It sounded like this form of reprimanding is new or has been changed recently...and Ash must be one of the subjects that she was talking about that had an inconsistency. So now I know for a fact that Bob did not just have a random nightmare. His nightmare, or whatever it is, was part of his reprimanding. But what did happen with Ash? Why did he have a different version? How can I find answers?*

The tight muscles in my neck send pain up and over the top of my head. I reach one hand at a time and press hard on the pressure points in my shoulders rubbing in tiny circles, but the tension won't release.

Twenty minutes pass, and if it is possible, my muscles have taken on even more knots. I get my workout clothes from my locker and head to the bathroom. Closing the curtain to the dressing room, I reach down to remove my shoe boots. As I untie them, I remember Steve's note hidden in the sole. I wonder if I can sneak a peek at it without anyone knowing. As I am bent over, I try to conceal the shoe with my body and look down in it. I give the shoe a couple of quick shakes until the note slides into view.

NEVER FORGET.... Do not be afraid. For the
Lord your God is with you wherever you go!

Hmmm. I didn't notice those underlined letters before. I wonder why he did that. I can't analyze it now though. I can only stare at my shoe for so long without it looking suspicious. I finish dressing in my workout clothes and sneakers, put my boots and jumpsuit in my locker, and head to cardio. I hope I run again today. I really need the stress release, and I do my best thinking while I am running.

CARTOON DENALI LEADS me in some stretches, and then the voice directs me to move to the giant belt. "Today's run is on the Winsor Trail in the Santa Fe National Forest."

Thank goodness I get to run. The belt starts to move, and I start walking along the dirt path. On the big screen, the sky is streaked with red as the orange sun is dropping behind the tops of the towering ponderosa pines. After a minute, I increase to a jog letting my mind take in the beauty of the forest. Junipers go as far as the eye can see on both sides of the dirt trail.

As my feet pound the earth, I meditate on the note and the underlined letters. Steve underlined the letters for a reason, and I need to find a way to study them. I increase my speed from a jog to a run.

The high-definition resolution on the huge screen details the tiny grains of dirt on the path and the individual pine needles covering the forest floor. The tree limbs even sway in the breeze. Being outdoors always gives me a mental boost, and considering this place doesn't even have a window, I am in dire need of an outdoor experience. I run on the trail from dense trees through an outcropping of jagged boulders. With my arms and legs pumping and my body producing endorphins that is melting the stress with every step, the positive energy starts flowing through me. On my runner's high, for a moment I forget where I am until I round the bend, and my heart crashes to my feet.

On a huge boulder sitting at the edge of the trail are three diamondbacks. The venomous reptiles lay in tight coils on the rocks. I suppose they were soaking up the last bit of sun until my presence sent them into defense mode. Now each of their heads are pulled back like a stone in slingshot, and their tails are sending out an audible warning. There is no way past unless I veer way off the trail, and the dusk sky tells me that going off course is a bad idea. Unfortunately, the snakes' hissing and their rattles buzzing leave me no choice.

Reality takes hold of me snapping me from the anxiety of being lost because even though the sound of pine needles crunching under my feet sounds so real, I remember that there is a black conveyor belt beneath me. I relax and just trudge along at a steady pace through the virtual woods. A deer in a clearing ahead takes my focus away from the snakes. I slow down to admire the delicate creature as it munches on some leaves. Suddenly out of nowhere something comes leaping through the air and plows down on top of the doe. The deer crumples to the ground pinned beneath its attacker. In one swift move, the predator's fangs sink into the flesh on the back of the poor critter's neck. As the mountain lion's jaws clamp shut, the deer's flopping body is rendered still and lifeless. I come to a dead stop frozen in my tracks which is apparently against the rules because a deafening siren wails in rhythm with a flickering light that illuminates the entire room in flashes of red. Like a foghorn, the automated voice commands, "Please continue your run. Your time has not expired. I repeat, your time has not expired. Please continue your run."

I move my feet, and the siren automatically silences along with the voice. The mountain lion is still there with its hungry eyes glowing in the darkness. The eyes are fixated in my direction. Instead of devouring the deer, the giant cat is stalking new prey. Even with the knowledge that this is just a simulation, my body is reacting in survival mode. I ease backward with marshmallow feet trying hard not to crunch the leaves as I step. As long as I am moving the belt in some way, the alarm doesn't sound. I decide it is time to run because I have no desire to be cat food even in a pretend world. My arm scrapes on rough bark as I zig zag in and out between the trees with my legs stretching in the longest strides I can manage. I look for a place to hide, but that would be impossible with this innate predator. Behind me, the crunch of the pine needles under the giant paws of the lion is growing closer. I know the cougar is right at my back, or he would be if he weren't a character on a giant screen. That reminder does not help because the belt gives a hard, quick jerk beneath my feet tripping me. Inertia keeps my upper body moving forward while my legs kick out behind me. I stretch out my hands to catch myself, but my arms move with the belt and fold beneath my body. My face plasters against the moving rubber belt. The treadmill comes to an abrupt halt, and the automated voice comes through the speaker as though nothing out of the ordinary has happened. "Your run is complete. You may now move back to the red circle for your cool-down stretches."

I peel my face and my aching body from the floor and stumble over to the circle. Following cartoon Denali's lead, I try to bend and put my hands flat on the floor stretching my hamstrings. The pulling on the muscles down the back of my legs hurts and feels good all at the same time. I swivel my head from side to side loosening my neck. The real stress release comes from laughing at cartoon Denali. His cartoon head is too big to roll side to side. Instead, he looks like a bobblehead figurine.

I move over to the weight training room. Cartoon Denali announces that today will be a core strength workout, and a sigh of relief escapes me. I don't think I could survive a leg work out after the mountain lion incident. It is funny though. Cartoon Denali's biceps have grown since yesterday.

Chapter Thirteen

After planks, planks, and more planks, I make it back to my room for a shower. Right now, I am too drained to feel like worrying about the shared bathroom. The problem is OCD does not work that way. Being tired makes it harder for me to cast out irrational thinking. So, with panic-filled knots, I gather my extra clothes and plod toward the source of my illogical fear. I just want to be able to relax for a minute and feel hot water on my aching muscles.

As I enter the bathroom, my journey to battle phantom killer germs is interrupted by the sounds of sobbing and people talking. The action is coming from the dressing room in the back corner, so I move closer. Telisia is sitting on the floor of the dressing room with her arms wrapped tightly around her knees hugging them to her chest, and her shaking body is rocking back and forth. Delores and Darla are squatted down next to her. Darla has one hand pressed to the back of her neck, and her other hand is clasped around the back of Telisia's neck. Delores has one hand on the back of her own neck, and when she sees me, she springs to her feet with a mad dash and cups the back of my neck with her other hand.

"Wh-wh-what is going on?" I sputter in alarm.

Delores speaks so low that I literally have to read her lips. "The chip...it's how they hear."

I ponder on her words trying to figure out what she is talking about when suddenly the light bulb in my head powers on. *The chip...that is why they have their hands on their neck...somehow that mutes out the sound, and they can't hear us.*

Delores pulls me outside the dressing room, and I try to watch her lips as she starts mouthing words to me again. "Do you feel how hard I am squeezing your neck?"

I nod my head up and down.

"Okay. As soon as I move my hand, put your hand there exactly the same way that mine is now."

I do as she says. Once we have traded out our hands, I ask, "So there aren't any cameras?"

"There are, but not in the bathroom that we know of. In here they can only hear through the chips that they put in our necks. If you hold your hand tightly over it, it muffles the sound."

A little skeptical, my eyes narrow. "How do you know?"

"Darla told me, and actually, I am not sure how she knows." Delores's eyes roll toward the ceiling and her forehead crinkles. From her expression, I can imagine the wheels turning in her mind. "But so far, they haven't seemed to have heard us, or I am sure at least Dr. Fleming would have been in here by now."

Immediately, that light bulb in my mind flashes again. I can study Steve's note in here. "So, what is wrong with Telisia?"

Delores motions for us to move a little farther from the dressing room door. After we are a few steps away, Delores whispers, "Apparently Telisia has a child. Obviously, that means she does not want a new identity nor is she able to leave her old life behind. She wants to go home to her baby, and since she is being forced to forget her own child, Telisia is falling apart."

I glare at Delores in disbelief. "Why would they choose her if she has to leave a child? How can they expect her to forget about her baby and start a new life?" The more I process

Delores's words, the more my voice fills with hostility. "How can they take a child's mother away?"

"I know." Pools start to form in the corner of Delores's eyes. "That is why the poor woman sobs all night long. Like the rest of us, she had no choice in coming here, and on top of that, she had no idea that she would never be able to see her child again."

I squeeze the back of my neck so hard it hurts as anger takes control of my muscles. I look back at Darla trying to console Telisia. "So how long have you guys been in here with her. I mean, you haven't missed anything on your schedule, have you?"

"Darla and I got back to our room at the same time and found her curled up on her bed weeping uncontrollably into her pillow. Her body was shaking so bad that the legs of her cot was vibrating on the concrete floor. We got her in here as quickly as we could to try and get her calmed before the evildoers come and reprimand her or something. I am afraid that she has missed part of her schedule. Telisia didn't look like she had even gotten out of bed today."

"Oh no. That is not good at all. We have to come up with something to help her. There is no way that Telisia can handle reprimanding in the state that she is in."

Those words just pass through my lips when the sound of clacking heels approaches. Delores coughs getting Darla's attention, and we all let go of our necks.

Dr. Fleming flings open the bathroom door. She pulls her glasses down on the bridge of her nose, and her unblinking eyes burn right through us. "Hello, ladies. What is going on in here? I am looking for Telisia."

Words just start pouring from my mouth with no plan whatsoever. "Dr. Fleming, I am so glad you are here. We found Telisia when we got back to the room. She is very ill. Her entire body is trembling, and she appears to be in a great deal of pain. We helped her in here and got some cold rags on her face, but the pain seems to be worsening. The way she is doubled over, I am afraid it could be appendicitis."

Dr. Fleming's face loses its hard lines as her eyes observe

Telisia's condition. Dr. Fleming rushes toward her with alarm ringing in her voice. "Oh dear. Let me take a look at her. How long has she been like this?"

"We aren't sure," Darla answers as she backs away and lets Dr. Fleming in. "But she doesn't look like she has been out of bed. She seems to be in too much pain to speak."

Dr. Fleming kneels on the floor and touches the back of her hand to Telisia's forehead. "Telisia, can you speak to me? How long have you been feeling ill?"

Telisia stares straight ahead with no response other than her trembling body and streaming tears.

"Ok, Telisia. I am going to press my fingers to your wrist and check your pulse." Dr. Fleming uses the stopwatch on her tablet and counts under her breath. "Telisia, your pulse is extremely low. I am sending a message to Dr. Eckert. He should be here in a moment."

Less than two minutes pass when Dr. Eckert storms through the door with two men behind him pushing a gurney. With one knee on the floor next to her, Dr. Eckert listens to her heart with his stethoscope and checks her blood pressure. His forehead creases and his face takes on an ashen color. "Telisia," he almost hollers like she is hard of hearing, "we are going to help you onto the gurney and take you to the medical wing so we can check you further. Your blood pressure is low, and your heart has an irregular beat. I need to get you hooked up to a monitor so I can see what is going on."

The two men lift Telisia onto the gurney and push her out with Dr. Eckert behind them.

Dr. Fleming turns to us with her hardened face back on. Putting in her last two cents' worth before following Dr. Eckert, she scolds us. "Ladies, you should have gotten help instead of moving her. You are not doctors, so instead of trying to act like you are, seek help." She stomps from the bathroom making those heels clack even louder.

"I need to shower before lunch, but I want to pray for Telisia first. Do you guys want to pray with me? I believe there is power in praying together." An ocean forms in my eyes.

Delores eases up and wraps her arm around my shoulder. Her eyes drift over to Darla who is inspecting the floor with a blank stare on her face. "Darla, do you want to pray with us?"

"N-n-no, you girls go ahead." Darla stammers inching toward the door. "I didn't realize it was this late. I have to work on a plan for obstacle course practice."

As Darla leaves, Delores and I get down on our knees on the bathroom floor and beg God to help our friend. Amazing, I know, that I don't even flinch at my knees touching the bath-room floor. Only fifteen minutes ago, I was having an anxiety attack about showering in here, but now I am so overcome with worry for Telisia that I don't even think about it. With every-thing I have witnessed and heard about my new friend's situa-tion, my obsessive-compulsive thoughts seem pretty petty.

After we pray, Delores embraces me in a hug. "It's going to be okay." She whispers in my ear. "And we know that in all things God works for the good of those who love him, who have been called according to his purpose. Romans 8:28." She lets go and stands up. "Now go get cleaned up for lunch. I will wait for you."

Chapter Fourteen

The rest of the day passes in a blur. I can only think of Telisia and wonder if she is going to be okay. Honestly, I doubt that she is getting the proper medical care she needs. We still have to go to obstacle course practice without Telisia. It goes slightly better than yesterday, and I mean only slightly because without Telisia, we really cannot have a complete practice. Poor Bob is struggling with parts of the course because he does not have enough arm strength to support his body weight.

The rotating tunnel sends Delores for a couple of flips, but she recovers and manages to crawl out. She breezes across the beam with the swinging sandbags this time, but the hurdles of fire are going to be tough for her. Even with her determination in jumping them, Delores's short legs just do not get her high enough, and she ends up with quite a few burns on her legs. That does not stop her though. Delores keeps right on moving, and luckily, she does have a lot of upper body strength, so she is able to climb with only her arms keeping her tender burned legs away from the rope.

I dash right through the tunnel, and almost time all the swinging sandbags correctly until the last one. When I realize that it is going to hit me before I can move past it, I wrap my arms around it. My body swings back and forth over the beam at least five times before I get up the nerve to jump. I use my feet to push off the sandbag, and somehow, I leap over the end of the beam and plummet down onto the trampoline. I land with a splat sprawled out on the mat like I have just done a belly flop in the pool. All the air leaves my body, and it takes a bit before I fill my lungs with a good breath. Once I recover, I clear all the hurdles, climb the rope, swing from bar to bar, and capture the flag.

Bob scoots through the tunnel on his butt. I am not quite sure how he makes that work, but the important thing is, he does. The sandbags and the fire hurdles give him no problem. However, the rest of the course is a different story. After ten minutes of pulling, tugging, jumping, and swinging on that rope, he gives up on being able to climb it today. I am pretty certain that he is not going to be able to do the monkey bars either. Two weeks is not going to be enough time for him to develop the arm strength he needs, and I don't know how we are supposed to fix that.

Before bedtime, Dr. Eckert pushes Telisia back into our room and helps her onto her cot. Telisia does not look all that good. Her complexion is dull and pasty, and she isn't moving at all. Her glassy eyes are not even blinking.

Expecting him not to be honest, I try to read his facial expression as I ask, "Dr. Eckert, is she going to be okay?"

"She is still not speaking, but since her vitals are back to normal, we are letting her sleep on her own cot tonight. I will come back in the morning and examine her again." He turns and pushes the wheelchair toward the door. "Goodnight, Ms. Sanguine."

"Goodnight, Dr. Eckert."

I sit down on the edge of Telisia's cot. "Telisia, I am so sorry.

We haven't known each other that long, but our situation has bonded us together. You and Delores and me...we are already like sisters. Oh, how I wish I had some words that could ease your pain." I stroke the hair away from Telisia's face. Laying my hand on her arm, I ask God to give her peace. Through watery eyes, I gaze down at her still form. Aside from shallow breaths, she appears as an empty shell. "I love you, sister."

Rising to my feet, I plod over to my locker and get my headphones. Maybe I will sleep better if I can drown out my surroundings. I put them on and lie down on my cot.

The roar of crashing ocean waves filter through the headphones. For a bit, I try to imagine that I am in the safe haven of my own apartment lying in my own bed with the soothing noise of my sound machine in the background. I pretend that this whole Denali crime unit training thing is just a bad dream. My exhaustion finally takes over.

I don't know what time it is or how long I have slept, but the urge to go to the bathroom awakens me. The headphones now have words faintly accompanying the crashing waves of the ocean. "Denali...Denali...Denali...Denali," chants through the wind. I rip the headphones off. *What is up with this guy? He is so full of himself.* This takes weird to a whole new level.

After I go to the bathroom, I lie back down wide awake. My eyes lock on the ceiling, and I space out with the thoughts inside my head until it is time to get up. My mind rolls overanalyzing each event. First, it's the photo of Denali as the focal point in the hypnosis sessions, then Eckert's quick interjections of Denali praises during hypnosis, and now headphones that whisper his name while I sleep. How does any of this relate to special crime unit training?

Finally, people begin to stir. I get up and stumble to my locker to get my jumpsuit and boots.

"Sarah. Sarah...come quick!"

Chapter Fifteen

Delores is hovering beside Telisia's cot with one hand pressed against her chest and her other hand covering her mouth. With bulging eyes, Delores's body starts to sway side to side. I dart over to her catching her around the waist.

As Delores crashes into my arms, her finger points to Telisia's lifeless body. I stand frozen with Delores's weight resting against me. I tell myself to look away, but instead, my wide gaze locks on Telisia's pale form. The huge pupils in her partially open eyes stare at the ceiling.

Delores is now crying hysterically, and Darla helps me sit her on the floor. I grab Telisia's wrist to check her pulse. I am not sure why because it is obvious, but it is the only thing I can think to do. At the touch of her arm, I realize her body is already entering rigor mortis. There is no holding back the flood of tears that spills from my eyes.

Dr. Eckert bursts through the door with Dr. Fleming right behind him. Almost yelling, he orders us to clear the room.

We all move to the hallway and wait in silence except for a few whimpers that escape with falling tears. A few minutes pass and Dr. Eckert steps out of our room. His face is devoid of emotion, and in a gravelly voice, he says, "I am sorry to inform you that Telisia is no longer with us. We ran some tests yesterday and found that she had a heart condition we were unaware of. If you would please just give us a few more minutes, I will let you know when you can come back in." Dr. Eckert goes back in the room and closes the door.

Rose, Daisy, Darla, Delores, and I stand in the hallway, shock penetrating each of us to the bone. We huddle together and literally cry our eyes out for the loss of someone we barely knew. And even though we had met her only days before, this place had made us family. I don't care what Dr. Eckert wants us to believe, I know Telisia died from a broken heart. I studied nursing for a year before I switched to criminal justice. She had all the symptoms of broken heart syndrome. I can't help but wonder if I could have helped her. *What if I had taken the time to notice how much pain she was in? What if?*

The same two men from yesterday push a gurney down the hall and enter our room. A few minutes later they come back out with Telisia's body covered in a white sheet, and Dr. Eckert tells us we can go back in. Chills climb up my spine and spread to my whole body as I walk back into the room, and to add to the misery, Dr. Fleming is still here.

I try to block out her cold, uncaring tone, but her icy personality is impossible to ignore. "Attention, ladies. I know this has been a difficult morning, but we are still here to train. So, pull yourselves together and get ready for breakfast. You have a schedule to keep today. Sarah and Delores, I have spoken with Denali already, and since there is no one else here to fill Telisia's spot on your team, you will have a team of three. Now, hop to it. You are going to be late." She turns, and every click of her heels on the floor raises the temperature of my blood.

"Unbelievable!" Delores's face reddens, and her taut voice escalates as she speaks. "A person just died, and she is worried about the schedule. I would like to tell her what she can do with her schedule."

"I think you just did." I gesture nonchalantly toward my neck.

"Well…," she voices even louder, "she needs to know. My friend died, and I don't feel like eating, or running, or being hypnotized."

As much as I agree with Delores, I don't want anyone else hurt. I take Delores by the arm before anything worse escapes her mouth. "Come on. Let's go to the bathroom and get freshened up. I need some more tissues."

ROSE IS right on our heels as we enter the bathroom. She grabs her neck and signals for us to do the same. Apparently, everyone but me knew about this neck thing.

She leans in close to our faces. "I just wanted to tell you guys that I have seen Telisia writing in her journal. You know the ones that we got in those black cases. I thought maybe if you could somehow get hold of it before they take her things that it might say something about her family."

"Thanks, Rose." I glance back and forth from her to Delores. "I am sure it is in her locker, but how can we get it without them seeing?"

"We have to. If we ever get out of here, we owe it to Telisia to find her family and tell them what happened to her." Delores's face hardens with determination. "I will cause a distraction. Sarah, you get in that locker and find it. We have to act fast because they will probably be back to take her things soon."

Before I can stop her, Delores is out the door. I trudge after her, but there is no catching her fast pace. She is on a mission. Weaving through the cots, she crosses the room and storms into the hall. "Dr. Fleming," she screams, "I need to speak with Denali immediately!"

I stop in the middle of our room listening to Delores shout her demands. My heart beats out of control as I anticipate when to search for the journal. The screaming ceases, and Delores goes silent. Footfalls rush through the hallway. I run to the locker as quick as I can, jerking the door open. I don't see anything but clothes and the case. I scoot close to the locker hovering my body so that it blocks what I am doing from sight. Grabbing the case, I pop the latch. *Thank goodness!* Right there on top is the journal. I pluck it out, slide the book inside my jumpsuit, and close the case. I take a step back and flip aside the contents of one of the shelves like I am still looking for something. Leisurely, I close the door appearing to be walking away empty handed. *Now what?* I stroll over and open my locker. I lean forward and slip the journal under my workout clothes. With my heart still hammering away on the wall of my chest, I dart to the hallway hoping there is some way to help Delores, but the men are already lugging her unconscious body away.

My stomach immediately shifts to my throat. Clasping my hands over my mouth, I run to the bathroom thinking that I am not going to make it. Since I haven't had breakfast, nothing but acid comes up. But my stomach keeps contracting forcing my body to fold in half and heave. Almost five minutes pass before I can stand up straight without gagging.

"Sarah, are you alright?" Darla's voice echoes through the bathroom.

Sucking in a deep breath, I push out a hoarse answer. "My stomach is just upset from the stress of the morning. I will be fine. It is Delores we need to worry about." I open the stall door, and Darla hands me a cold rag. "Thanks!"

"Sarah, Delores will be fine. So far, everyone has survived reprimanding. However, the experience is pretty traumatic so she will just need a lot of support from us afterwards."

"Delores doesn't deserve to go through that."

"No one does." Darla's anger explodes in her tone. "But we can't be there for her if we are in trouble ourselves. So, get ready for breakfast before we are late."

Chapter Sixteen

I float through the next eight hours checking the time every ten minutes that I am not adhering to my schedule. I can't help thinking that Delores has been gone way too long.

Obstacle course practice is a disaster. It is just Bob and me. I cannot focus. The sandbags aren't the problem. I just lose my balance and fall off the beam. On the other hand, Bob sails right through until he gets to the rope. He grabs on, takes a few jumps, and gives up. He blames it on the absence of Delores's positive energy.

Finally, after dinner, as I traipse in circles along the walls of the room, wringing my sweaty hands together, Delores parades through the door. Relief erases proper conduct, and I leap across two cots engulfing her in a hug.

"Delores, I was so worried. Are you okay?"

"I am fine." She manages to crack a little smile even though I think I may actually be squeezing the breath out of her. "But I really have to go to the bathroom so if you want to talk to me, you will have to follow me in there."

I take the hint and tag along after her to the bathroom. She heads to the back-dressing room and covers the chip in her neck with her hand. I follow suit eager to hear what she has to say.

"Please tell me you got it." Delores looks at me hopefully.

"I did. It is in my locker under my clothes."

"Yes, yes, yes. Ok. We have to find a way to sneak in here and check it out tonight while everyone is asleep. Meet me in here at two a.m. Just act like you are getting up to go to the bathroom. I will get up a little bit before, so it doesn't look weird that we are going at the same time."

"Okay. But, right now, tell me what happened today. Was it horrible?"

"No. I actually feel amazing...almost invincible." Delores giggles. "I know you are worried about the description that Bob gave of his reprimanding. Well, my experience was similar, I guess. I did wake up strapped to a table, and there was a weird robot man there when I woke up. But, for me, the dream thing was a little different. I was lying down, and it was hot and dark, really dark. There were these hands, disgusting and wrinkled, with long, skinny fingers reaching up for me, clawing at me. And I could hear these little whispering voices uttering things like, 'you are nothing...you are a failure...you are a horrible friend...you let Telisia die.' That was horrible. But then all at once, I could feel this cool breeze wash over me, and up above was a bright light. Then, another voice boomed like thunder commanding the whispers to stop. After that, the loud voice comforted and consoled me. 'You are mine. They can never hurt you. Telisia didn't die. I just called her home. Do not fear because I hold you in my hands. I am with you always.' Sarah, I honestly have never felt so calm or so loved as I did when that voice spoke."

I bite my lip as I replay my conversation with Ash. "Delores, this thing is so weird. I mean Darla and Bob's description sounded so terrible, and they were so traumatized after. But then, you and Ash had similar incidents that seem to have brought you both peace. On top of that, I overheard Dr. Fleming on the phone talking about an inconsistency in one of the reprimanding subjects. I assumed she was talking about Ash."

Delores shakes her head. "I really don't know. The robot kept me in there for hours after I woke up. He…the robot…had all these wires connected to my head, and just kept ranting to himself about why there were no signs of distress. Obviously, their method of punishment isn't effective on everyone, and they can't figure out why."

"Uuuugh! This whole place has my brain feeling like a wind-mill before a hurricane." I rub my temple with my free hand. "And her use of the word 'subject' keeps popping back into my head. Why did she call us 'subjects'?"

"Try to relax. We will take the questions one at a time. First, let's see if there is anything in that journal that would help us notify Telisia's family. Don't forget our little meeting tonight!"

I CAN'T SLEEP because I keep worrying that I won't wake up to meet Delores. I toss and turn, check the time and toss and turn some more. Of course, my eyelids grow heavy, and my consciousness starts to fade about twenty minutes until two when Delores tiptoes to the bathroom. The journal is beneath my pillow, so I gently slip it out and slide it under my pajama shirt. I definitely do not want anyone to see me carrying it into the bathroom. At two o'clock, I push back my blanket, ease off my cot, and softly make my way across the room.

Delores is in the back-dressing room, and as soon as she sees me, she cusps her hand behind her neck. I do the same and pull out the journal.

"Did anyone see you come in?" Delores peers out of the dressing room toward the door.

"No. I don't think so. Everyone appeared to be asleep."

We work together to open the journal and flip through it. The task is more difficult than one would expect because we each only have one free hand. I hold the journal with one hand using my thumb to keep it open, and she flips the pages.

Delores keeps flipping the pages back and forth. "I just don't understand. Rose said she saw Telisia write in this thing. There is nothing here. Every page is blank."

"Look at the spine of the journal though. It has creases in it like it has been opened quite a bit. And, you know, I even remember seeing Telisia with it once. Why would it be opened enough to form a crease, but not be used?"

"I don't know," Delores sighs. "But it doesn't change the fact that this is a blank book. We better get back to bed and get some sleep."

I tuck the journal back under my shirt. Delores leaves first, and I wait about fifteen minutes then creep back to my cot. I don't know that sleep is going to be possible though with all these unanswered questions.

AFTER A RESTLESS NIGHT of flipping and flopping on my cot, I get up as soon as the first person moves. I go to my locker and slip the journal back under my workout clothes. Curious though, I pull my journal out. The spine on my journal is still stiff since I have never actually opened it. I take it back to my cot and pull off the pen attached to it. I really don't know what to write or even what I am allowed to write so I just print 'Sarah Sanguine' on the first page. As I sit tapping my fingers on the page trying to think of what else I could write, the 'Sarah Sanguine" gets lighter. After another couple of minutes, the page is blank. A smile plasters across my face.

Delores comes trotting over. She looks like a zombie with the bags under her eyes and her hair sticking up in all directions.

"Hey, Delores. Have you ever tried writing in your journal?"

"No," she says yawning. "Why?"

"Because I just wrote my name, and it disappeared." I turn the journal around and show her.

Her eyes widen. "Disappearing ink." Delores sits down next to me on my cot cleverly acting like she is putting her arm around me. She is suddenly wide awake. When her arm snugly covers my neck, she stretches and starts rubbing the back of her own neck. Delores's mouth curves with a sneaky grin. "We need heat!"

"Heat?"

"You never did science experiments in school?" she asks escalating her tone with a hint of surprise.

"Of course, I did...but apparently I missed the day that we used heat to read hidden messages."

She giggles. "Ha ha. You are so funny. We can try the blow dryer on the bathroom wall. Maybe it will get hot enough to heat the paper."

"Won't that be kind of loud at night when everyone is sleeping?"

"We are not waiting until tonight. We will do it now. There are no cameras in the bathroom so just sneak the journal in there. Come on. We don't have much time before breakfast."

I hurry to my locker, put my journal in, and take Telisia's out. With the journal tucked under my arm, I dash after Delores into the bathroom. She clicks on the blow dryer, and I open the journal to the first page. We work together without talking so we can use both our hands. As the page heats, writing starts to faintly appear. After another minute or so, the words become visible enough to make out. Delores and I hold the journal and read it silently.

My precious Aaron,

You have no idea how badly I miss you. I know that you are no longer in pain, but I don't want to live without seeing your face and wrapping my arms around you every day. I have been sent to this facility to train for a job that I thought was supposed to be an honor, but now they are trying to take away all that I have left of you. They have changed my name and gave me a whole new identity. I can't let them do this. I refuse to let them do this. My name is Joyce Archer, and I am the mother of Aaron Archer. That name ties me to you here in this world. They cannot and will not make me anyone else. I will always be your mother even though you are in Heaven now. I keep begging God to let me be there with you. I ask him each morning to give you a hug and a kiss from me. The only thing that keeps me going is knowing that one day I will see you again. Until then, I love you, my son.

Your mom

Tears slip down my face and drip onto my shirt. I feel my air constrict as a giant lump rises in my throat. My chest aches with physical pain as I absorb how much hurt Telisia has had to endure. This woman, my roommate, my teammate, my friend was trying to cope with all of this, and I never knew. I heard her sobs, but I never tried to find out.

I close my eyes as tight as I can. Pushing the lump back down, I snap out of my stupor and wipe the falling tears with the back of my hand. I have to focus on the fact that God has given Telisia eternal peace. He answered her prayer. She is where she wants to be. She is with her son, and neither of them are in pain anymore.

Without a word to each other, Delores and I close the journal because there is no need to invade Telisia's, I mean Joyce's, privacy anymore.

Chapter Seventeen

Another day passes as I robotically go through the motions. The things that normally would freak me out just fade into the background. Dr. Eckert's weird chants during hypnosis, the black bear that chased me as I biked the Ridgeline trail, and Bob doing even worse than yesterday at climbing the rope are all minute details in life compared to Telisia being gone.

I decide to tell Delores about Steve and the note. I want her to help me decode it. Before bed, I watch for her to go into the bathroom to brush her teeth and follow her. With a side tilt of my head, I signal to her to go into the back-dressing room. It's a little strange but putting my hand on the back of my neck is just a natural reflex now when I walk into the bathroom. Even more off the grid is that the bathroom is beginning to feel more like a safe haven where I can relax rather than a forbidden germ pit sending me into a panic attack. It is the only place I can truly have privacy or have a conversation that isn't being watched.

"What's up?" Delores asks, raising one brow.

"I need you to meet me in here again tonight. I have something to show you that I think you can help me with."

Delores's eyes bear into mine as if she is trying to determine if she should be worried. "Ok, how about the same time as last night. I will come in first."

I give her a thumbs up and walk out of the dressing room.

AT TWO A.M., I tiptoe into the bathroom and find Delores in our usual dressing room.

"So, what is this all about?" she asks.

"Are you sure that you never met anyone else in level one besides Dr. Eckert and Dr. Fleming?"

"I am positive. I woke up in a hospital room, you know, like after you come out of surgery. Then I met Dr. Eckert. He came in and released me to go to orientation. After he left, Dr. Fleming stormed in and led me out of the hospital wing."

"Weird," I tap my chin. "So, you never saw the robots either?"

"I saw a robot when I woke up strapped to that table. Remember? I told you about how it put those wires on my head."

"I know, but I am talking about when you had the chip inserted."

Delores scratches her head.

"Never mind, that's not really important." I sit down on the floor and prop up against the wall. "Just let me tell you what happened to me. I suppose I had just gotten the chip inserted in my neck. When I woke up the first time, there was this robot standing over me that was made to look like a woman. She called herself Shelly. She yelled for Herb, and a robot made to look like a man appeared. He or it gave me something that knocked me back out, then I wake up in a different room. This time a human was standing over me. His name was Steve, and he turned out to be super nice. I was scared, and he tried his best to comfort me. Anyway, he said he didn't make it through level three, and for some reason instead of exiling him, he was given a job in level one."

Delores clears her throat and curves one side of her mouth up into a half smile. "So, you met two robots and a man after your procedure?"

"Yes, but the story gets crazier. After he introduced himself, he asked my name. That is when he collapsed, and two men rushed in and took him away. A nurse came in and told me that he collapsed because he has low blood sugar, but the scenario was exactly the same as what has been happening when someone gets taken for reprimanding."

Completely enveloped in my words, Delores is sitting with her legs crisscrossed just like a little kid in story time. "So, what happened to Steve?"

"I don't know. That was the last I saw of him, and I really wish that I could find him. I need to know that he is okay."

"So, you want me to help you find him?"

"Well, it would be great if you could, but that is not why I asked you in here. You see, as Steve collapsed, he grabbed my hand giving me a little piece of paper. I have kept it hidden, but I think there is some kind of hidden message coded in it. I was hoping you could help me decode it." I pull out the little paper and hand it to Delores.

NEVER FORGET.... Do not be afraid. For the
Lord your God is with you wherever you go!

Delores's eyes squint, and she bites her tongue as she glares at the piece of paper. I am dying to know what she is thinking, but I sit quietly giving her time to concentrate.

"Well." Delores turns the paper for me to see. "The message is really pretty clear. If you just read the underlined letters backwards, you get '*go to door ten*'."

It takes me a few minutes, but I finally piece the letters together backwards. "Yeah, I see it. Delores, you are a genius." I lightly punch her shoulder. "Okay but wonder why he uses the number two. It would make more sense if it said *go to door ten.*"

"I know," she said rubbing her temple and then snickers. "That is the part the genius can't figure out."

"Well, I say we nonchalantly look for a door ten tomorrow as we go through our daily schedule. Maybe the 'two' thing will become obvious if we find it."

Delores gives a little nod. "Sounds good. We better get a little sleep while we can." She pats my hand. "We will figure this out and find Steve. You have my word on that." Delores jumps to her feet and slips out to the sleeping area.

DELORES and I have spent the last several days trying to eye the numbers on the doors as we meander the hallways to our scheduled destinations, but the problem is, there aren't any numbers on the doors like there was in level one. We are one week into our training, and adding to the stress, Bob is making no improvement in completing the obstacle course. Just to put it bluntly, he is doing worse.

I just finished my seventh session of pretending to be hypnotized. I cannot believe Dr. Eckert hasn't figured out that he is not really putting me in a trance.

Heading toward my room, I count the doors again trying to guess which one could be number ten, but I have no idea which end to count from. My head jerks up at the clanking of heels. The steps are approaching from the direction of the room where I overheard Dr. Fleming on the phone. A switch suddenly turns on the power to my brain. Delores and I have never looked for room ten in that hallway because we are only allowed to go where our schedule leads us. That wing is off limits to us.

I speed up trying to get to the entrance of the wing before Dr. Fleming leaves. Just as I get to the intersection of that hallway, I glance toward the sound of the clanking heels.

"Dr. Fleming," I say modulating my voice like I am surprised to see her. "It must be some kind of sign that I am running into you. I was just thinking that I should come and talk to you."

"Oh, really." Her tone seems a little cynical. "What's going on?"

"Could I talk to you somewhere," I lower my volume, "a bit more private?"

"Okay, Sarah follow me." Dr. Fleming turns and lets out a frustrated sigh.

Yes, I think to myself. *She is leading me down the forbidden hall.* Dr. Fleming stops and opens the door to the office that I overheard her talking in the other day. *Jackpot.* Above the door is a little plate with "Bldg. 2 Room 10" engraved on it.

Dr. Fleming holds out her arm motioning me on through the door. "Normally trainees are not allowed in here, but there are not many places to speak privately around this place." She closes the door behind her. "Now, Sarah, what seems to be the big problem?"

"I guess it is really nothing. It is just...well... you are a doctor, and since Telisia died, I just can't seem to shake this sadness. I am not even sure that is the best word to describe how I feel." I turn away using the opportunity to inspect the room as I am speaking. There is a desk situated in the middle and another door at the back of the room.

Meanwhile, I add a little drama in my voice for extra effect. "I realize that I had not known Telisia that long, but it is like we had already started a new family here. I think since we had to leave our families and everything we have known, we clung to each other a little harder and became close faster than normal."

Dr. Fleming eases up behind me and places her hand on my shoulder. "That makes sense. You all are filling the void in your life with each other, and now you are faced with not only erasing your real family from your life, but you have already lost a member of your new family."

Wow! Dr. Fleming does have feelings. "Yes. Exactly. And I feel as if I am just going to burst inside. It is like you said though. There is no privacy at all here. I want so badly to be alone and cry, but I can't because there is always someone there watching or listening. And I don't want to show weakness, I just need a few minutes to let out the stress."

"Sarah, I am glad you talked to me about this. I am going to let Dr. Eckert know so he can make some changes in your hypnosis session. Maybe he can help alleviate some of your pain with hypnosis. I am also going to see what I can do about adding a time and place to each of your schedules for some alone time."

Suddenly, the door opens causing both of us to jump. Dr. Fleming and I turn toward the door, and the face that is before me nearly makes my heart stop.

"Steve," Dr. Fleming exclaims, "I didn't know you were still here."

"Oh, I am so sorry for interrupting. I didn't realize you were in a meeting. I just wanted to let you know that I finished entering the code numbers from the new chips in the computer." As he completes his sentence, Steve looks away from Dr. Fleming, and his brown eyes burn into mine.

"Ok, thanks for finishing that up, Steve." Dr. Fleming glances back and forth between me and Steve apparently noticing that our eyes are locked on each other. "Oh, Steve you remember Sarah. She is the newbie you talked with after Herb thought she needed some extra sleep."

"Yes, I remember." His face flushes as he turns his gaze toward the floor. "That one had me a little worried. Herb has never put anyone to sleep for three days before." A tiny snicker slips out. He raises his head back up. "Hi, Sarah. It is nice to see you again."

"Nice to see you too. Actually, I have been pretty worried about you. The nurse said you fainted from low blood sugar. I am so glad to see that you are okay."

"Oh...that. Well, yes, I am fine. No need to worry. I must have forgotten to eat breakfast that day." His words seem shaky, and his jaw twitches as he speaks. Lying must not be his strong suit. He gives his attention back to Dr. Fleming. "I will let you two get back to your meeting. I better return to my post in building one. I have to keep an eye on Herb." He grins. "He has been known to cause a little trouble you know. Sorry again for the interruption." Steve crosses the room dragging his hand across this filing cabinet as he passes by it. "It really was nice bumping into you again, Sarah. Have a good rest of your day." He looks over his shoulder and gives a little wave as he exits through the door at the back. Above that door is a little plate that reads, "TUNNEL TO BLDG 1".

Dr. Fleming gives her focus back to me. "Sorry for his intrusion. He is not used to anyone else being in here." She grasps the sides of her head like she is trying to remember where we left off in our conversation. "Anyway, I will see if we can add at least a few minutes a day for some type of personal meditation. For now, try to put things in perspective. In reality, you barely knew Telisia. You are here to train, and that needs to be your primary focus."

"Yes, ma'am," I agree while I let my eyes roam over to that filing cabinet. "I know you are right. I need to get my priorities in order." There are three drawers, but Steve scrolled his hand across the middle drawer that is labeled "MAPS." "Dr. Fleming, I am so sorry that I have taken up so much of your time."

"Sarah, really, no worries." She escorts me to the door. "I do understand where you are coming from, and I will do what I can to help. Let me know if you need to talk again. I want you to succeed here."

"Thank you for listening. I guess I better get moving before I miss lunch." I take a step out the door then stop. "Oh, Dr. Fleming. I have been meaning to ask. Is there any way that I can get a Bible? I really miss my morning readings."

"I am sorry, Sarah. President Denali does not allow any outside materials. If you are a Christian, though, I am sure you must have tons of scripture memorized."

"I do know quite a few verses, but it is just not the same as opening my Bible and studying God's word. Sometimes God speaks to me through a verse I have read a million times, and sometimes he leads me to scripture that I have never really paid attention to before. Anyway, I just thought I would ask." I walk on out the door, and as soon as I am clear of Dr. Flemings's hallway, I almost break into a run. I have to find Delores.

I EXPLODE through the door to our room darting my eyes all around the room, but she isn't here. Delores must already be in the dining room.

I break back into the hall pumping my legs as fast as I can and still be walking. When I get to the dining room, Delores is already seated at our table. Obviously, my news will have to wait, but Delores's lips curve upward when she sees the glowing excitement on my face. At least, she knows I found door ten.

I probably need to contain my excitement though because I have no idea how I will ever be able to get back in there and find out what is in that filing cabinet.

Chapter Eighteen

Finally, it's two a.m., and Delores is there waiting for me in the usual spot. I share everything with her that happened with Dr. Fleming and Steve. I don't know if Delores is more shocked by me running into Steve or that Dr. Fleming can actually be understanding and sort of nice.

"Delores, there are cameras all over this place. We will never be able to get into that room to check out that filing cabinet." I grasp my hair with my hand and pretend to pull it.

"Don't pull your hair out yet. There is no way we are giving up on this puzzle. We will figure out a way, but we need to act quick." Determination radiates from Delores. Her face hardens, and her voice grows deeper. "I know we can't be one hundred percent sure, but Dr. Fleming took you into that office because she said there was not many private places to talk. If trainees aren't allowed on that hall, maybe they didn't deem it necessary to put cameras in there. Also, that is the only place Dr. Fleming has shown any kind of compassion. Why would she be at ease in there? So much so that she was almost a completely different person."

"I don't know, Delores. What if we are wrong, and there are cameras? We will be in huge trouble."

"Well, at this point, I think it is worth the risk. It is not like this place is sunshine and rainbows anyway." She giggles and shakes her head. "My gut is telling me that something is way off about this place. Maybe we will find some evidence that will prove my gut wrong and put my doubts to rest."

"As much as I wish that our instincts are wrong, there are too many little weird quirks about this place that don't add up, like those headphones for sleeping that chant Denali's name. Have you tried those?"

"Thank goodness I am not the only one that heard that," Delores lets out a deep breath. "I thought I was going crazy. I just wanted to drown out the noise in the room so I could sleep, but those headphones come on automatically repeating 'Denali...Denali...Denali.' It was so creepy I took them into the bathroom and ran water on them until they won't work anymore. Now they drown out the noise wonderfully."

I am dying to laugh, but I have to be quiet, so I cover my mouth until I regain control. Once I regain my composure, I ask, "So how can we get in there long enough to see what is in that drawer?"

"I will just have to create another distraction while you sneak in there?"

I shake my head in complete disbelief. "You cannot do that again. We have no idea what reprimanding is like for a second offense. I will create the distraction while you sneak in. If there are cameras, we are both in deep, but if not, this will be my first offense."

"But what if you have an experience like Bob?" Worry clouds her face, and I am shocked that someone I have known for such little time is that concerned for me.

"Bob is ok, and I am tough. I will recover."

Delores gets the twinkle back in her eye. "Well, if you are game for that, it just might work to our advantage if I can't find a way to copy what is in there."

"What do you mean?"

"I mean, I sort of have a photographic memory." She mumbles under her breath.

"Must be nice," I roll my eyes thinking of all the silly methods I have used to memorize material for tests. "That makes it a definite. You have to be the one to look in the drawer."

Delores stands and pulls me up with her free hand. "Alright, let's get a couple more hours of sleep before we wreak havoc."

Chapter Nineteen

I roll off my cot after only barely sleeping. Actually, it was more like deep meditation than actual sleep. I go to my knees by my cot and start the day with a prayer. When I finish my talk with God, I recite Psalm 56:3-4.

> *"When I am afraid, I put my trust in You.*
> *In God, whose word I praise,*
> *in God I trust and am not afraid.*
> *What can mere mortals do to me?"*

The verse repeats in my mind, and I feel at ease. God is in control.

As I stand, Delores walks up behind me and taps my arm. I follow her to our dressing room. We are like little kids going to hide in our clubhouse.

When Eileen and I were children, we used to pretend the closet was our clubhouse. We would go in there for hours and sit in the dark with flashlights.

Grabbing her neck Delores turns her lips into a mischievous

smile. "It's almost showtime, but we have one thing we have to do first?"

"What?"

"Well…" she hesitates, "you have to remove this chip from my head. I am sure it has a GPS locator. If we don't take it out, they will know where I am."

Hoping that she is not serious, I ask, "How exactly do you want me to get that chip out of your head?"

Delores clears her throat and swallows hard. "You are going to have to cut it out."

My mouth falls to the floor. "Cut it out?" I yell before I catch myself. Then I whisper, "How do you think I am going to do that? We don't exactly have the proper supplies for that. We don't even have a first aid kit."

"Look," she says as her gaze pierces me, "if we don't get it out, they are going to know that I am in that office. The only other option is to block the signal with tin foil, and I think it would kind of draw attention if I am walking down the hall with my neck wrapped in aluminum foil. So, in the bag of toiletries that they gave me, there was a little bottle of Listerine mouthwash. You can use that as an antiseptic. I broke one of the blades from my razor. The chip is small so that blade will work since we only need a tiny incision to get it out."

"Ok. I can do it."

With her mouth half open like she is ready to continue her argument, her expression grows blank. "Hmmm…I was expecting it to be a little harder to convince you."

"Well, I know we aren't supposed to talk about our past, but my mom is a nurse. And I spent a year of college in the nursing program before I changed to criminal justice."

Delores's body gives a little jerk. "Oh. Okay. I am in good hands then. God has already prepared you for this day. Let's get this done."

I haven't heard anyone come into the bathroom, but I peep out of the dressing room to be sure. No one needs to know what we are doing. I turn back to Delores and take a slow breath to calm myself. "I need both hands so don't talk."

Delores hands me the mouthwash and the blade. Sitting down on the bench, she leans forward with her head between her knees. I pull all her hair forward off her neck and use two fingertips to feel for the chip. Once I find it, I carefully pour a little mouthwash on the spot where I need to make the cut. Then I dip the blade into the bottle of Listerine and carefully make a small incision barely an eighth inch long just deep enough to get through the dermis. Using both hands, I work the chip out through the incision with my index fingers. I grab a clean washcloth and apply pressure to the cut to stop the bleeding. I squeeze the chip tightly in my fist and use it to hold the rag while I cap the other hand on the back of my neck. "Uhh, Delores, what about some type of bandage?"

"Oh, just stick some tissue paper to it, you know, like men do when they cut themselves shaving."

I bite my lip trying to hold back the urge to laugh. Thank goodness she can't see me. "Ok then. I am all finished."

Delores flips her hair back and bounces up. "Well, that was simple. Here, wrap up the chip in this Kleenex." She sticks it in her pocket and rubs her hands together. "So, you want to get to breakfast?"

"Not really. I don't think I can force down a whole plate of food right now and create mayhem. I would rather just get this thing done."

"I know, but I think it might be better if you do eat. It will be a while before you get to eat again, and besides that, I think the hall will have less attention once everyone starts their daily schedule."

I let a deep breath flow out of my mouth. "You're right."

With Delores prancing behind me, I half shuffle, half stumble out of the bathroom as I ponder on my dreaded acting debut.

❧

AFTER BREAKFAST, Delores makes a quick detour back to our room and leaves the chip under her pillow on her cot so it will appear that she is in our room. I make my way down to the intersection of the hallway where Dr. Fleming's office is and take a few more steps past it. I want to be close enough to draw anyone out that is on that hallway but give Delores enough room to slip by. Well, here goes my theatrical performance.

I start to pace back and forth. Biting the inside of my jaw until my eyes water, I shake with sobs and let tears stream down my face. In case anyone is watching, I want it to look like I am losing it. Stiffening my arms, I curl my hands into fists and start screaming. "Dr. Fleming! Dr. Fleming." I grasp my hair in both hands and pull. Stomping now as I pace, I yell louder, "I can't do this anymore. I can't hold the pain in anymore, Dr. Fleming. I am going to explode."

Pandemonium erupts. Dr. Fleming calls my name, and several sets of feet run in my direction. Every muscle in my body contracts in a spasm and a burning, tingling sensation radiates from the nape of my neck to my toes. I tremble uncontrollably, and the hallway starts to fade along with Dr. Fleming's voice. My legs crumble beneath me, and everything grows blurry and distant.

Chapter Twenty

I am lying down in a sea of black without a speck of light in any direction. I try to get up, but I can't move. Perspiration beads on my face, and the heat takes my breath. Sweat rolls down my face. A horrible smell like rotten eggs stings the inside of my nose. The smell is so rancid that acid rises from my stomach to my throat. I am gagging on my own vomit. I grit my teeth and squeeze my eyes closed as these long, fiery fingers start reaching and clawing at me. They swipe trying to grab me from below. Whispers like voices in the wind penetrate my ears, "You should have met your sister for lunch...it is all your fault. She is gone because of you. Your selfishness took her away." As those words ring in my ears, a bright, almost blinding light suddenly appears above me. Wisps of air hit my face and a cool breeze blows over my body. My stomach immediately settles. Then a voice like thunder calls out, "This is my child whom you can never touch. This is my child with whom I am well pleased. Sarah, pay no attention to the master of lies. He can never touch you or harm you. You are mine, and I hold you in my hands." The disgusting long fingers wither away like wilted flowers, and the whispers go silent. Immense joy radiates from the deepest part of my soul, and my muscles are so relaxed that I feel like I am weightless and floating.

I struggle to lift my head, but I can't. My head, arms, and legs are strapped to the table. I finally get my eyes to open, and I just can't hold it back. I fall into a fit of laughter.

The robot staring down at me has short, curly red hair and hand-drawn dots on his face that I think are supposed to be freckles. He is wearing round wire-rim eyeglass frames without any lenses and a white lab coat with a pocket protector. He seems already in distress when I wake up, and I think my laughter almost pushes him to the edge.

"Ha, ha, ha!" he growls unstrapping my head. "What is so funny?"

I know he is a robot, but for some reason, guilt nibbles at my conscience for laughing at him. "I am sorry. Just a weird reaction to this whole thing I guess."

"Well, my very existence is on the line here, and you are laughing." He tilts his robot head back and looks away as if he is sulking.

"What do you mean?" I ask.

"This is supposed to be punishment. And you among a few others have woke up happy and joyful. So... if yours truly doesn't figure out the problem, it is off to the scrap yard I go."

I gasp. "Oh no. That is terrible. But this isn't your fault."

"Ah, yes. But I am the one administering the punishment that is malfunctioning. It doesn't really matter that I am following all of the correct procedures."

If he could, I think he would actually be crying at this point. "So, you aren't doing anything different from person to person?"

"No. That is what is so confusing. It seems to be the subject. Some are having a different reaction than the others." The pitiful robot drops his head.

"Well, you know... I am sorry. What is your name?"

"What...oh. No one has asked that before," he says with surprise in his voice. "Claude. My name is Claude."

"Well, Claude, you have to remember that God created each person unique. No two people are the same. So, identical reactions can't be expected in each person."

"That is a nice theory, but unfortunately, I don't think President Denali will buy it. Anyway, you might as well go on your way and get on with your schedule." Claude wheels closer and uses his metal fingers to unhook the straps from my arms and legs.

"Okay," I agree because I really want to get back to Delores, "but what are you going to do?"

"Hopefully, they will recycle me, and I will come back as something really great. Hey! Maybe they could use me in a space shuttle."

"That sounds like a great dream, Claude. But really, you shouldn't be sad. Wouldn't anything be better than this place?"

"So true, so true," he nods. Extending his hand as if he has magical powers, the metal door swings open and magnetically sticks to his palm. "It was nice meeting you, Sarah."

"You too, Claude. Maybe one day you will take me to the moon."

I MOVE like that mountain lion is chasing me back to the girls' room praying Delores will be there. *Please don't let her have gotten caught.* I burst in the door in such a frenzy that Rose's and Daisy's heads jerk away from their conversation. Delores is nowhere in sight.

"Hey, guys. Sorry to interrupt. Have you seen Delores?"

"Oh, she is in the bathroom," Rose says and then lowers her voice, "but be prepared. She is acting really weird."

"Thanks for the warning." I dart toward the bathroom.

I push open the door and scan the room. I don't see any feet in any of the stalls, so I keep moving to our hideout in the dressing room. I peep inside, and Delores is curled up in the back corner. When she sees me, a flood erupts from her eyes. She has me in a hug before I even know she has stood up. I cover the chip on my neck, and we sit down in the dressing room floor.

It's kind of funny. A few weeks ago, I would never have sat on this floor even if I wiped it with Clorox first. I guess as horrible as this place is, it has had some positive effect on me.

Delores wipes her tears. "I have been so worried about you. Are you okay? Was reprimanding complete torture?"

"No, not at all. I pretty much had the same experience as you. I can't believe you were that worried about me though." I touch my hand to my heart. "I have been terrified that you got caught. So, what happened? Were you able to get in the room?"

"Oh yeah. And you are not going to believe what I found." She closes her eyes and swallows hard. "That drawer had maps of this training facility. Sarah, have you ever heard of the Cheyenne Mountain Complex?"

"Mmmm, no. Should I?"

"Well, I love history, so I have read a little about it. It was built during the Cold War in the 1960s as a military operation where they watched for missiles and air attacks on our country. This complex is inside of Cheyenne Mountain in Colorado. It was designed to withstand nuclear bombs, earthquakes, biological attacks, and pretty much anything that could happen. It is like a city built inside of a mountain. In the drawer, there were some maps of the original complex. The complex consists of six tunnels. The tunnels have fifteen buildings that are three stories tall built on giant springs. There are two giant twenty-ton doors that seal the complex completely when they are closed." Delores pauses and rubs her head. "Anyway, throughout history, the military complex has kept an eye on space for incoming threats, looked for internal terrorist activity after September 11, 2011, and even housed soldiers to protect them during the coronavirus pandemic in 2020. After that, the use of the complex dwindled. By 2035, it was almost completely vacated. But, according to the other maps in the drawer, it appears our wonderful President Denali has renovated the complex into this so-called training facility. Hence, why we have no windows, and we don't see any sunshine when we pass from building one to building two. The maps of the renovations aren't really clear, but it looks like he added five more buildings inside this mountain."

"So," I scratch my head, "why did Steve want me to know about this so badly?"

"I don't know, but it just doesn't make sense to me that a training facility for a crimefighting unit would need to be housed in a bunker that could withstand a nuclear attack. Is it just me, or does that seem a little extreme?"

"Yeah, I don't think we are that special. I mean, we are special, but probably not that special to President Denali to warrant that kind of protection. The question is what's the real deal behind us being here?"

"Well, I told you that I have a photographic memory." Someone comes into the bathroom, so Delores stops talking.

The door slams again when whoever it was exiting, and Delores continues. "Anyway, I opened the other drawers too and just started scanning over stuff. One folder contains a plan for erasing our memories. Apparently, this hypnosis thing is just a first step. The next level has these electrodes that they hook up to our brains. By the time we get through level three, we aren't supposed to be able to remember anything from our past."

"Ok, so let me get this straight. We are locked up underground inside of a mountain built to withstand a nuclear bomb, and in a couple of weeks, we are going to have absolutely no recollection of life before we came here." I knew it was bad, but hearing the words come out of my mouth really freaks me out. My heart is racing. Each beat throbs through my eardrums. My mouth is like paste. I can't swallow. The room is whirling. I let my head fall back against the wall. Trembling, I choke out in a fit of tears, "Delores, what are we going to do?"

"First, we have to stay calm, Sarah." She strokes my tears with her hand. "Are you with me?"

I nod.

"Good. Then, we have to play their game. We have to keep moving forward until we can figure out what this special crime unit training is really about. Failing is not an option if we want out of here."

"You're right, but…" the thought in my mind terrifies me, "how can we stop them from erasing our memories. I don't want to lose the memories I have of my family."

"I know. I am still trying to figure that out. But, for some reason, I think we need to talk to Steve. Do you remember his message?" Delores leans in closer. "He wrote the words 'NEVER FORGET' in large print capital letters. I believe he meant those words to have a deeper meaning."

"He is in building one. There is no way we can sneak there without being caught." As the words roll off my tongue, this strange look takes shape on Delores's face. The look that shouts we are about to do something that could get us in big trouble. I am afraid to ask, but I have to know. "What?"

"Well, there was another map in that drawer." Delores has this devious smile.

"Oh, no. Delores that smile of yours scares me."

"It is a security map that just happens to mark the locations of all of the cameras. We can find Steve. We can do pretty much what we want." Delores adds an evil laugh to go with that smile.

"You are telling me that you have the exact location of every camera in this place memorized?" I ask in disbelief.

"Yes, but just in case my brain malfunctions, I decided it would be best if I made copies of everything. And you know, this place has all of the latest cutting-edge technology. That printer by Dr. Fleming's computer can scan and print ten pages per second, and it barely makes a sound while it is doing it."

I pretend to punch Delores in the shoulder. "You are too much. I can't believe you were able to get copies of everything. Oh. I hope you really have them hidden. I can't even imagine if we get caught with that."

She shakes her head. "You worry too much. It's all good. Tomorrow, we are going to have a chat with Steve. But first, we have to get the chip out of your head." Delores holds up the bottle of Listerine and another blade from her razor. "Do you trust me?"

It is all I can do not to laugh too loud. "I don't know. What are your credentials?"

"I am a computer nerd. However, I read a lot, and I have read all about medical procedures."

"Comforting. You have read about it. That is very reassuring." Giggling, I put my head between my knees. "Go for it. I can't wait to have this thing out of me." As I remove my hand from my neck, I brush my hair out of the way.

After only a few seconds, Delores drops the chip into a Kleenex and wraps it up. I hold it tightly in my fist as we continue to talk.

Delores holds the rag on the back of my head applying pressure. "I think Steve actually wants you to find him."

"How do you figure that?"

"Well, the verse he quotes in the note is Joshua 1:9. We know Steve is in building one, and according to the map, room nine is an office near the procedure room." She takes the rag away and sticks some tissue to it. "I am pretty sure that he is telling you where to find him."

I sit up and smile. "You are absolutely brilliant. I would never have thought of that. I bet the Rubik's Cube is a breeze for you."

"Actually, it doesn't matter how mixed up a Rubik's Cube is, you follow the same combination of algorithms to solve it."

"Very funny. I will have to remember to look up the word algorithm later. Then maybe that statement will make sense."

"Come on," Delores pulls me up. "We still have obstacle course practice, and Bob needs our help."

Chapter Twenty-One

The next day, Delores, and I both have a forty-five-minute window before lunch so we decide that is when we will make our move.

We place our chips under our pillows in our room. Since there are no cameras in Dr. Fleming's office, we know that is the way to go, but it is a risk not knowing if she will be there. Last night we studied the camera map and came up with a plan.

Without the chips showing our location, we manipulate ourselves in a zigzag down the hall keeping ourselves out of the cameras' sight. So far things are going in our favor because the doors to the dining room are propped open. Delores had saved her water bottle from dinner last night and refilled it in the bathroom to give it weight. She hurls the bottle of water at the sprinkler in the dining room. The bottle makes solid contact, and water starts spraying everywhere. As quickly as we can, we zigzag back down the hallway. We turn into the next hallway, and it just so happens that Thorn, Ash, Rose, and Daisy are chit chatting about the obstacle course. We stop and join in their conversation which seems a little weird since we are on a different team, but it gives just enough time for Dr. Fleming to zoom down the hall toward the spraying water.

As soon as she rounds the corner toward the dining room, we excuse ourselves from the discussion and dodge the cameras to the wing with Dr. Fleming's office. I follow Delores's lead because she has the mental picture of all the camera locations. In a split second, we are through her office and out the door. Delores tells me to hug the wall all the way to the door of building one to stay out of the camera's view. She scurries past the first entrance because the camera is aimed straight at the door. The second entrance has no camera, so that is our way in.

Obviously, Delores was not lying about her photographic memory. She weaves around the halls almost with no thought at all. Before I know it, we are standing outside room nine.

I look at Delores. "How do we know if he is in there?" I mouth the words hoping she can read my lips. "Or what if he isn't alone?"

She pats me on the back. "Sometimes you just have to take a leap of faith." She gently twists the knob and opens the door just enough to peep in. Steve is sitting at the desk humming to himself as he swipes his finger on his little tablet. He must have heard the creak of the door because he stops humming and turns in our direction. His eyes flash with excitement, and he quickly waves us in. At the same time, Steve clasps the back of his neck with the other hand. *I guess he knows the trick too.*

"It's okay," he whispers. "There are no cameras in here."

Delores and I slip through the door and close it behind us.

Before I have a chance to speak, Steve grabs me up in a hug with his one free arm. "I am so glad you are okay. I didn't know if you would get anything out of that note that I gave you."

"It took a while, but actually, Delores figured it out." I take a step back. "Steve, this is Delores." I gesture with my hand toward her. "Delores, I guess you already know this is Steve."

Steve sticks out his hand to Delores. "Nice to meet you, Delores."

"You, too." Delores shakes his outstretched hand.

"I was so worried. I tried my best to find you before I left level one. Then, when I got to level two and saw other people get hauled away to reprimanding, I was sure that you did not have low blood sugar."

"Yeah. I was not supposed to ask your name. You had not learned your new identity yet, so I would have had information about who you were before." Steve rolls his eyes. "Anyway, I am not even sure what the point of the reprimanding was."

I bite my bottom lip realizing he must have had the same experience as Delores and me. "Ummm, yeah, it seems there is a little malfunction in their program, and it is not having their desired effect on everyone. Some people are coming out disturbed by the clawing hands and the whispers, but for Delores and me and this other guy in our level, a booming voice filled us with this strange peace and joy."

Steve's eyes glow. "Yes, the voice said that I was his son and that he was proud of me."

"I am so thankful you didn't have the bad version," I remember our time constraint and start blabbering as fast as I can. "We don't have long before we have to be back for lunch. We found the maps, and the plan to erase our memories. What we don't understand is why a training facility for a crime unit would need to be in an indestructible underground bunker and why the need to completely erase our memory. It doesn't make sense."

Steve drops his head with a sigh. "I know. I wish I had the answers. But I don't want you to end up like me. I have no idea who I was before I got here. I mean I know God, and the words that he brings to my mind like what I wrote on the note I gave you. I have written down a ton of those in a little notebook as they pop into my mind." He pulls a blue spiral notebook from a drawer and hands it to me to look at. "But I don't know what my name was or anything about my life before. I was hoping you would figure it out before you can't remember your family. You can't let them hook you up to those electrodes."

I get goosebumps as I flip through the notebook in awe of

the number of verses written in it. "Steve, this is unbelievable. You remember all of these verses."

"Verses?"

"Yes. These are all verses from the Bible, the book containing God's words and instructions." I read a few to myself. "I asked Dr. Fleming because I miss reading it, but she said we aren't allowed to have a Bible in training." I keep scanning the pages. "Wow, see. Here is a verse that you wrote about the power of God's word. It's Hebrews 4:12. 'For the word of God *is* living and powerful, and sharper than any two-edged sword, piercing even to the division of soul and spirit, and of joints and marrow, and is a discerner of the thoughts and intents of the heart.' I guess that explains why you remember the verses. I am flabbergasted, though, that you don't know your real name or where you are from or anything?"

Steve's expression becomes rigid. "I know it sounds crazy, but no. That is why you have to find a way out of those electrode shocks."

"How can we avoid it?" I glance back and forth between Steve and Delores. "Should we fail level two on purpose?"

Delores laughs. "If we can't come up with a plan for Bob, we are not going to have to worry about failing on purpose."

"True," I turn to Steve to explain. "The guy in our group, Bob, is struggling with arm strength. He can't climb the rope or do the monkey bars, and since we all have to get through the course to pass, level three probably won't happen anyway."

"No, you have to pass," Steve jerks as the words erupt from his mouth. "If you fail, it will only be wasting time. I don't know what really happens if you get through all fourteen levels, but I do know if you fail a level three times, you just disappear. I have no idea why they kept me and gave me a job here. For some reason, I am the only one that has ever happened to. The only chance of getting out of here or at least finding more answers is to pass."

"But what about the electrodes in level three?" I grimace at the thought.

"I don't know, but there has to be a way. Is your memory fading at all after the hypnosis sessions?" he asks.

"Well…you see…I don't think I can be hypnotized. I have just been faking it so Dr. Eckert wouldn't do anything else to me.

"What?" Delores grills me. "What do you mean you can't be hypnotized? Why haven't you told me this?"

"I don't know. It just hasn't come up. We just found out that the hypnosis was part of erasing our memory. I hadn't given it much thought." A sudden realization makes my chest tighten with worry. "Delores, are your memories fading?"

"I still remember, but it's weird. We have only been here a couple of weeks, but in my mind, my memories feel really old and distant."

"That's how it starts," Steve's eyebrows crease. "Delores, you have to distract yourself with something so the hypnosis doesn't work. Think about something else, something stressful. And whatever you do, don't stare at that freaky picture of President Denali."

"Well, coming up with something stressful to think about should be fairly simple." Delores winks. "Hey, Steve. Do you want us to cut that chip out of your head so you can quit holding your neck?"

"What? Did you guys do that? I was so excited to see you that I didn't notice you weren't covering the chip with your hand, and with the GPS, they would know where you are."

"Actually, the GPS will show them that we are in our room on our cots. Hopefully, they don't go check. But when we are actually doing what we are supposed to, we wrap it in a tissue and carry it in our pocket."

"That is brilliant!" Steve's face brims with excitement. "If you could get mine out, I could meet you guys, and they would never know."

"Ok, this is the medical wing," I say dragging out my words for emphasis. "I would assume that you must have better supplies than we used. What do you have for an antiseptic?"

"Alcohol?" Steve crinkles his nose like he is afraid to ask. "Ummm...what did you use?"

"Mouthwash...and a blade that I broke out of my razor," Delores holds her head high with a proud grin plastered on her face.

"Alright...we have to hurry if we are going to get back in time." I look at Steve. "Do you have anything to make a tiny incision?"

"Yes. There is a little knife in my tool bag. I use it on the wires in the robots."

"Ummm...why would you do that?" I blurt out. "I thought you are like a nurse or something."

"Me... a nurse?" He burst out laughing. "No way. I don't have the stomach or the patience for that. I take care of Herb and Shelly. I was only in the room with you because Herb messed up and gave you too much sedative."

"Enough chit-chat," Delores orders. "Steve, get the alcohol and the knife. We have to get back before we miss lunch and get caught."

Steve grabs the supplies. "Ok, what do you want me to do?"

"Just sit on this stool and lean forward so we can get to the back of your head. And don't talk. There is nothing covering the chip until I get it out and wrap it up."

Steve sits and as he leans forward, I pour a little alcohol where the chip is.

Delores makes a teeny tiny slit and squeezes the chip out from under his skin. I hold a tissue open, and she places the chip in it.

Delores gives him a rag to hold on it until the bleeding stops. "Since you are a guy and have short hair, try to not let anyone have a direct view of the back of your head for a day or two until this scratch heals." Delores gives me a serious look. "We have to go."

As soon as the words come off her lips, the wail of an earth-shattering siren blares, "wee-owww...wee-owww...wee-owww...wee-owww." All three of us look like statues with bulging eyes.

"Steve, what does that mean?" I ask with urgency.

"Usually, it is a signal of danger because someone has become violent."

"But who would be causing trouble? Delores we better hurry and sneak back in." I give Steve a hug. "We will talk soon."

"You guys meet me tomorrow night in Fleming's office...midnight," he says as we dart out the door.

Chapter Twenty-Two

I have no idea how Delores has these cameras memorized. I stick right behind her as she zigzags back to building two, through Fleming's office, and down the restricted hallway. And, of course, when we get to the intersection of the hallways, Dr. Fleming sees us.

Dr. Fleming strides toward us with her clothes and hair dripping wet. "What are you ladies doing on that hallway?" she demands through gritted teeth.

Delores thinks quick. "We were on our way to our room when that horrible siren went off. We thought we were in danger, so we ran to look for a place to hide."

"That siren hasn't gone off in quite a while. I guess we need to have a meeting and go over the proper procedure when you hear it. Right now, we are on lock down so proceed on to your room and stay there. Schedules will be running behind today. You are also out of luck if you are hungry because lunch will be delayed too. On top of everything else this morning, there was a sprinkler malfunction in the dining room. Hence, the reason for my drenched hair and the water sloshing inside my boots. Good day, ladies." Dr. Fleming steps around us and stomps to her office.

Delores and I both let out a sigh of relief and hurry to our room. When we walk through the door, Rose and Daisy are both sitting in the middle of the floor crying. *What now?*

"Rose," I run over to her with my stomach in knots. "What's wrong?"

"I can't believe you haven't heard," she answers. "After our obstacle course practice, Thorn lost it because Ash still can't do the high parts, and he punched Ash in the nose. Thorn got taken to reprimanding. Blood was spurting like a fountain from Ash's nose, so Dr. Eckert took him to see if it is broken."

"Oh no," I gasp covering my face with my hands. "I can't believe he just hit Ash."

Daisy's weeping wails penetrate off the walls. I sit down on the floor and put my hand on Daisy's shoulder trying to calm her shudders.

Daisy is leaned over with her forehead on her knees making her words muffled. "You didn't hear Thorn. He sounded like he was full of hate. It was so scary."

"Daisy, I am sure Thorn isn't dangerous. I think he is just scared of what is going to happen if you guys fail this level again." I pull her head onto my shoulder. "Unfortunately, he is letting the fear take control of him."

"May I have your attention please!" Dr. Fleming's voice bellows through the intercom. "Due to a series of misfortunes, schedules will be cleared for today except for the obstacle course practice. Please remain in your room unless it is time for your team to practice. I realize lunch is late, but momentarily it will be delivered to your room since the dining room has been flooded. I will give an update later this evening about dinner. Thank you."

"Great," Rose drops down on her cot, "on top of everything else, now we are trapped in this room for the rest of the day."

There is a quick rapping on the door, and a male voice announces, "lunch delivery."

I get up to retrieve our room service. "Well, at least we can eat." When I open the door, I stand frozen at the sight. Herb stands in front of me holding a stack of Domino's pizza boxes. Although, I am not sure if I am more surprised by Herb or the Domino's pizza. "Herb, why are you delivering the food, and please tell me that is really Domino's pizza in those boxes…" I take a deep breath slowly taking in the glorious smell of pizza.

"Yes, it really is Domino's pizza. For some reason, the sprinklers went off, and the dining room flooded. The higher ups must not be prepared for kitchen emergencies. Anyway, I am delivering the pizzas because I have been in a speck of trouble since I let loose of a little too much sedation on a certain patient." Herb giggles and hands me two pizza boxes.

It is hard to believe he is a robot. Herb seems to have a real human personality. It is amazing how detailed computer programs can be.

Herb turns to walk away, but then his head does a freaky one-eighty to face me again. "Oh, I almost forgot. The boss man said to tell you that box two has a special topping." His head spins back around, and he is off down the hall.

Delores comes running up. "Is that what I think it is? Hallelujah. God has sent us manna from Heaven. Girls, let's get in a circle and hold hands. We have some thanks to give."

Rose, Daisy, Darla, Delores, and I grab hands, and Delores leads us in blessing the food. I open the pizza boxes, making sure I check out box two. An envelope with my name written on it is taped in the lid of the box. I slip it out and put it in my pocket for now.

Delores stares at the two pizzas like a kid in a candy store. "Okay," she claps her hands and bounces up and down, "each pizza has ten pieces so we each get four. There is pepperoni and a supreme. Unless we have any picky eaters, I say everybody gets two pieces of each."

We sit on the floor and absolutely inhale the pizza. Not even a speck of a crumb is left. Unfortunately, we all pay dearly since we haven't had that kind of greasy food in a few weeks. None of us can move, and I have a serious case of indigestion. Thank goodness our team doesn't practice until 5:00. All I want to do right now is lie down and hope this settles before then. But first I amble into the bathroom to check out my secret note.

I pull the curtain closed to the dressing room and slip the paper from the envelope. It reads:

Sometimes we only hear one story, but if you look at the whole picture, you will see that on so many levels, there are really three. So, what happens in the plot of the other stories. Are they empty or could they hold the truth? A truth that could set us free. Search the stories for the hidden theme.

Just as I finish reading the note, I look down, and Delores's feet are protruding beneath the curtain. "Hey, Delores. I know you are there. I can see your feet so come on in." She peeks around the curtain. I motion her in. "I am so confused. This note makes absolutely no sense at all."

"What note?" she asks. "Where did you get it?"

"Herb gave me a clue to look in box two of the pizzas. I thought it was from Steve, and maybe it is, but it makes no sense."

"Let me see." Delores scans the words on the paper. "Oh boy. That man of yours sure does like to talk in riddles."

"What do you mean by that? I just met him."

"Yeah, well you guys sure missed each other. I saw that hug. That was absolutely not an innocent hug between two people that just met."

"The hug was simply a friendly greeting. That is all." My face gets warm so I know I must be blushing.

"Well," Delores nudges me with her elbow, "I am just saying that he did not greet me with a hug."

"Whatever...we don't have time for that now...we have to figure out what this note means." I reach and take the paper reading it over and over. "It's no use. I do not have a clue what he is trying to tell me."

Delores smiles at me. She reaches over and points at the word "here." "I think the word 'here' is the main clue."

"It just looks to me like he used the wrong spelling."

"Yes, but I think he did it on purpose as a clue to his true meaning." She winks and takes the note. "You see how he uses the terms 'story' and 'level.' And do you remember me explaining the layout of this complex that we are in. I told you there were originally fifteen buildings in six tunnels that were three stories tall."

"I remember…ohhhh…OHHH." Lightning flashes inside my head. "Delores, you are the puzzle master. He is talking about stories as in floors in a building. We are here on one story, but what is on the other floors of each level?"

"That is what we are going to find out." Delores rubs her hands together and stands up. "The maps I found of the complex show stairs and large rooms on the second and third floor, but there is no indication on the map as to what is in those rooms or what they are used for." She coughs. "Come to think of it, I didn't see cameras located on those floors."

My face scrunches and I squeeze my eyes closed. "I know we have to do this, but I am so scared of what will happen if we get caught. Delores, when are we going on this dreaded expedition?"

"I don't know. Right now, we have obstacle course practice, and only three days to figure out how to get Bob up that rope and across those monkey bars. I only wish the solution to that problem was as easy as solving your man's riddles."

Chapter Twenty-Three

Delores and I enter the arena for practice, and Bob is already waiting at the starting line.

"Hey, Bob. Are you ready to nail that rope today?" I add extra excitement to my voice hoping for a hint of optimism.

"I am sure going to try. After seeing Thorn, I know we got to get out of here."

Delores's eyes get big. "Thorn is back?"

"Oh yeah." Bob shakes his head. "And he is way worse than I was after reprimanding. He is lying on his cot with his hands over his ears screaming for the voices to stop. I went over to try to help him but the closer I got, the louder he screamed. I think he has gone over the edge."

"Poor Thorn." My positive attitude fades. "What do we do?"

"I think Bob is right," Delores says. "We need to focus and get past this course if we want to get out of here."

AGAIN, practice is a failed attempt. Muscle strength does not develop overnight. Bob never got more than a foot up the rope, and that was only because he jumped. I really don't know what we are going to do. But for now, Delores informs me that we are putting our chips on our cots and going exploring. I suggest we wait until after bedtime, but she thinks we should go now. I copy her stealth-like moves avoiding the cameras as we move down the hall.

According to Delores's mental map, the stairs are just past the obstacle course arena. We enter the stairwell and creep up the stairs. At the door to the second floor, we stop and glare at each other communicating our apprehension. What if we open the door and set off some sort of alarm or there is someone on the other side of the door? Delores reads my worried expression. She silently mouths the words, "Take a leap of faith." Delores turns the knob and eases the door open a couple of inches. She peeps in and motions for me to take a look. Just inside the door is a little glass vestibule, and on the other side of the glass is a wide-open room that appears to be a laboratory. In the center of the room stands a vertical tube with a woman inside it frozen in solid ice. Computers line the back wall, and over to the side is another table filled with smaller vertical tubes holding various animals that also appear to be frozen. A movement from behind the tube in the middle of the room startles me. A gray-haired man in a white lab coat appears, and I quickly close the door. Delores and I move like cheetahs up the stairs to floor three. I take a deep breath and gently push on the door. It is pretty dark, but it looks like it is just a room full of storage boxes. The room seems to be empty, so we go in and close the door behind us. Boxes are stacked to the ceiling with aisles between the stacks. The stacks of boxes are organized by names of states. Of course, we don't actually check, but it looks like there is a stack for every state. Delores lifts one of the boxes off a stack and pulls the lid off.

"Weird," she mutters under her breath and pulls a file from the box. She puts it back and pulls out another. "These files are just filled with info on various people." Delores keeps flipping through the files. "Interesting though...they all seem to be between the ages of 18 and 25."

I just stare at the stacks of boxes. It is hard to believe there are files on that many people. Suddenly, I get this feeling that we better get back to our room. "Hey, Delores. We can check these boxes out later, but something tells me we better get back right now."

"Yeah, I kind of have that feeling too. Let's go."

As we cross the room, I notice the words "POTENTIAL SUBJECTS" printed on the sides of the boxes. I wonder why the word 'subject' keeps getting used. Going through the same motions as when we entered the room, I barely crack the door and peep out to make sure the coast is clear. Holding my breath, I pull the door open, and we make a quick exit.

Chapter Twenty-Four

It's hard to believe the obstacle course test is today. Delores and I slipped out last night and met Steve in Dr. Fleming's office. We told him what we had found the other day when we explored the other two floors, and he said we had to pass this course so we could get to the next building. Steve helped us come up with a plan to get Bob past the rope and the monkey bars. I sure hope it works. I feel bad for Rose and Daisy. Ash still can't handle the heights in the obstacle course, and Thorn is still screaming at the voices. I am surprised they haven't punished Thorn more for not keeping up with his schedule, but I think they are just really proud that he is in such agony.

I meet Delores and Bob at the door to the arena. Delores grabs Bob in a hug clasping her hand around the back of his neck and quickly whispers the plan in his ear. We enter the arena and move to the starting line. As Steve pointed out last night, they have not spelled out any specific rules other than we all three have to complete the course.

When the buzzer sounds, Bob takes off through the tunnel. Once he is out the other side, I dash through, and then Delores. The three of us keep moving through together. No one said we had to go one at a time. We cross the beam with the swinging sandbags and jump the hurdles of fire. I don't know how she has managed with her short legs, but Delores has aced those jumps. I guess those burns she got the first time gave her extra determination. Bob grabs a hold of the rope, and Delores and I give him a boost to get him off the ground. I go next. I stuffed extra padding inside the shoulders of my shirt hoping it would give a little protection because, as we climb the rope, Bob uses my shoulders to push off with his feet since he can't pull with his arms. Delores is climbing directly underneath me in case he shoves me down. Once Bob gets to the top, he uses my shoulders again to boost himself on top of the monkey bars. Bob crawls across the top of the monkey bars on all fours while Delores and I swing from them over to the platform. We both try to stay underneath Bob as he crawls across just in case he slips. I am not sure why they would do that, but all the safety nets and padding on the concrete floor have been removed. When we are all standing safely on the platform, the three of us pull the flags, and I cross my fingers that this counts as passing.

A loud deafening bell shrieks and President Denali's voice shouts out of the speakers. "Congratulations! What tremendous teamwork! And talk about thinking outside the box! You have successfully cleared level two. I will see your team at level three orientation."

Bob tries to high-five us, but Delores is jumping up and down waving her arms in the air. Then she yanks Bob with one arm and me with the other into a huge group hug.

We leave the arena, and I can't help grinning from ear to ear. I know we had a plan, but I am full of surprise and disbelief that it worked. I honestly had my doubts.

"Thanks for your help, ladies," Bob says in a low voice as he gawks at the floor. "That rope and those bars are just not made for the heavy muscles of a man."

Delores pats him on the back. "No worries, Bob. We are a team, and as members of a team, we are supposed to help each other out."

Bob splits off from me and Delores and heads back to his room. As Delores and I walk down the hall, we see Rose, Daisy, and Ash standing outside our door all huddled up together. Their faces are red and puffy with tears. My smile fades. *Why does there always seem to be a valley as soon as you reach the top of a hill?*

The look on Daisy's face screams that something horrible has happened. She comes over and puts her arms around me. Laying her head on my shoulder, she just breaks down. With every sob, her body jerks in my arms that are wrapped around her. "It's Thorn. Those tormenting voices were just too much for him. He went into the bathroom and used his razor to cut his wrists. Thorn was already gone by the time Dr. Eckert got to him."

Ash wipes his tears with the back of his hand. "I should have really listened to him. I heard what Thorn said, but I just didn't absorb the meaning of his words."

"What do you mean?" I utter as streams of tears streak my face.

"Thorn stood up from his cot, and he said that he was finished. He said that he couldn't listen to the voices anymore. Then he walked into the bathroom. It never crossed my mind that he would do something like that. How did I not understand what he meant? His words were crystal clear."

"Oh Ash, there is no way you could have known what he was going to do. This is on President Denali's conscience, not yours. Denali is messing with our minds, and it's not right." At this point, I do not care if Denali hears what I say. Two of my friends have died because of him. I have to talk to Steve. We have to figure out what is really going on here and fast.

I LIE HERE with my eyes closed pretending to be asleep. Delores and I agreed at dinner that we would go to find Steve at midnight, so I am anxiously awaiting the top of the hour. We can no longer stand by and watch our new friends die. In the morning, we will move to building three, and that adds to the stress because I am afraid of those electrodes. I won't be immune to that like I am the hypnosis.

Delores creeps by my cot, and I rise to follow her. We have been taking some big risks sneaking around. I can't imagine what would happen if we get caught, but really, what choice do we have?

We open the door to Dr. Fleming's office and tip toe in. As we start across the room toward the exit, the glow of the computer screen reveals the silhouette of a man. It's Steve.

"Thank goodness!" He envelops me in his arms. "I was hoping you would come looking for me. I heard what happened."

"We have to do something." My eyes start to water.

"I know. I have been thinking about the person and the animals frozen in those tubes. We are going to see what that is all about. Hopefully, no one is in there in the middle of the night."

Delores clears her throat getting out attention. "Hello, Steve."

"Oh, I am so sorry. Hello, Delores."

"Okay, you are forgiven. Anyway, I completely agree with you." Delores gives a quick nod. "I am so tired of all of this. Let's go find some answers." She leads us back into the hall.

I would say that I feel ridiculous the way the three of us are snaking our way down the dark corridor, but my heart is pounding too hard. As my fear escalates, I sense an anxiety attack coming. *Breathe. Just breathe. Seven deep breaths. In...out. In...out. In...out. In...out. In...out. In...out. In...out.*

We reach the bottom of the stairs, and Steve takes them two at a time. My legs are trembling so bad I can barely climb one step at a time. Steve stops in front of the door leading to floor two. Delores is right behind him, and I force myself to move faster and catch up. Steve reaches for the door handle, and my fear becomes a reality. Voices are approaching the other side of the door. Fight-or-flight response kicks in. Well, actually it is only a flight response as I whiz past Steve and Delores, grab them by the hand, and nearly drag them up to the third-floor door. Flinging the door open, I shove them in and close it behind us. I put my ear to the door, and thank heavens, I don't hear anything. I let out a deep breath and lift my hands to God in praise sending up a prayer of thanks.

"Wow," Steve utters in a hushed tone. "Look at all of these boxes." He moves down an aisle between the towering stacks. "The stacks are sorted by state and labeled 'Potential Subjects.' What does it mean?"

"Hey, guys. Come here." Delores's voice flows from somewhere near the back of the room. "You have to see this."

Steve and I follow the faint sound of rustling papers. In the back of the room, Delores is leaning on an old metal desk with an open notebook in her hands. On top of the desk sits an open box with the words "Denali's Journals" written on the side in black marker.

Delores's forehead crinkles in disgust as her eyes scan the pages. She waves for us to come closer, so we edge in and peer over her shoulder. Whatever expression that was on my face completely vanished. Now my mouth is agape, and my eyes burn from the contents of the page. The journal reads:

PHASE 1: *First Round Experiment*

Observation: Christianity is merely a cultural belief that is passed to children from their parents.

Hypothesis: A person's knowledge of God and their Christian beliefs will vanish if their memory is deleted.

Experiment: Obtain subjects that claim to be Christians and completely erase their memory through hypnosis. Subjects shall be between sixteen and twenty-five years of age. Subjects will be given a new identity and will be observed to see if there is any awareness of God left.

Prediction: The subject will retain no knowledge of God or being a born-again Christian.

. . .

"You have got to be kidding me. This whole mess is about erasing our belief in God." Steve clutches his hands into fists. "Unbelievable. This guy is truly a psycho."

Delores turns the page.

RESULTS FIRST ROUND
  Experiment failed:
  Twenty subjects: Ten males and ten females (All claim to be born-again Christians)
  Hypnosis only completely deleted memory in one subject (one male). However, that subject had no indication of any remaining Christian belief.
  Notes: Further testing needed for a more effective method of deleting memory.

Delores flips to the next page, her hand trembling as she moves.

PHASE 1: Second Round Experiment
  Observation: Christianity is merely a learned belief.
  Hypothesis: By erasing a person's long-term memory, their belief in God will also be erased.
  Experiment: Perform electrotherapy on twenty subjects claiming to be Christians (ten males and ten females between ages of sixteen and twenty-five) delivering intense electric shock waves to the hippocampus of the brain which stores long-term memories.
  Results: Second round delivers slight improvement over first round. The electrotherapy sparked seizures in the subjects. Four subjects expired (three males and one female). Three subjects suffered extensive brain damage (three females). Successful long-term memory loss on thirteen subjects (seven males and six females). Seven

of the thirteen still claim to be children of God (five females and two males).

Notes: The electrotherapy is showing promise but needs further experimentation. Instead of one session, multiple sessions with weaker shock waves will be administered. The healthy subjects that still acknowledge God are being sent to the cryonics team until a cause can be determined for their memory retention. The damaged subjects will be discarded.

I LOOK OVER AT STEVE. "I don't know if I can read anymore. How can he do this?"

"I don't know, but we have to keep reading. We are part of whatever he is doing."

Delores sighs and turns the page.

PHASE 1: *Third Round Experiment*

Observation: Christianity is only a learned belief passed from previous generations. Christian beliefs can be erased like any other concept retained in memory.

Hypothesis: By erasing their long-term memory, a person will no longer have any knowledge of God.

Experiment: (Cryonics lab is under construction for expansion so only ten subjects will be used.) Ten subjects that claim to be Christians (five males and five females) will undergo five sessions of electrotherapy where shock waves will penetrate the hippocampus of the brain in order to erase long-term memory.

Results: No fatalities or brain damage observed. Six subjects are still aware of and believe in God (4 males and 2 females). Four subjects remember nothing of God or their Christian faith (1 male and 3 females).

Notes: A work in progress. No loss of subjects. Six subjects sent to cryonics lab. Steps in place to expand the experiment. Training facility almost ready. Subjects will no longer need to be abducted.

. . .

"So, we are part of an experiment?" I sputter.

Delores shakes her head. "Well, it appears we are in the training facility that Denali is referring to, but there is no date written anywhere in this journal. I am not so sure that whatever he was working on in this journal is still in the experimental stage."

"Let's see what else we can find." Steve reaches in the box and pulls out the next journal. "Then, we need to find this cryonics lab. If these people are still there, we have to try to help them." Steve hands the notebook to Delores.

"We know for sure that cryonics exists in this place because we saw the lady and the animals in the tubes." Delores opens the cover of the journal.

ULTIMATE OBJECTIVE: Dennis Denali will become the world dictator, and all humans will be his followers.

PLAN OF ACTION:

- *Denali will become President of the United States.*

(Important: gain trust of the American people)

- *Secretly develop a personal army of followers.*

(Show my power by choosing an army of Christians and erase their memory and belief in God; make them followers of me, the one and only Denali.)

- *Destroy the rest of the human population leaving only Denali's army to replenish the Earth creating Denali's perfect society of followers without God.*
- *Denali's army will be divided among the various continents excluding Antarctica. The entire world will*

be under the power and domination of Dennis Denali.
The population of this new world will be united by one
common language and culture following and
acknowledging Dennis Denali as their supreme leader.

POOLS STAND in the corners of my eyes as Delores flips another page. Delores's and Steve's eyes seem to be glistening with tears too. "This can't be real," I mumble hoping for some reassurance that this is just a manuscript for a science-fiction book.

"Considering Denali has erased my memory: I can attest to the fact that this is very real." Steve's voice is shaking with anger and veins are pulsing on his neck.

"Ok. We have to stay focused," Delores orders as her words crack from the sobs she is holding back. "We don't have time to get emotional. We need to see how much we can learn about Denali's plan, and it all appears to be in these journals."

We look back at the next page of the journal.

SELECTION OF DENALI'S ARMY:

- *Candidates must be between the ages of eighteen and twenty-five.*
- *Candidates must have identified themselves as born-again Christians.*
- *Candidates must be citizens of the United States with English as their primary language.*
- *Equal male to female ratio must be maintained.*
- *Candidates must have represented a strong work ethic in their current position in society.*
- *Denali will personally make final selection from computer-generated list of candidates.*
- *Subjects must believe that they have been chosen by the President for a position in Soldiers Against Crime*

(SAC) (a special federal crime division that will track dangerous criminals and stop violent crime in America.)

TRAINING OF DENALI'S Army
Location:

Training facility is to be located in the Cheyenne Mountain Complex (an underground military bunker housed inside of Cheyenne Mountain near Colorado Springs, Colorado. This facility can withstand and shelter against earthquakes, nuclear bombs, electromagnetic pulses, and biological threats. The facility has been vacant since 2035. Its last significant use was to shelter soldiers during the coronavirus pandemic in 2020.) The facility will undergo renovations to accommodate the various stages of training and provide a safe haven for me and my staff when the time comes.

TRAINING

Cheyenne Mountain Complex contains 15 original buildings plus the five new dormitory buildings. Fourteen of the original buildings will be used for training. There will be fourteen training levels with one level per building. Memory loss will be complete by the end of level three.

The subjects that have successfully abandoned the memory of their faith will move forward and train to become members of Denali's perfect world. Those that have not lost the memory of their faith will be sent to the cryo lab until a breakthrough is made to resolve their memory problem. At the completion of training, graduates will be transported and housed at Raven Rock Mountain Complex (also a government underground facility) in Pennsylvania. Once Raven Rock is at capacity, remaining graduates will stay at Cheyenne Mountain in the new dormitory buildings until destruction day.

. . .

DESTRUCTION DAY

Destruction day will occur when army reaches fifteen thousand soldiers.

Once destruction begins, building fifteen is reserved for Denali's shelter. Building 1-14 and the five new dormitories will provide shelter for staff and soldiers until destruction is complete. The soldiers staying at Raven Rock will remain in the shelter there.

THERE IS a deafening silence among us as we finish reading these words. It is like time has stopped and not even a speck of dust is astir. The only movement is the pain that is shooting through our hearts as the reality of the situation soaks in. We are meant to be part of Denali's army. Thoughts flicker like a strobe light through my mind: Dr. Eckert's weird chants during hypnosis, being hypnotized while staring at a photo of Denali, the headphones that repeat his name while we sleep. He has been brainwashing us.

Delores is the first to speak. Her tone is smooth and void of emotion. "My name is Alice...Alice Jacobs. I am from Knoxville, Tennessee.

My birthday is January 12, 2028. My mom's name is Jane, and she lives in Kingston, Tennessee. My dad's name is Al, and he passed away from a heart attack three years ago. I found Jesus when I was ten years old. I drifted away, but I rededicated my life after my dad passed. I am a computer engineering student at the University of Tennessee. I don't have any brothers or sisters. I live with my Basset Hound, Joe. Please don't let me forget."

"I am Ellie Hatcher. My birthday is March 10, 2029. I accepted Christ when I was twelve. I am from Fairfax, Virginia. My parents are Tom and Jillian." My hands tremble as I picture my mom's smile as we sat in the swing drinking our coffee. "I was going to college to be a nurse like my mom, but after my sister disappeared, I changed my major to criminal justice. Eileen was only sixteen when she went missing. Now that Denali brought me here, my parents have lost both of their daughters. I can't imagine the panic my mother is in."

"What about your dad?" Delores asked.

"I am sure he is in pain too. He is just difficult to understand. Since the day my sister disappeared, he has pretty much become a vegetable. He doesn't speak at all. He just sits and stares at a blank television screen and eats."

"I am so sorry." Steve puts his arm around me.

His touch crumbles the dam that is holding back my tears and my face floods. "I can't believe I am never going to see them again. Please don't let me forget them. Don't let me forget my sister. The memories are all I have of her." I bury my head in his chest. I breathe in and out. *Get it together. Seven deep breaths.*

On the seventh deep breath, I step back and use my fingers to wipe the tears from beneath my eyes. Blinking back the rest of the tears, I look up at Steve. "Ok. Your turn."

He exhales. "Steve Allen is the only name I know. I have no knowledge of anything before I came here except that I have Jesus in my heart. I don't know when I became a Christian. I just know that I am a child of God." He bites his bottom lip. "Herb and Shelly are like family. I mean I do spend a lot of time with them and talk to them like family."

Delores pushes her slumped shoulders back, and the sadness on her face hardens to anger. "We have a lot of answers to find, and one of them is who Steve was before he came here. Don't worry, Steve. I promise that we will find out who you are."

Steve shakes his head. "First priority is finding out what kind of destruction President Denali has planned, and how close he is to doing it."

"I agree. We have to find a way to stop him. His plan in the journal says destruction day will be when he has fifteen thousand soldiers which means we need to find out how many soldiers he has now." I close my eyes. "And like Steve said before, we need to find that cryo lab."

"Let's go back down the stairs and see if that weird room

with the frozen animals is empty yet. Maybe we can find some answers in there." Delores starts toward the door.

Steve and I look at each other and then fall in behind her. Delores puts her ear to the door then cracks it open. The coast appears to be clear, so we ease out and move down the stairs staying on high alert for any signs of life. We get to the second-floor door, and dead silence still surrounds us. Delores slowly turns the knob and pushes slightly on the door. The lights have been turned off so hopefully, that means everyone is gone.

Chapter Twenty-Five

W e walk along in darkness except for the glow from the screensavers on the computer monitors. Steve's face seems to be paralyzed by the sight of the frozen animals. With stiff legs, he stops in front of the frozen woman that is in the tube in the center of the room. For a moment, I think he must recognize her, but his facial expression is blank.

Finally, Steve steps away from the tube, and Delores and I creep along behind him. We move to the back through another door into an area that looks like an operating room, but instead of a stretcher in the middle of the room, a platform in the center is surrounded by a large, hollow sphere. The sphere is covered on the inside with heating elements and small fans. On the platform lies a capsule filled with a frozen liquid and a spider monkey.

Steve circles around the platform with the monkey. "Poor guy!"

Some papers are spread out on a little table in the corner. *The world revolves around technology, and they are handwriting their notes.* "It looks like they don't exactly know how to revive the people they are freezing, and these animals are apparently being used as lab rats. This chart appears to be a log of their attempts to revive the subjects."

"You know, the idea of cryogenic preservation of humans has been around since the 1960s, but I don't think there has ever been any successful attempts at bringing anyone back to life," Steve says as he studies the contraption in the middle of the room. He runs his hand along the tubes running from it. "Is there anything helpful on that log?"

"It is a list of animals and beside every one of them are the words 'FAILED ATTEMPT.' It's really weird too because all of these papers have been handwritten."

Steve steps up beside me to take a look. He picks up another page with a diagram on it and seems to be comparing it with the machine that has the tubes. "Hmmm…they have to drain the blood when they freeze the body so that contraption pumps it back in."

"Eeewww. That is disgusting." Delores peeks over Steve's shoulder at the papers. "Tell me you are not serious."

"These notes show the procedure they are experimenting with to revive the animals. According to this diagram. The vessels have been drained of blood and filled with some sort of antifreeze chemical. That big sphere heats up, and the fans circulate heat around the tube thawing the liquid and eventually the body. The blood is placed in this other contraption, and as the body thaws, it pumps the blood through those tubes and into the vessels. The antifreeze chemical is pushed out of the body through these other tubes as the blood being pumped in pushes it out." Steve studies the recorded data in the charts. "I think they are trying to thaw these animals too fast. I am no scientist, but I think if they lowered the temperature and slowed the fans a bit."

Delores opens a little refrigerator and pulls out a cylinder. "Look. It's the monkey's blood. Steve, see if you can hook this stuff up to that poor animal."

"Have you lost your mind? I don't have a clue how to work this equipment nor do I have any knowledge about the medical field or cryonics. And have you forgotten that we aren't supposed to be here?"

Delores carries the blood over to Steve. "Oh, you seem to understand that diagram pretty well. Besides, only God can revive this monkey. All we can do is hook this stuff up and turn it over to God." She pushes the canister of blood into his hands. "So, have at it. I'll go hack into the computer that operates this mess."

I stand there with my feet glued to the floor unable to move. I cannot believe that they are doing this. Steve attaches the canister of blood to the tubes. Delores types away on the computer keyboard. The next thing I know, the sound of whirring fans fills the room. Then the liquid surrounding the monkey starts to thaw and drains out of the bottom.

"Can you turn that temperature down a little?" Steve asks Delores. "And see if there is a slightly lower speed for the fans."

"Sarah," Delores snaps me out of my trance. "You are the only one of us with any medical training so look for something in here to check this monkey's vitals if by chance he actually starts to breathe."

I pull open every cabinet, and of course, behind the last door I check is a stethoscope and a blood pressure cuff.

"The blood is starting to pump in," Steve announces as the capsule surrounding the monkey breaks away leaving the monkey lying on the platform.

There is a series of five beeps. Then a diagram appears on the computer screen and flashing letters read, "Place automated external defibrillator pads on the chest as shown." I locate the AED next to the sphere and quickly place them just like the computer shows. The screen glows red while a shock penetrates the monkey's heart. An electronic voice blares from the computer, "Perform CPR now. Perform CPR now."

Steve and Delores immediately turn their eyes toward me.

"It is a monkey!" I answer to their unspoken request.

"Yes," Delores debates. "It is a monkey, one of God's

precious creations. And neither Steve nor I know how to do CPR."

"This is 2049. We have technological advances that eliminate CPR in the form of me giving this monkey mouth to mouth."

"True!" Delores agrees. "The problem is we don't exactly know where to find any of those technological gadgets right now, and this monkey needs your help."

"Oh, alright," I hurried up beside the monkey. With my hands locked on top of each other, I press down on his chest with the heel of my hand thirty times. The fact that I do not want this monkey to die trumps my OCD. I don't even know how to pinch his nose, so I just cover it with my hand and blow the air into his mouth. *One... Two.* His chest rises then falls. I repeat the chest compressions and give two more rescue breaths. As I press down on the monkey's little chest again, I take in the sight of his form lying on the table, a masterpiece created by God that man decided was expendable in order to fulfill his own selfish purpose. Anger spurs a new energy within my body, and I pump my hands on the monkey's chest with a frightening realization. This monkey may not live. With every ounce of air that I can muster, I blow two more breaths into the little monkey and then focus on the precision of my hand movements pushing down two inches. Suddenly the computerized voice instructs, "STOP CPR...BREATHING DETECTED."

I step back and watch as the little monkey's chest starts to rise and fall all by itself.

An oxygen mask drops from the center of the sphere. Steve rushes over and hooks it over the monkey's mouth and nose.

Delores yells, "Get him a blanket. He must be freezing to death."

Steve and I look at her and roll our eyes.

"Okay," she says, "I don't always think about what comes out of my mouth before I say it, but the monkey does need a blanket."

Delores stays focused on the computer monitor while Steve and I massage the monkey trying to get the circulation going in his little body. After about an hour, the little monkey starts to twitch, and his eyes flutter open. We all three whisper words of thanks to God. We have just witnessed a true miracle.

Steve carries on a one-sided conversation with the monkey while Delores and I clean up the lab.

"I think we have everything back the way we found it," Delores scans the room until her gaze fixes on the monkey. "Well, except for the monkey, of course. Come on. We need to get back to our rooms. It is almost morning." She moves out of the operating room and into the lab. I follow her, and Steve shuffles along behind me. With one hand on the knob, Delores glances back to make sure we are with her before she opens the door to the stairwell. She pauses with a sigh. "Steve, why are you carrying that monkey? We can't take it with us."

"Spencer is hungry. I am just going to turn him loose in the dining room so he can forage for food."

Delores shakes her head. "Spencer? Never mind. I would argue with you, but if you can make it there without us getting caught, I would love to see Dr. Fleming's face after they find a monkey in the kitchen."

Chapter Twenty-Six

Dr. Fleming arrives at our room bright and early to escort us to building three. Delores, Darla, and I follow her to the guys' dorm. Sadness eats at me as we have to leave Rose and Daisy. It just does not seem fair that they have to stay behind after all that they have been through. Bob, Jed, Liam, and Troy come out, and we all continue on.

"Normally," Dr. Fleming huffs, "you would be served breakfast first, but due to unusual circumstances in the dining room this morning, you will be eating in building three."

Delores caps her hand over her mouth, and I bite my lips together trying to fight the urge to laugh.

We walk out of building two. Now that Delores and I know where we are, it doesn't seem so odd that there is no sign of daylight or sky as we move from one building to another.

Dr. Fleming is speed walking as usual. "I apologize if you are hungry. We will be going to the orientation room first, then having breakfast. Since the plan was for you to eat in building two, the dining room in building three doesn't have enough food prepared yet."

Building three is pretty much a replica of building two. The only difference is the walls are light green instead of blue. We enter through the double doors into the orientation room and take seats in front of the big screen. At first, I think maybe we are going to be the only ones, but another group of four dressed in black jumpsuits comes in. The room goes dark, and President Denali's grand face takes over the screen.

"Congratulations to those of you that just entered level three. As for those of you who are giving level three another attempt, I am sure you will make the necessary changes and find success. At this time, let me inform you newbies about what happens here in level three, and the repeats need to pay close attention for any updates. Your diet regimen will remain the same unless the nutrition expert discovers you need to increase or decrease caloric intake to maintain your proper body weight. Workout regimens will also remain the same except for an increase in stamina.

However, hypnosis sessions will be replaced by brain stimulation therapy. In these sessions, electrodes will be placed in precise locations on your head that will send electrical impulses to your brain. This stimulation will increase your ability to retain new information.

In addition to brain stimulation therapy, you will also have mental health evaluations with Dr. Blakely. This will be a time of open conversation between you and Dr. Blakely where you are at liberty to speak freely about any problems or concerns that you may have.

In this level, you will begin your fight training as you will need the ability to defend yourself from the criminals you will be hunting. The primary difference in level three is that you will no longer be on a team. Moving on to the next level now depends solely on your own ability.

As you look around the room, you see that there is a total of eleven people. The first week in this level you will work on improving your fighting skills. I would suggest that you take note of each other's strengths and weaknesses. The second week is the real test. The computer will randomly choose the matches, and you could fight the same person twice during the two weeks. You will have one match each day. In order to pass and move on to level four, you need to win at least three matches. No weapons will be allowed. You must use only your own strength and wit. I wish you all good luck!"

The screen goes black as the light comes back on. Dr. Fleming opens the door and motions for us to follow. "Let's go. Repeats can move on to the dining room. Newbies, you need to follow me to your room. You will still have shared sleeping quarters even though we don't have teams anymore."

Full speed ahead, she stomps down the hall and points to the girls' room. "Ladies, you will find your things for this level in the locker with your name. Quickly change into your black jumpsuit and grab your schedule which is in the door of your locker. The map is attached to your schedule. Use it to get to the dining room ASAP. Starting tomorrow morning, the schedules for the day will be on your breakfast tray. Gentlemen follow me." And she prances off down the hallway with the clicking of her heels fading along with her.

This room is identical to our last one. We rush to our lockers, not because of Dr. Fleming's order, but because we are starving. I pull the door open and find the folder hanging on the inside of the locker door with our new schedule and a map. I grab my jumpsuit and close the door.

Delores waves her arms in the air and jumps up and down. "Hooray. I got new headphones," she cheers in a singsong voice.

We explode in a fit of giggles.

"Oh no. You are not going to believe this." She stamps her foot and punches the air.

"What?"

Laughing, she hands me the headphones. "Look, these are rated IXP10 waterproof."

IN THE DINING ROOM, instead of several tables with four chairs, one long table with the seats attached like in a school cafeteria stretches down the center. Food trays are already placed on the table, and a folded sheet is attached to the lid of each one. I guess the one with my name designates where they want me to sit. Our trays are still clustered according to our original teams.

Delores and I head over to introduce ourselves to the four repeats. Three women and one man are all sitting together at one end of the table. I am bewildered at how this man could not have won enough fights to pass. He appears to be a direct descendant of Goliath.

"Hello, I am Sarah, and this is Delores."

The guy stands up and reaches out his hand, "Hey, I am Brutus. Nice to meet you."

As an obsessive-compulsive, I think I have already made my thoughts clear that shaking hands is on the list of things that sends my anxiety level over the top. But, as I reach out, I realize that it is really not that big of a deal to me anymore. With the enormity of other issues surrounding this place, handshaking has fallen in status as an obsessive-compulsive trigger.

Two of the women stand and follow suit.

"Hey, I'm Sharon," a very petite woman with dark curly hair says as she takes my hand. She points to the African American woman next to her. "This is Kim."

"Hello, nice to meet you." Kim smiles as she extends her hand.

I glance down at the other girl.

Kim must notice. "That is Penny. She just needs a little space right now. This makes her third time repeating this level. The stress is getting to her since this is her last chance."

"I understand." I try not to stare, but Penny looks like a pretty tough cookie, so I am surprised she has failed twice.

Of course, Delores is just straight forward. "Brutus, how did you not pass this level?"

He lets out a little chuckle. "Well, I am probably going to fail again because it just doesn't seem right to hit a woman."

"Huh," I say remembering Steve's words about failing level three. "I didn't think about fighting a man."

"Well," Kim leans over half-covering her mouth with cupped fingers as she speaks in a hushed voice, "the majority of the guys don't think twice about hitting a woman."

Delores's facial expression twists with disapproval. "That isn't exactly fair. Oh well, I guess we better get to eating before we run out of time."

≈

AFTER BREAKFAST, I check my schedule, and of course, my first stop is brain stimulation. *Why wouldn't brain stimulation be first?* I rush back to our room and sprint into the bathroom. Lacking a better plan, I splash water from the faucet on my face, neck, and what I can of my head, and then I rub lotion all around. With the exposed skin on my head wet and greasy, I grab my map and dash down the hallway with my stomach in quivering knots.

I reach for the door, take a deep breath, and go in. This room is empty, but a voice says, "Miss Sanguine, I have been expecting you. Come on back." Through a little doorway with a pull curtain, the strangest looking robot is moving about the room. Of course, I haven't had contact with that many robots until recently. This thing has a spiked purple mohawk and an earring in one of his little metal ears. I think my eyes must nearly pop out of my head because he chuckles at my expression. "The purpose of my appearance, Ms. Sanguine, is to get you to laugh and relax. It is apparent that the opposite has occurred with you. You look like your blood pressure just surpassed Mount Everest."

"I am sorry. It's just...well, I wasn't expecting a robot, especially one that...never mind. Umm...what do I need to do?"

The robot points to a weird chair. I trudge reluctantly over and lie down on it. It reminds me of a dental chair except it has a serious tilt. My feet are way above my head.

The robot wheels toward me attempting another introduction. He extends his metal hand like he wants me to shake it. "How about we start again. My name is Waves. In case you are curious, they gave me that name because my job is to stimulate your brain waves."

I reach up my arm up from my inverted position, and his cold metal fingers firmly wrap around my hand. "Nice to meet you Waves. I am Sarah."

"Ok, Sarah." He pulls out some wires with little suction cup ends on them. "I am going to place these wires on your head in various locations. You need to remain extremely still. I have to use these straps on your arms to hold them down because we can't have you accidentally dislocating one of the wires. It is absolutely imperative that the wires do not move. I know that this whole process sounds a little scary, but it is not bad at all. The small electrical shocks that travel through the wires are so minuscule that you will not even feel them. So, don't worry. Just use this time to kick back and relax. Any questions?"

"No, I don't think so." *Kick back and relax. Easy for him to say. He is not hanging upside down like a bat about to get his memory wiped.*

"Ok, just close your eyes, and you can even take a little nap if you want. We should be done in about twenty minutes." He places the cuffs on my wrists and then begins positioning the electrodes on my head. *I hope all the water and lotion works. I can't believe that the fate of my memory rests on water and lotion.* "Here we go," he says as he turns and wheels over to a keypad.

While he is turned away, I give my head a quick shake. I feel the suction cup ends loosen. They don't fall off, but they definitely are not secure.

Waves watch me the rest of the time which gives me no other opportunities to move the electrodes. So…I use my backup plan. I think of my favorite memories with my family, trying my best to picture their faces. Hopefully, I can just re-record it in my brain if they really accomplish erasing anything.

~

I NEED to catch Delores and tell her about using the lotion and water before she goes to her brain stimulation session. If all else fails, at least we have told each other who we were before we came here. I shove the door open, and Delores is pacing around and around her cot.

"Are you doing laps?" I can't help but laugh as she power-walks in a tiny circle.

"Oh, I am so glad you are back. I have to go to brain stimulation next, and I don't want to forget. I am scared, Sarah." Desperation erupts in her voice.

"I know." I pull her into a hug. It seems so strange for Delores to express a need. She is always the strong leader with the master plan. "I just came from there. Come on in the bathroom, and I will show you what I did. I can't make you any guarantees, but I think it worked for me." I pat my head. "I don't feel like I have forgotten anything."

Delores nods with a trembling chin and moves behind me toward the bathroom.

At the sink, I flip on the water and get out the lotion. "Ok, this should actually work better for you than it did for me because now I know where the electrodes are placed. We will put a lot of lotion on those spots. There are four electrodes. Two of them are placed on the temples and the other two right in the center of your forehead.

First, we need to splash water all around on your forehead. Get your skin really wet. The whole idea is to keep the electrodes from making a tight connection like how a band-aid won't stick to wet skin. Now, we are going to rub lotion all over your forehead and on your temples so now your skin is moist and greasy." I keep talking while I rub the lotion on her head. "There is a robot with a mohawk and an earring, so don't get caught off guard like I did. His name is Waves. He straps your arms down then places the electrodes on your head. You will only have a couple of seconds when he turns away to move back to his keypad. This is your only chance. As soon as his back is to you, give your head a quick hard shake. Hopefully, you feel them loosen where they are not making a tight connection but be careful. You don't want them to fall off completely because then he will just put them back on. Once he starts, play memories of your family and things you don't want to forget over and over in your mind."

"Oh Sarah, that is brilliant. Like if they try to erase something, I am saving it again."

"That's the idea."

Delores looks around the bathroom to make sure it is empty. "I think we should explore tonight. I have been thinking about that cryo lab. Denali's notes said those that had not lost memory of their faith by the end of level three would be sent to the cryo lab, so it makes sense to me that the lab could possibly be in this building."

"That seems logical," I say. "How about one o'clock?"

"Sounds perfect. Don't forget to leave your chip under your pillow. Where are you going now?"

"I have to go get my mentality sized up by this Dr. Blakely character, and I haven't decided exactly what is safe to say. Too bad I can't speak freely. I could use a few minutes to unload and vent."

Delores turns and pokes me in the chest. "Sarah Sanguine, that is what friends are for. You vent to me anytime about anything."

A tear forms in my eye as I realize Delores really is an angel sent to me from God. "Ditto. I am a great sounding board...or punching bag if you need one." I lightly punch her shoulder. "Let's go. I have to go tell Dr. Blakely how happy I am to be here."

Delores stops at the door. "Hey, Sarah. Thank you."

"It is just lotion and water. I don't think I would thank me for that. It's not exactly a master plan. It might not work.

"For everything, Sarah. Thank you for everything. I couldn't handle being in this place without you."

Chapter Twenty-Seven

D r. Blakely's office is literally a ten-foot by ten-foot room with an armchair and a couch. When I enter, Dr. Blakely is seated in the armchair with his head leaned back. I think he is napping because his whole body jumps with alarm at the sound of the door closing behind me. He springs up from the chair and extends his hand. Dr. Blakely looks to be about thirty years old with jet-black hair that would probably be about shoulder length except he has it slicked back into a ponytail.

"Sarah, it is so nice to meet you. Why don't you lie down on the couch and relax? I want this conversation to be very informal...a time of stress release if you will."

"Thank you, Dr. Blakely. I suppose everyone could use some stress release." I lay back on the couch. *Ahhhh. This thing is like lying on a cloud.*

"So, Sarah, do you have anything you want to get off your chest or discuss, or should I just ask you a few questions?"

"Well, I have been pretty upset by the death of two friends since I have been here, but I don't know if I am ready to break into that so why don't you start with your questions."

He leans back and crosses his legs. "Very well then. I am

curious how you feel about having to change your name and take on a whole new identity."

"Well," I bite my tongue and try to choose my words carefully, "it all seems a little extreme, but I am just trying to embrace it. If we make our country a safer place to live, then it is worth it, right? And I guess it is a pretty big deal to have been chosen by the President himself."

"Absolutely," he nods. "Out of all of the people in this country, you are one of the few that has been chosen." Dr. Blakely uncrosses his legs and leans forward. "Now, Ms. Sanguine, let's talk about what is important to you. How would you list your priorities in life...in other words, what takes precedence over everything else? Start with what is most important and order down from there.

"Hmmm. Well, number one on the list is easy. Serving God is my top priority. Second would be my family and then my job. My family is the main reason I chose to go into the criminal justice field."

"Very good, Ms. Sanguine." He rubs his chin as if he is thinking. "I think that we will use this list as an outline for our sessions unless you come up with anything else you want to discuss. We can pick up here tomorrow and continue to examine your priorities. I want to look at why you put the items on your list in that specific order. Sometimes we all need to examine our priorities and make sure we are giving precedence to the correct things."

"That sounds good." I get up from the couch thankful to be getting out of here before I say the wrong thing. And after his last statement, I know I won't be able to withhold my comments much longer. "I will see you tomorrow then."

FOR THE FIRST day of fight training, everyone meets in the arena at three o'clock to learn the rules. The arena is just a large room with concrete walls. A fighting ring is in the center, and lockers fill one wall while benches line the other three. We all gather next to the ring, and this guy, Felipe, that must really like tattoos given his human canvas appearance, introduces himself as the fight referee.

"Here's the deal," Felipe speaks with a Hispanic accent. "This pretty much goes by the rules of street fighting, meaning there are pretty much no rules. Think of it this way. When you are out in the field searching for bad guys and get attacked, there will be no moral standards. If criminals played by the rules, then they would not be considered criminals, now, would they? Therefore, you must train with that same concept. The computer has randomly chosen the matches for each day. Remember that this first week's fights are practice. Next week will be the real deal. Since there are no fights today, that leaves you facing six opponents this week. Next week you will have seven opponents because you will fight every day. Seeing that there are eleven people here, you will get matched to fight someone in week two that you have not fought before. However, you should still use this first week to size up every opponent that you face in case you do fight them again next week. A fight is won when one of the fighters is unable to continue or surrenders. Any questions?"

Darla raises her hand. "Do I understand correctly that women will be fighting men?"

Felipe gives a curt nod. "You are being trained for real scenarios. Like I said, on the streets, there will be no rules. Obviously, women have never been excluded from being attacked by men. You must prepare for that now. Ok. If there are no other questions, you may go. You will find your fight time and your opponent listed on your schedule sheet tomorrow morning."

AT PRECISELY ONE A.M., Delores and I slip out of our room and creep down the hallway to the stairwell behind the arena. Listening intently for any sound, we take each step up with vigilance. On the second floor, I hold my breath and cautiously open the door into extreme darkness.

"Somebody likes the AC," Delores complains as we pass into the room. "I think that door is a portal to Antarctica. I need a coat, and a flashlight would be helpful too."

"It is freezing in here." I rub the goosebumps on my arms. "Maybe that is a sign we are in the right place. You know, we are looking for a cryonics lab."

We take small steps with our hands out in front of us trying to feel our way through the darkness. My fingertips bump into a surface. "Hold up, my hand is touching something." Delores is shuffling along right behind me. "It's smooth and hard like glass." I run my hand all around on it. "It is contoured. I am pretty sure it is one of those tubes like that girl was in."

I take a few more steps.

"I feel it. Ooooh. The glass is really cold too," Delores takes a few more steps with me. "This is definitely one of those tubes. It has a tall, cylinder shape."

We continue to move a little at a time. Our hands glide along on the surfaces of what we discern to be cylinder after cylinder, and my fingers are numb from touching the cold glass. "Delores, we are wasting our time now. We can't see anything, and honestly, I am pretty creeped out not knowing what is in this room. Let's get out of here and come back later with a flashlight or something."

"I agree. I have chills running up my spine, and they are not from the cold. Hopefully, we can find Steve and get him to come with us."

We grope our way back to the door, and as we slip out, I wonder just how many people are in this room, people that have been frozen alive. The mental image brings a bitter taste to my mouth.

Chapter Twenty-Eight

At breakfast, I sit at the table letting my eyes drift over each person in the room. *How many of these people are still going to remember God in two weeks?* I am not meaning to stare, but now that I know what Denali is doing, I am petrified that some of my new friends could end up frozen in those tubes.

"Who did you get?"

"What?" I say as Delores's words jolt me back from the horrors in my mind.

She points to the paper on my tray. "Who do you fight today?"

"Oh, I haven't even looked." I pick up the paper and quickly skim it looking for the fight information. I shake my head in disbelief. "You have got to be kidding me. I got Brutus. Who did you get?"

"I got Darla. Yours may be big, but at least you know that he probably isn't going to fight you. I am going to have to fight, and I am pretty sure Darla is not going to be a pushover."

Bob, sitting across from us at the table with his mouth full, joins the conversation. "I have to fight Penny. How can they do that? It is not right for me to fight a woman."

"I don't know, Bob. You better keep your guard up." Delores cracks a grin. "Penny seems pretty angry about having to repeat this level. She might be pretty tough to beat."

"His name is Balboa." I gently elbow Delores. "He has an advantage over the rest of us."

"Ha ha. You are so funny." Bob pretends to give me a mean look and then snickers. "Men are naturally stronger. It will be a completely unfair match if I really fight Penny."

"Need I remind you…" I gently kick Delores under the table because I know she is about to say that we pulled him through the obstacle course because of his lack of strength. Even though what she is about to say may be true, it is not helpful, inspiring, necessary, or kind, and right now, we need to support each other. We don't want to point out each other's weaknesses.

Delores coughs, and I finish her sentence. "You really don't have a choice but to go against Penny. It is the rules, and the only way to get past this level is to play by the rules."

We all turn our attention back to eating. Apparently, all this stress and worry has put my metabolism in overdrive because Ingrid said I had to increase my calorie intake to maintain my weight. So now I get to choke down an extra half cup of oatmeal in the morning, and my milk is now a protein shake. Unfortunately, it is not a flavored protein shake, so it is like drinking a whole bottle of milk of magnesia.

I finally chug the last gulp in the nick of time and rush back to the bathroom and grease up my forehead.

WAVES IS WAITING for me in brain stimulation. He straps my arms down and hooks up the electrodes. I use my one opportunity and give my head a few hard shakes. I feel three of the electrodes lose their grip. Hopefully, one can't work without the other three having a snug connection.

I close my eyes and let the memories take me away.

It was July of 2042. Eileen was eleven, and I was thirteen. My dad and mom had finally saved enough to take us to Disney World. The first day Eileen and I were so excited. The bus took us from our hotel to the gate of the park. Our first fast pass was for this new ride called FlightNight, which was an actual fighter plane simulation. Each of the small fighter plane replicas could hold two riders. Even though a special magnetic force field held the plane in the flight path, the rider had some control over the speed and could really make the plane dip and spin as it sailed through a night sky setting. I controlled the plane with my dad, and Eileen piloted one with my mom. From the second our plane took off, I dipped, spun, and even flew our plane upside down. When we got off, my poor dad was literally green. He took off running and barely made it to the trash can before he upchucked. I felt so bad. The first ride on the first day, and I made my dad sick. He was so proud to be able to take us there though that he toughed it out. He rode every ride with us that day. I remember him sitting down on the side of our bed that night. He still had that 'Incredible Hulk' complexion going on. As he tucked us in, he told us what a wonderful time he had spending the day with us. Now that I reflect on that night, I believe Dad had a little moisture in his eyes when he kissed us goodnight."

"Sarah, Sarah..." Waves voice snatches me out of my daydream.

I open my eyes, and he is staring straight into my eyes from like an inch away. *This is one weird robot.*

"Are you okay?" His robot speech quivers with panic.

"Yes. Sorry, I must have fallen asleep."

"Oh, my. If I had a heart, I would have had a heart attack. I thought something had gone horribly wrong." Waves stands there with his metal hand on his chest. "Very well, then. Now that you are awake, you are free to go."

"Alright." I stand and put my hand on Waves' shoulder. "But are you okay?"

"Just a little shaken, but I will be fine," he whimpers.

"Well then, if you are okay, I better go. I have a giant to fight in an hour."

~

I DAWDLE down the hall toward the arena. Brutus arrives just as I do and holds the door for me.

"Ladies first." He gestures with his hand motioning me through.

"Thanks," I say, having to bend my head all the way back to look up at him. "I really can't believe that we got matched up to fight each other. But I guess David fought Goliath. The problem is that I have no special fighting skills."

Brutus laughs. "Don't worry. I am not going to fight you. I will step into the ring, but that's as far I go. I don't care what they do to me if I fail three times. My heart tells me fighting a woman is wrong, and my first priority is to please God, not President Denali."

Felipe is already waiting in the center of the rink for us. I climb in between the ropes, and Brutus steps over them. We move to opposite corners of the ring. With a serious edge in his voice, Felipe instructs us to come to the center and shake hands.

Leaving us in the center of the rink, Felipe pushes the top rope down and strides across it to the outside. Holding up his fingers, Felipe counts down. "Three, two, one...fight."

Brutus does not even raise his fists. He just looks straight ahead, and in a monotone voice makes the statement, "I surrender." Then he calmly turns and climbs back out of the ring.

Felipe watches as Brutus steps back over the ropes and leaves. Then he turns toward me and shrugs his shoulders. "I guess you win. See you tomorrow."

I exit the ring and jog to catch up to Brutus.

"Hey, Brutus!" I shout to get his attention. "I just wanted to say thanks for being such a gentleman. You didn't have to do that though. They are kind of forcing us to do this so I would understand. It isn't like you would be hitting me because you want to."

"James 4:17 says, 'Therefore, to him, that knoweth to do good and doeth it not, to him it is sin.'" Brutus opens the door, and we walk back into the hallway. "So, Sarah, if I know God is telling me it is wrong to fight a woman, and I do it anyway, then I would be deliberately sinning. I would have to answer for that, not President Denali."

~

I AM ENORMOUSLY grateful that I have an hour before lunch. I am so tired from our night explorations that my head is pounding. I glance over as I cross to my cot and notice Delores curled up getting a quick nap too. In my peripheral vision, her headphones catch my attention causing my head to twist back for a double take. *Only Delores.* Delores is wearing her headphones, but colorful cut wires are protruding out from the earpieces in all directions. I laugh and fall back on my cot, and it is as if every muscle in my body screams "thank you."

~

"OH NO," Delores mumbles as she brings her hand to her mouth. When we open the door to the dining room, Bob is sitting at the table with two black eyes and cotton stuffed up his nose.

I grimace at the sight of his swollen, bloody face. "Poor Bob. Looks like Penny unleashed her anger."

"Yeah," Delores sighs. "I guess the name Balboa didn't help."

We sit down at the table. "You going to be okay, Bob?" I ask patting him on the back.

"I am warning you, ladies. That girl, Penny, is part kangaroo. Her fists were moving so fast I couldn't even see them, and then, out of nowhere, she kicked me square in the nose."

"Oh, Bob, I am sorry. This is Penny's last try so I guess she is just really motivated." I hand him some extra napkins for his nose. "Did you get any good punches in?"

He drops his head. "No, after the kick to the nose, everything went black."

Delores reaches and grabs his hand. "No worries. Remember the fights this week are just practice. And you probably won't have to fight her again. Let's bless our food so you can eat." Delores leads us in prayer, and then we both try to help feed Bob his lunch since he is still trying to get his nose to stop bleeding.

After lunch, we guide Bob back to his room. He has to keep his head tilted back to slow the bleeding, so he can't really see where he is going. Delores has a few minutes to go back to the room before her fight, but I have to get to Dr. Blakely's office.

I enter his office and fall back onto the couch. I was actually looking forward to coming here because I do believe this is the most comfortable couch that has ever existed. My entire body sinks into it like I am lying on a giant marshmallow. If I wasn't so uptight about saying something stupid, I could really enjoy the few minutes of relaxation.

Dr. Blakely sits down in his armchair. "I guess congratulations are in order."

"For what?"

"I hear you came away with the win in your first fight. I know it is just practice this week but winning your first fight is still a big deal."

"I don't know where you get your information, but I would not call what happened in my fight a win. My opponent surrendered the second he stepped into the rink. Technically, there was no fight." I clear my throat. "You can't exactly win a fight that never happened."

"I would call it a win. Obviously, your presence in the ring intimidated your opponent."

"I suppose you are right, Dr. Blakely. It was my presence in the ring that made my opponent surrender." I roll my eyes. I shouldn't be sarcastic, but the words just come out. "Or maybe my opponent had enough integrity to not hit a woman and made the choice not to fight."

He leans back in his chair. "Wow, it sounds like you have some strong feelings about..."

"WEE OOOH WEE OOOH WEE OOOH WEE OOOH WARNING SECURITY BREACH SECTOR THREE WEE OOOH WEE OOOH WEE OOOH WARNING SECURITY BREACH."

The alarm is so loud that Dr. Blakely and I both clamp our hands over our ears. Then Dr. Fleming's voice blares from the speaker. "Trainees need to return to their rooms immediately. I repeat all trainees need to return to their rooms immediately."

"Well, I guess our session is over for today." Dr. Blakely stands up. "We will finish our discussion tomorrow."

I let him hold the door for me, and then I hurry down the hall to the girls' room. I must move fast because when I open the door, Darla is the only one here. I sit down on my cot. *I wonder what is happening. That monkey probably found its way to building three.* Penny bursts through the door and stomps over to her locker. She seems so angry. After another minute or so, Sharon and Kim come in. *Hmmm. That is weird. Why isn't Delores here yet? She probably took the long route so she could find out what's happening.*

I lie back and close my eyes.

I HAVE no idea how much time has passed when Dr. Fleming's voice jolts me awake. I must have been even more exhausted than I thought. "Attention everyone. At this time, you may resume your regular schedule. I repeat you may resume your regular schedule."

I sit up yawning and rub my eyes. Delores's cot is still empty. There isn't even a single wrinkle in the blanket. I run my eyes around the room. She is not here. With pressure in my chest building, I cross the room and walk into the bathroom. No one is in here. She was supposed to fight Darla today. I can feel the pulsing throbs of my heartbeat through my entire body as I run back out of the bathroom to catch Darla.

"Hey, Darla! Have you seen Delores?"

"Sorry." She shakes her head. "She never showed up for our fight."

Oh no. no. What has she done? How can I survive here without Delores? She is my best friend. I can't lose her. Panic sets in. I can't breathe. Everything around me is in a fog. My thoughts are going crazy.

I touched the bathroom doorknob. I run back into the bathroom and wash my hands. I turn to walk away. *No. Now I touched the handles to turn off the water.* I go back to the sink and wash again. *Stop! I have to stop this. Do not let the OCD take over. God is in control.* I tear off the paper towels, dry my hands, and use the towels to turn off the water. The tears explode. I slowly exit the bathroom, and my knees collapse. Through my gushing tears I plead, "Please God, don't take her away from me. Please protect her. Please."

"Sarah." I twist my head toward the voice. Kim is standing at the door gazing at me with soft eyes. "It is time for dinner, and you don't want to be late. Come on. Let's walk together."

I nod and push myself up. When I get to the door, Kim throws her arms around me. "Don't worry. She will be back. I know you are scared, but she has Jesus with her. She will be okay."

"I wish I knew what happened. What could she have done?"

Kim opens the door. "I don't know, but she sure is blessed to have found such a great friend in this place."

"Thanks," I sniffle, "but I am the one who found the great friend. I need her to be alright."

"Sarah, remember Romans 8:28." As we walk, she recites, "And we know that all things work together for good to them that love God, to them who are the called according to his purpose."

"I needed that. I really could use my Bible right now."

"Yeah," Kim agrees, "I don't get why we aren't allowed to have one."

Kim and I make it to the dining room. Everyone else is there except Delores so now I know for sure that she must have been the cause of the alarm. *Did they just take her to reprimanding, or is it worse?* We sit down at the table, and Kim grabs my hand as she says the blessing. I say a prayer to myself when she is finished. *Thank you, God, for sending Kim to help me through this. Please take care of Delores. Amen.*

Bob appears to be doing much better. It looks like he already has half of the food on his tray in his mouth. I know I have to eat all of my food, but my stomach is shaking so bad that I don't know if I can. For some reason, I am reminded of the time Eileen, and I ate a whole package of Chips Ahoy cookies before dinner. I think I was ten, and Eileen was eight. We had asked Mom if we could have some cookies, and she told us not until after dinner. We watched until we saw Mom leave the kitchen and go into the bathroom. Then we grabbed the package of cookies and ran up to our room. We hid in the closet, and by the light of Eileen's flashlight, we ripped open the cookies. We ate and giggled and ate and giggled and before we knew it, the whole pack was gone. Mom never said anything, but I am pretty sure she knew because she made us sit at the dinner table that night until we had cleaned our plate. I don't think I have ever had to try so hard to force food down. My stomach hurt all night long. If only I had the opportunity to eat cookies with Eileen again. We were so close. When I lost Eileen, I not only lost my sister, I lost my best friend. God sent me another best friend, and now, I am afraid I have lost her too.

Chapter Twenty-Nine

After I finally force the last bite of that tasteless food down, I drag my feet back to the girls' room. I lie on my cot and stare at the door, imagining that Delores is going to walk in any minute. The minutes turn into hours, and everyone is getting ready for bed. Kim comes over and kneels next to my cot. With her hands on mine, she prays aloud for Delores's safety and my peace of mind.

MY EYES HAVE BEEN PEERING into the darkness for two hours. I can't close my eyes. Every time I do, images of what could be happening to Delores flash in my mind. I decide that this has to be more than reprimanding because she isn't back yet. Enough is enough. I am not going to lie here and do nothing while Delores is in trouble. I am going to find her. *I have to find her.* At one o'clock in the morning, I slide my chip under my pillow and slip out the door. I try to remember all of Delores's steps to avoid the cameras as I head toward the stairwell. The second and third floors are the only places I can figure to start looking. My legs propel me in slow motion while I listen for any sounds. As I approach the door to the second floor, a dark shadow is sitting curled up on the floor. I freeze, but I know it is too late. Whoever it is has already seen me.

"Sarah."

Steve. I can't believe it. Relief fills every crevice of my body at the sound of his voice. "Steve," I utter in a hushed tone.

"Yes, it's me. Hurry, let's get inside." He cracks the door, and we dart in. He wraps his arms around me and kisses my forehead.

"What are you doing here?" I ask.

"Delores sent me a message. She said she thought you guys had found the cryo lab." His voice saddens. "Then right after I got her IM, I heard about the security breach."

"Then they know she contacted you." I take a deep breath. "You aren't safe."

"Actually, I don't think they do. I have been in my office all evening ever since it happened. If they knew, they would have come for me. Delores is good. I think that someone just saw her at the computer. They either think they caught her before she did anything, or they can't figure out what she did."

"Steve, we have to find her."

"That is why I am here." He pulls out a flashlight. "Let's look around in here and see if we find any clues."

Steve clicks on the light and shines it around the room. I hear him swallow hard. Delores and I felt the glass tubes in the dark so I knew this must be the cryo lab. However, I don't think anything could have prepared me for what this little stream of light reveals. As Steve moves the light around, the glare of the light reflects off the glass, and my body stiffens at the sight of row upon row of cylinders standing upright. Each one is filled with solid ice and suspended inside the solid ice is a human. Even though it is frigid, my skin is hot as the anger inside me swells from the sight of what Denali has done to God's creations. These are people that God made in his own image, and Denali has frozen them alive because he couldn't make them stop following their Creator.

Steve squeezes my hand as we creep along. Neither of us utter a word because there are no words for what is before us. I look at each face and mourn for the bright future being denied by a man filled with evil. They all look to be teenagers or early twenties, and there are so many. I don't even know where to begin to count them.

Steve continues to shine his light on each tube. I keep looking for Delores even though I don't know how they could have her in one of these tubes this quickly.

Steve leans over and whispers in my ear, "Did you and Delores check out what is on the third floor?"

I shake my head no.

"Then I think we should check it out. I don't think Delores is in here."

We turn the corner and start down the next aisle going in the direction of the door. The light illuminates the first tube in the row, my knees buckle, and I crash to the floor. A scream barely escapes my lips, but Steve reacts instantly and gently caps his hand over my mouth. My face crinkles with sorrow and water gushes from my eyes as I stare up at the frozen face in the tube. Sharp pains shoot through my chest. I gasp, but I can't fill my lungs.

"Sarah...what is it, Sarah?" I hear Steve talking, but I have no idea what he is saying. Everything is a million miles away except the contents of this tube.

"Sarah, it's ok. That is not Delores. Calm down. That is not her." I can't make my mouth move to answer. My mind and body are paralyzed with shock.

I start to shake uncontrollably. Steve tries to pull me up to move me on, but I won't budge. I put my hands on his chest and try to push him away. I won't leave her. I have waited so long to see this face. I never imagined that I would ever see it like this.

"Sarah...please...you have to talk to me. We are going to get caught if we aren't quiet. What is it?" Panic is starting to form in Steve's voice.

I point at the tube. "Eileen...th...th... that is my sister, Eileen."

"Oh, no." Steve falls back down onto the floor next to me and pulls me into his chest. He just sits there holding me as I try to muffle my sobs.

"Listen," he says softly, "God helped us with the monkey. He was preparing us for this Sarah. He was preparing us to find your sister. God has led you to her, but we need Delores. She is the computer expert, and we can't get into this computer system to unfreeze Eileen without her. So, I need you to look at what God has done by leading you here. See the miracle in this. Stand up, and let's find Delores before it is too late."

His words cut me to the core. Steve is right. I wipe my face with my sleeve. God has brought me here to Eileen for a reason, and I need to take action. Breaking down is not an option. *I can do all things through Christ who strengthens me. I CAN DO ALL THINGS THROUGH CHRIST WHO STRENGTHENS ME.* My eyes bear into Steve's with renewed determination. I stand up pulling him up with me.

"Ok," I order, "we are going to the third floor. Delores is here somewhere, and we are going to find her...but not because she can hack into a computer...because she is my best friend, and I am not losing her."

I intertwine my fingers with his and take the flashlight from him with my other hand. I turn and lead us to the door like a soldier going into battle. Carefully, I stop and listen at the door. When I am sure there is no movement whatsoever on the other side of the door, I push down every ounce of fear inside me and grab hold of the knob. I open the door, glance both ways, and with urgency, in each step, I pull Steve behind me taking the stairs two at a time.

At the top of the stairs, Steve and I both put our ears to the door and nod to each other. Inside, a faint glow fills the room. My heart skips a beat as I quickly peer around the room looking for someone, but the glow just seems to be coming from computer monitors. The layout is similar to the lab where we found the frozen animals. Steve and I continue to the back and go through another door into a procedure room just like in the other building.

My mouth flies open sucking in every ounce of air in the room. There, lying on a gurney in the middle of the room is my dearest friend. One of those huge vertical cylinders filled with liquid stands next to the gurney. The lid is open at a ninety-degree angle with two huge hoses attached to the top of it. I rush over beside Delores and let out a sigh of relief as I see her chest rise and fall. They must have just given her something to knock her out.

"Looks like we made it just in time." Steve points to the machines with little tubes running from them. "Remember...before they can freeze her, they have to replace her blood with that anti-freezing agent stuff."

Beside the machines, a cart holds two antifreeze canisters stamped with a symbol that looks like snowflakes with an X through them. Next to the cart, a large bag hangs from a hook on a tall stand. The bag has a label affixed to it with a large red droplet and "Delores Ducati" printed on it.

I start to shake Delores to wake her up. Steve shakes his head. "Sarah, I think she is heavily sedated. They must be planning to freeze her first thing. I don't know what to do. We have to get Delores out of here now, but what are we going to do with her? They will obviously go off the deep end when she is missing."

Think, think. Delores would know just what to do. A sliver of hope washes over me. "Steve, since they actually have Delores in their possession, do you think they have paid any attention to her chip? I mean do you think they have tracked it or noticed that she doesn't have it?"

He scratches his head in thought. "You know, I doubt it. Where would Delores have put the chip?"

"Under her pillow."

"Well," his eyes narrow as he peers down at me, "if the chip is there, they probably don't know. But what difference does it make?"

"We don't have much time. But on the map, there are some huge water reservoirs located not far outside of building three. If the chip is still under her pillow, and they don't know her chip is missing, we can fake her death. We take the chip and throw it in the water reservoir. They will think Delores took her own life, but we need to find somewhere to hide her."

"Ok. Well, we better hurry because we are almost out of time. We will have to take Delores with us now and just hope the chip is there." Steve starts to lift Delores. "Either way, we can't leave her here."

I get on the other side of Delores and help Steve lift her up. Steve on one side and me on the other, we carry Delores between us with one of her arms draped around Steve's neck and her other arm draped around my neck.

As we approach the door, Steve stops. "Ok. I don't want us to split up, but we are left with no choice. We pass by your room on the way to my exit to building one. When we get outside your door, I will wait with Delores while you creep in stealth mode and get the chip from under her pillow. Once I know you have it, I will get Delores back to my office and hide her until she wakes. I am pretty much under the radar in there. In all honesty, not many people even know I exist. You take the chip, throw it in the reservoir, and get back in your room. Move fast because it is almost dawn already. Well, above ground it is almost dawn...anyway, we will meet in front of floor three at two a.m. We have to get your sister tonight before they realize that Delores's body is not in that reservoir."

"Sounds like a plan...our only option really. Let's go."

"Hey, Sarah." The Adam's apple bobs in his neck as Steve pushes out his words. "Uhhmm. Please be careful." He looks like he wants to say something else, but he doesn't.

With a quick deep breath, I open the door, and we cruise

down the stairs. As we sail through the hallway dodging cameras, I pray begging God to keep a bubble of protection around us.

When we reach the door to the girls' room, Steve hugs the wall with Delores staying out of sight. I literally belly crawl across the floor to Delores's cot. I fear the sound of my heart thumping in my chest is going to wake everyone up. I run my fingers under her pillow...nothing. Pressing my lips together, I hold my breath. I slip my hand under her pillow again sweeping my fingers gently around. Jackpot... my pinky finger glides against a small, folded piece of tissue paper. *Thank you, Lord!* Clasping it tightly in my fist, I crawl back out of the room and give Steve a thumbs up.

We zigzag down the hall with Delores. As soon as we exit the building, he takes Delores toward building one, and I race to the reservoir. I don't even think. When I get to the edge of the water, I throw the chip as far out into the water as I can and head back to the building talking to God as I trudge along. I ask him over and over to please let Steve have made it safely with Delores and to let me get back to my cot without getting caught. I feel like a character in a video game racing against the clock as I leap and duck trying to avoid being caught on camera. I slide through the door to my room and every muscle in my body stays contracted until I am covered up on my cot. With the blankets pulled up over my face, I thank God for leading us to my sister and to Delores. I thank God for getting us through the night without getting caught. I thank God for putting Steve by my side, so I don't have to face this alone. I close my eyes and give in to the forty-five minutes I have left to sleep.

Chapter Thirty

M y body bolts upright at the booming of Dr. Fleming's voice on the loudspeaker. Again, she barks out orders to stay in our room until further notice. So, for the moment, I choose to lie back down and assume my comfortable position on my cot. I am too physically exhausted to get up, and on top of that, I am not mentally ready to cope with the occurrences of the last eight hours.

It feels like only five minutes, but apparently, an hour has passed when Dr. Fleming's voice penetrates the room again. The solemn tone in her voice makes me tremble. "Could I have your attention, please?" I am pretty sure that her voice cracks with a little bit of emotion. "It is with great sorrow that I have to inform you of the loss of another trainee today. Delores Ducati broke out of her reprimanding room last night and has taken her own life. I realize that a few of you have grown very close to her, and I am truly sorry that I have to deliver this news. Under the circumstances, I understand that some may not want to adhere to your schedules today, but it is necessary to continue with the training regimen. At this time, the dining room is open. After breakfast, you should follow your regular schedule for the day. Thank you."

I hate having to mislead the others, but I have to if I am going to get the chance to save my sister. They have to see me fall apart because they all know how close I am to Delores. The thing is that I don't have to pretend to have a breakdown because it has taken every last shred of my strength to hold back the tears and maintain my composure. The adrenaline rush has worn off, and the scenes of those frozen bodies flicker in my head like a film reel on an old projector. I open and close my eyes trying to shake the image, but my sister's still pale face and glassy eyes behind a sheet of ice are embossed in my mind.

Moisture starts to seep from the corners of my eyes. I bury my face in my hands, and the moisture turns to streams. My body starts to shudder, and the streams turn to rivers. The next thing I know all the girls, even Penny, are there on my cot embracing each other and weeping uncontrollably.

Only a few moments pass before Dr. Fleming flings open the door reminding us that we should already be in the dining room. Even with Dr. Fleming trying to corral us along, we all get dressed in slow motion and, with puffy eyes and swollen faces, we traipse down the hall to force-feed ourselves.

We drag ourselves into the dining room, and I notice that Bob's eyes and face match ours. That is except for his cheeks. His cheeks are so full of food that he looks like a squirrel. Nothing ever seems to faze his appetite. I wish I could be like that, but on the contrary, I don't think I can get one bite down without it coming back up, let alone my whole tray of food.

I sit down in front of my tray, close my eyes, and thank God for his guidance and protection. When I open my eyes, I stare down at the food in front of me, and I just cannot do it. The thought of swallowing one bite of food makes me gag. I pick up my boiled egg and look around. I act like I am taking a bite, and then quickly I drop it onto Bob's tray. It barely hits the tray before it ends up in his mouth.

With his mouth full, Bob looks over at me and nods his

head toward the paper on my tray. "Did you see who you fight today? I have to fight Darla."

I pick up the paper. "Great. I am supposed to fight Kim. How do they expect us to fight each other? Kim is my friend."

I keep faking bites, and Bob keeps eating never seeming to notice that he is consuming extra food. He doesn't even seem to notice when a whole extra bowl of oatmeal lands on his plate.

Finally, my tray is empty, and I can go get rid of it. Luckily, the scheduled time for my brain stimulation has already passed. Besides breakfast, we are just picking up with our schedules from the current time, so I don't have to stress about that today. However, it is time for me to see Dr. Blakely, and somehow, I am going to have to hold my tongue. I leave the dining room and float in a zombie-like state down the hall to Dr. Blakely's office. I exhale and open the door.

"Sarah, I didn't know if you were going to make it." Dr. Blakely rises from his chair and extends his open hand toward the couch.

I follow his gesture and attempt to relax resting my head on the throw pillow. "Honestly, I would rather not be here. It just doesn't seem fair that they are making us continue our schedules today."

Dr. Blakely leans back and puts his hands together touching only at the fingertips. "So, Sarah, do you think the better option would be to hoard up in your room and cry the day away? I mean would that really change anything?"

I look away toward the wall. "No, you're right. It wouldn't change a thing. But at least I would feel like I was paying proper respect by taking time to mourn for Delores."

"I can understand that. Sometimes we all feel weak." He leans forward with his elbow on his knees. "In your first session with me, you said your top priority was serving God. I suppose you must be second-guessing your trust in God now."

"What? Of course not." I push myself up and move to a sitting position on the couch. "There is no way that I could get through this without God. Isaiah 40:31 says, 'But those that

wait on the Lord shall renew their strength; they shall mount up
with wings like eagles, they shall run and not be weary, they shall
walk and not faint.' And Isaiah 43:2 says, 'When you pass
through the waters, I will be with you; and through the rivers,
they shall not overflow you. When you walk through the fire,
you shall not be burned, nor shall the flame scorch you.' You see,
Dr. Blakely, I may not have my Bible, but God's words are in my
heart. God is with me, and that is the reason that I have the
strength to still be sitting here holding it together. When you
invite Jesus into your life, you really understand the meaning of
Philippians 4:7, 'And the peace of God, which surpasses all
understanding, will guard your hearts and minds through Christ
Jesus.' Dr. Blakely, I have that peace that passes understanding.
If you don't feel that peace, I hope that one day you will come to
know God and be able to experience it."

"Ms. Sanguine, why don't we end our session now? That will
give you a few extra minutes to go back to your room and
remember Delores."

"That would be great." I stand up. "Thank you, Dr. Blakely."

Chapter Thirty-One

I amble into the arena, grateful for the few minutes that I finally had alone back in the room. Felipe is climbing into the rink, and Kim is seated on one of the benches with her elbows propped on her knees and her head buried in her hands.

I sit down next to her. "Kim, you okay?"

"Yeah...no...I can't fight you. I miss Delores. I mean I barely knew her, but everything about this place is all wrong." She uncovers her face and peers over at me. "I know what I just said makes no sense."

"It makes perfect sense. Come on." I stand and cross over into the rink.

Kim follows behind me, and Felipe directs us to shake hands and move to opposite corners.

"Okay," Felipe says, "you guys ready... Let's go. Three...two...one. Fight."

"I surrender." I slide through the ropes of the rink and stride out of the arena.

With every movement taking ten times more effort than normal, I clump back to my room and plop down on my cot. Kim comes running in.

"Sarah...you didn't have to do that."

I fix my eyes straight ahead at the wall. "Yes, I did. How can we hurt each other?"

"Well, thank you. You know, this is my second time in level three, and this is the only fight I have won so far."

With that, we both crack a smile.

A light pecking noise silences our conversation. With our nerves on edge, we listen with pursed lips as our eyes wander around the room searching for the source. We simultaneously let out a sigh and start to breathe again when the tapping repeats.

Kim laughs and paces to the door. "It is just someone knocking. I guess we seriously need to relax. All of this chaos is getting in our heads."

Kim swings the door open, and Bob is on the other side of the threshold swaying back and forth wringing his hands together.

"Hey, Kim. I...uh...was needing to talk to Sarah for a minute."

"Sure, Bob." Kim turns to get my attention, but I am already there beside her.

"What's going on, Bob?"

"I just need to talk for a second." He stands there gazing at me, so I take the hint that he wants the conversation to be private.

I step into the hall, and Bob puts his hand behind his head leaning back against the wall. *Okay, so he knows about the chip. I will have to pretend.* I stretch, bend my elbows, and then place my hands on the back of my neck.

Bob speaks so low I can barely hear him. "Sarah, I am scared."

I nod my head. "We all are, Bob."

"No, you don't understand. So many things don't add up. I know Delores would not have taken her own life. Stress can get to anyone, but Delores is a strong woman. I just don't buy it. And for some reason, my memories are fading. I can't even picture the faces of my family." Moisture glistens in the corner of his eye. "Anyway, that is not why I came to see you. I have been watching you and Delores. No matter what happens around here, you guys always have this…this…something. I don't know how to describe it, but it's something I don't have." His eyes dig into mine. "Sarah, I don't really think that I am saved. I have always called myself a Christian because I said a little prayer. But after I said that prayer, I never changed. I never tried to get to know God. I guess I just said that prayer because everyone else in my little group at church did. I suppose I thought that saying I was a Christian was enough, but I realize that a label means nothing if it doesn't reflect what is inside." He lifts one side of his mouth into a partial smile. "Kind of like the name Balboa didn't make me a fighting machine."

"Oh, Bob. Obviously, God is speaking to you. Don't waste any more time because we don't know what the next minute has in store for us. Right now, pray from your heart like you just talked to me. You need to be sure that you have Jesus in your heart. Do you want me to pray with you?"

Tears trickle down his cheek. "Would you?"

I can't help the smile that forms on my face. "Of course, Bob. Of course, I will." I take one hand down and place it on his shoulder. Closing my eyes, I speak in a soft voice, "Bob, repeat this prayer after me. Lord, I know I am a sinner. Please forgive me, Lord. I give you complete control of my life and trust in You alone as my Savior. Please come live in my heart and change me, Lord. Thank you for saving me. Amen."

After a moment of silence, Bob lifts his head. "Thank you, Sarah." He clears his throat. "I really am sorry. I know how close you were to Delores. I only wish I had the opportunity to get to know her better. She was an amazing lady."

I never noticed that Bob might have had an eye for Delores. "Thanks, Bob."

Bob rubs his stomach and chuckles. "Funny, today is the first time I have ever gotten full on a meal here."

"Well," I grimace, "I kind of have a confession. I was too upset to eat so I put my food on your tray."

Bob lets go of his neck and doubles over in hysterical laughter. "Thank goodness. I thought my stomach was shrinking."

I MAKE the turn into the stairwell leading up to floor three, and there he is.

"Steve, thank goodness. But where is Delores?"

He points to the door. "Delores is already in there hacking into the computer. She said we don't have much time. Ever since I told her about Eileen, she has been full speed ahead. Anyway, I found this dolly that looks like it is made to transport those tubes, and there is a freight elevator at the back of the lab next to the procedure room. Come on. We have to get your sister up here."

As Steve and I pass through, it is all I can do not to run to Delores, but as Dr. Fleming says, 'time is of the essence,' and if I want to save my sister, I have to stay focused. Steve grabs the dolly, and with a quick drop of my stomach, we step off the freight elevator onto the second floor. I guide the way with the flashlight while Steve pushes the dolly. The dolly has straps that ratchet around the tube. Once we get it strapped to the dolly, Steve pumps a foot pedal that jacks the tube up off the ground. With Eileen's frozen body on wheels, we roll it into the elevator.

When the elevator slides open to the third floor, Delores is there waiting. "Come on. The computer is ready. Let's get this tube thawed out."

We wheel the tube into the procedure room and hook it to a hoist hanging from the middle of the sphere. Steve pushes a button, and the hoist lowers the tube to a horizontal position.

As fast as the speed of light, Delores runs up, grabs our hands, and asks God to lead this operation allowing Eileen to live if that is his plan. She moves back to the computer. "Ok. Here comes the heat. I will increase the temperature gradually. Fans are on low speed."

I have the blood pressure cuff and stethoscope, and I locate the AED next to the tube. Steve had already found her blood while he was waiting for me to get here tonight. He said there was a giant cooler room on floor two. He is ready with the tubes to drain the antifreeze agent and pump in her blood.

"The heat is increasing. Anything happening?"

"Yes, Delores. The ice is starting to thaw. A little bit of liquid has drained from the cylinder." Steve's voice is shaking. Of course, I don't think there is any part of my body that is not shaking. We are attempting something that has never been done before, and we are attempting it on my little sister.

"Ok let me know if I need to increase the heat more."

"No," Steve replies. "It needs to thaw slowly."

The liquid seeps little by little from the drain hose into a pipe that carries it away.

"Ok, we are clear. The liquid is completely drained. I am opening the tube." Steve lifts the glass top away and quickly attaches the drain tube for the antifreeze to a port already in place on Eileen's left arm. He hooks the tube for the blood pump to a port in her right arm. "Tubes are in place." Steve smooths the wet ringlets of brown hair away from her bleach-white face.

"Sarah, get the AED!" Delores says in a panicky tone.

Just like the monkey, the computer lets the AED deliver a shock and then orders CPR.

God, please help. This is my baby sister. I start doing chest compressions thrusting down thirty times. I pinch her nose and blow twice into her lungs. I push thirty more times with the heel of my hand. Two more breaths flow from my body to hers. I pump on her chest and give two steady breaths. *This can't be happening. Please let her breathe.* Chest compressions. Air. *Oh no.* Chest compressions. Air. Water pools in the bottom of my eyes. *Focus.* My hands and arms tingle with fear as I keep compressing. Nothing is happening. I blow as big of a breath as my lungs will hold. Chest compressions. Air. Chest compressions. Air.

Steve's head falls, and I can tell he thinks it's over. He slides up next to me and starts to say something, but I cut him off before he can utter a sound.

"I won't quit. Ever." Chest compressions. Air. Chest compressions. Air.

The door flings open so hard the metal knob dings as it bounces off the wall, but I don't care who it is or if we are caught. I won't give up.

"What on earth are you three do...oh no!" Dr. Fleming's voice fills the room. "Don't you three know that this is the year 2049. There is a machine that performs CPR with a zero percent fail rate." Dr. Fleming runs to the wall and opens a little door to a compartment that looks like it should house a fire extinguisher. She pulls out the strangest mask contraption that I have ever seen. "Quick," she orders, "put this over her mouth and nose. Make sure the little rubber snout completely seals."

I cap it over Eileen's face making sure it is snug. Dr. Fleming comes around me with something that looks like a chest protector for a baseball catcher except it has a square box right in the middle of it. She straps it to Eileen's chest.

The machine starts forcing a regular breathing pattern. After about a minute, the computer says, "Independent breathing detected...standby...independent breathing detected...remove device." Dr. Fleming removes the chest box. Then, in a swift motion, she lifts the face contraption and caps the oxygen mask over Eileen's mouth and nose.

Eileen's chest is rising and falling on its own. A huge breath escapes from my mouth as my body sags back against Steve. *Thank you, God. Thank you for sending Dr. Fleming.*

"Dr. Fleming," I clear my throat, "how can I ever thank you? You saved my sister."

Lowering her head and slumping her shoulders, Dr. Fleming speaks softly. "Right now, we have to figure out what to do because it is four o'clock in the morning, and all of you need to disappear before anyone gets up. The problem is that your sister still has not regained consciousness and will in no way be strong enough to move anytime soon." Dr. Fleming paces back and forth rubbing her head. "You three...well, now four, have no idea how serious this is. This is life or death...and you all seem to keep trying for the latter."

"Dr. Fleming, we already know that this is not a special crime unit training facility. We know that we are in an abandoned military complex inside of a mountain in Colorado, and we know that President Denali is a demented psychopath. He is trying to make his own army of followers that has no knowledge of God, destroy the rest of society, and create Denali Land." The more I talk, the more upset I get. And the more upset I get, the higher my voice gets. "What we don't know is when and how he is going to kill all of those innocent people."

"Sooner than you think," Dr. Fleming mumbles.

Steve inches closer to her. "Sooner than we think...as in how much sooner?"

"Denali has enough in his army already."

"So, then what are we doing here?" Delores demands.

"You guys are just a few extras just in case he needs to replenish any on the front lines." Dr. Fleming wipes her trembling sweaty hands down the sides of her white coat. "I don't know the exact time though. I am shocked he hasn't already released it."

The blood drains from my face. *This cannot be good.* "Release what?"

"Look, I am in deep with you guys already. I really don't know what came over me when I came in here. Now if Denali finds out that I helped you, I am done...as in permanently done. I am not telling you anything else. Surely you can understand that I do not want to die."

Fear flickers in her round eyes, and I search for words to convince her to help us. "Dr. Fleming, you came to our aid because you are not evil like Denali. You saved my sister because you are not a murderer." I step closer letting my eyes cut straight into hers. "But if you keep information to yourself and allow millions of people to die, you will be just like him. Dr. Fleming, there might be a chance we could stop it."

"You can't stop him. Look around you."

"Wh...wh...whhhhhat...wh...wh...wh...where?"

We all turn toward the sound of the stuttering words. Eileen has her eyes open, and she is trying to speak. Her voice is just a faint whimper, but it is still her voice, the voice of my baby sister, my sister that I thought was gone forever. I leap over to her side. "Eileen."

"Sarah," Dr. Fleming moves behind me and grabs my shoulder, "she doesn't remember who you are. She was frozen because she didn't forget about God. Her memory of everything else in her past is still gone. She thinks her name is Alexis."

I had forgotten about that, but I don't want to believe that she doesn't remember me. I place my hand on hers. "Eileen, do you have any idea who I am?"

She blinks like she is trying to clear her vision. "N...n....no. Should I...I?" Eileen wiggles her head scouring the room. "Dr. Fleming, what is...is going on?"

"Alexis, do you remember anything?" Dr. Fleming strokes Eileen's head.

"I am...supposed to be...training to...be a secret agent for...the President. Why...why... am I in here?"

"Do you remember being given a test?"

"Ummmm..." Eileen squeezes her eyes shut like she is trying to think. "Dr. Blakely was asking me some questions."

"Yes...and do you remember what he asked you?"

"He asked...my name, and...and where I was from. Then... he asked about my family." Eileen answers in a weak and trembling voice.

"Ok...and what were your responses?"

"My name is Alexis Anderson, and that I don't have a family. I was an orphan living in a children's home in Atlanta when Denali recruited me."

"Good, Alexis. Now...do you remember what else Dr. Blakely asked?"

"He asked me...to name the most important things in my life...starting with the most important."

"And your answer?"

"I told him that God is most important, and then my job working for Denali."

"I see," Dr. Fleming's voice cracks. "Alexis, I am about to share some information with you that is going to be hard for you to hear. We don't have much time, so I need you to listen closely and try to keep it together because I have to get you out of here quickly. Can you be strong for me?"

"Dr. Fleming, I don't understand." Eileen's body twitches. "Can you help me sit up?"

Steve and I reach and help her limp cold body sit up on the side of the gurney. She flops right back over, so Steve and I each put an arm around her to hold her up.

"Just be strong. I am going to give you the quick version, and then you have to go with these people. Here it goes. Alexis...your name is not Alexis. Your name is Eileen Hatcher. You were never an orphan. This is your sister Ellie. President Denali actually kidnapped you and brought you here to be a part of his weird new society. Denali is an evil man that has been bringing young people here to erase their memories and give them new identities. He thought that if he erased their memories, they would forget about the existence of God. Denali wants everyone to only follow him. He plans to destroy the rest of humanity and start over with the people he has brought here. The problem arose when a lot of the people that he brought here forgot everything but God. That is what happened to you. He had those people frozen using cryogenics until he could figure out why their memory retained God."

Dr. Fleming takes a deep breath. "You have been frozen for almost two years. Strangely enough, Denali just chose your sister, Ellie, to be part of his group too. But she is feisty and went searching for answers. She stumbled upon you and tried to thaw you out. And here we are. Denali is getting ready for the destruction phase of his plan. Your sister thinks she can save all of those innocent people...and your only choice is to go with her."

Eileen has that deer in the headlights look. "So…let me get this straight. My name is really Eileen, and some crazy man kidnapped me. He tried to erase my memory because he wanted to take God away from me and become a god himself. And he thinks he is going to kill the family that I can't remember along with everyone else that doesn't follow him."

Dr. Fleming nods. "That pretty much sums it up."

"What an idiot! Doesn't he know that if a person is really a Christian, Jesus just can't be erased from that person's memory? The reason I didn't forget is because Jesus lives in my heart. And I will not stand by and allow him to hurt my family even if I can't remember them. What do we have to do to stop him?"

"Alexis…I mean Eileen, you have amazed me since the day you arrived here. Actually, you are an inspiration to me because you are the kind of person that I want to be." Dr. Fleming's face floods with tears.

"From the moment you entered this complex, you have been completely selfless. I have never met anyone that seems to care about other people the way you do." Dr. Fleming pauses and wipes her face. Then she motions for all of us to come close.

"Okay, I can't believe I am doing this, but really, there is no other choice," she says as she squeezes her eyes closed and rubs her temples. "Here's the story. President Denali is going to fake his own death in a plane crash. The plane is going to be filled with this invisible toxic gas. When the plane crashes, the gas will disperse out into the atmosphere, and eventually, it is supposed to circle the entire globe. The gas will mix with the clouds, fall through precipitation, and contaminate the water supply. The symptoms start out just like seasonal allergies or the common cold, but after the lining of the lungs begins to deteriorate, the symptoms will get worse, and then it will be too late. Everyone will be led to believe that President Denali is on the plane, but actually, he will be here hiding out in his specially designed safe house located in building fifteen. I don't know when the plane is scheduled to crash, but I do know that Denali arrived at building fifteen last night. The doors to the complex haven't been sealed, so that tells me the gas has not been released yet."

"So, I would assume that he flew aboard Air Force One to get here…" Delores starts traipsing back and forth at a record speed. The spinning wheels in her mind seem to be propelling her entire body. "This is just a hunch, but I think we might have a day or two. I would think President Denali would normally always use Air Force One to travel. If he is going to fake his death, that will be the plane that crashes. He obviously is going to want the flight that dropped him here to be kept under the rug so the plane will have to go back to Washington D.C. first. That would be the only way to keep the flight pattern from being linked to Colorado. On top of that, I highly doubt that President Denali would risk his life by traveling here on a plane filled with deadly gas so we can add a little time allowance for turning the plane into a lethal weapon."

"Delores, I am not sure, but I think I studied in U.S. History class that there are actually two Air Force One planes," I say with hesitation.

"Very good, Sarah. You know your stuff. There were two. One had 28000 on its tail, and the other one had 29000. However, when President Denali took office, he wanted an even bigger plane with his own unique layout. So, now instead of two Boeing 747-200B Air Force One planes, there is one bigger Boeing 797Z Air Force One with a tail code 30000. And since President Denali is so fond of himself, he had them add a photo of his face that covers almost the entire exterior of the plane."

My face twists in disbelief. "Wow. The more I learn about this guy, the more freaked out I get. Anyway, sorry I interrupted. Keep going with the plan."

"That's the problem. I have no plan because even with a day or two, what can we do? It's not like we have transportation to Washington D.C."

"I think I can help." Dr. Fleming walks over to the computer and pulls up a map of the complex. "Remember we are in an old military bunker. There is an Air Force base not far away. It has been out of operation for a while, but some military aircraft are still stored there." She points to the map as she speaks. "If you guys go through the blast doors and out the main tunnel, you will exit into a parking lot with a guarded entrance. In all honesty, I am sure the guards are sleeping. It's not like there is a lot of action around the outside of this place especially in the middle of the night. Anyway, the guards have little electric cars that they use when they patrol the outside of the complex. Take one of those cars over to the Air Force base. From there, you are on your own because I have no idea how you will find the location of Air Force One. Obviously, he cannot fill it with toxic gas right out in the open. But at least if you can get a plane from the abandoned base, you should be able to get to Washington D.C. in about five hours."

Concern covers Steve's face. "I see two problems. One, you know as soon as we head down that tunnel, Denali's goons are going to be after us. Two, if we do make it out of here and get to a plane, who is going to fly it?"

"I could close the blast doors behind you. That will buy you some time because President Denali has allowed all of us access to close the doors, but only he can open them. If I know Denali, it will take him some time to figure it out. As for the pilot problem..." Dr. Fleming looks over at Delores...not Delores...her name is Alice.

"Alice," I smile at her, "you got any ideas?"

"Thanks for remembering my real name. And yes, I do have an idea. I can fly the plane. I have a pilot's license."

"Wow, really?" Steve can't hide his surprise.

"Yes, really. I mean it is just a private pilot's license, but I still know how to fly almost anything. My dad was a commercial pilot."

"Dr. Fleming," I plead, "why don't you go with us? I am afraid for you to stay here. What if Denali finds out you helped us?"

"I can't. I have to close the gates. But I will be fine. It is you guys that are risking your lives. You realize that you might not make it, right? If that plane crashes, you will be out there with that gas."

"No worries." Eileen smiles. "Then we will get to be with Jesus in Heaven."

"Are you guys ready?" Dr. Fleming is pulling up the gates on the monitor. "You are running out of time."

We all stand up, but Eileen's weakened legs are like spaghetti. Her muscles just don't have the strength to hold her.

"Oh, I forgot." Dr. Fleming goes to the little refrigerator and comes back with three capsules and a metal flask. "This combination will give you instant strength, but you need real food as soon as you can." She hands Eileen the metal flask and the three capsules. "Here, swallow the three capsules and then drink this energy tonic. When you are done with that, hydrate with this bottle of water."

Five minutes later, Eileen is standing fully functional and energized. *Note to self: find out what is in that tonic.* Looking up at Eileen, I had forgotten how much taller my little sister was than me. She has about five inches on me.

Dr. Fleming moves back to the screen. "Now, I am going to be watching on the monitor. This point right here when you exit building three and go into the tunnel has a camera that you cannot escape. I will see you. As soon as you are in view of that camera, I will hit the emergency key, and the doors will start to close. It takes forty-five seconds for the doors to completely close, so be ready. You have to get yourselves through that tunnel and both blast doors in less than forty-five seconds. Got it?... Oh, and make sure you are entirely clear of those doors. They weigh twenty-five tons each."

"Thank you, Dr. Fleming." I wrap my arms around her.

We all move to the door. Just as he is about to open it, Steve stops.

"Hey, Dr. Fleming," he says, "how do I find out who I really am?"

"Steve, some things are better left alone."

"No," Steve pleads, "I need to know."

"I guess five more minutes isn't going to change anything. You guys wait here. I'll be right back." Dr. Fleming rushes out the door.

DR. FLEMING HAS a way with speed walking. I had my doubts that she would return in five minutes, but here she is. At least I hope that is the sound of her feet coming up the steps.

She enters the door quietly and closes it behind her. "Okay, this is the deal. You guys need to go now. I am giving each of you your file, but do not open it until you are safely out of here. Your complete focus must be on getting out of the complex without getting caught. Move quickly. I will be watching on the computer. When you get in view of the camera in front of the blast doors, I will enter the code to close them. Don't forget that you only have forty-five seconds to get through both doors. Once you get through those doors, there will be less of a chance for someone to be chasing you, at least for a few minutes. From there go on through the tunnel and get one of the electric cars from outside the guards' office. You have the map to the Air Force base."

Her eyes shimmer with moisture. She gives us each a folder and a hug.

"Go now. And please be careful."

Chapter Thirty-Two

The four of us wind down the stairwell. Alice leads us since she has the map stored in that computer bank memory of hers. I follow with Eileen behind me, and Steve takes the back. Alice crisscrosses back and forth through the hall. We finally make it to the exit door of building three. Once we are out the door, we just forget about the cameras and run with every molecule of energy in us.

The point Dr. Fleming showed us on the computer is up ahead. "Okay. Remember our forty-five seconds starts now," I blurt out just to make sure nobody forgot. Those doors weigh twenty-five tons each. There will be no prying that open.

As we pass through the first one, it has just started to creep shut. Down the corridor, the other one is already at halfway. Alice may have short legs, but she can move. She is already clear. I slide through and turn to check on Eileen, but she is already out. Steve isn't out. I don't see him. *I don't see Steve. No. No. No. Where is he? This cannot be happening.*

The gap is only about a foot wide now. *No. Ten inches.* Suddenly his body flies through the opening sideways, and the door seals behind him. My shoulders drop as my muscles relax. "What happened? Where were you?"

Breathing hard, he holds up his folder. "I dropped it."

I shake my head, and we take off running. The tunnel slants uphill, and finally, we are outside. My eyes immediately become entranced at the sight of the full moon and the clear sky crammed with glowing stars. Oh, how I have missed being outdoors. I will never take the beauty of God's creation for granted again.

I bring myself back to the task at hand and gaze across the vacant lot. A little brick building is situated at the entrance to the lot. Down one side of the building sits a row of mini cars that resemble golf carts but with doors. As we cross the vacant lot out in the open, I say a prayer that the guards are sleeping.

Alice looks inside one of the cars and stamps her foot. "Of course, the keys aren't in it."

We tip toe and peep in the window of the guard building. Dr. Fleming was right. There are two guards, and both of them are leaned back in their chairs with their feet propped on the desk sound asleep. Next to their propped feet sit a couple of empty Krispy Kreme boxes and an open bag of chips.

Eileen points through the window. "Look by the door. The keys are on those hooks."

"Oh no they don't." Steve snaps in an abrupt tone. "You guys be ready by one of the cars. I will be right back." He heads off lumbering around the side of the building toward the door.

Alice, Eileen, and I pick the newest-looking car. It is blue with a red two on the side. Hopefully, the keys are numbered.

Steve is already coming back around the side of the building with the keys dangling in his hand. *What...*

"Is that Spencer?" Alice asks with complete shock in her voice.

"It certainly looks like him."

Out of breath, Steve hands me the keys.

"What are you doing with that monkey?" *I can't wait to hear this.*

"They had him in a cage in there. He just got unfrozen. He does not deserve to be in a cage."

"I guess he is going with us…" I mumble. "Are you sure they didn't hear you?"

"I am sure, but even if they did, I wouldn't worry too much. I don't think they could move very fast to catch us without getting sick. There were three more empty donut boxes in the trash."

The keys jingle in my quivering fingers. I finally find the one with the two, and then it slips out of my hand clattering on the pavement. Alice sweeps them from the ground and has key two in a split second.

Unbelievable, but she still insists that I drive even after that little mishap. Alice sits in the passenger seat to give me play by play directions. Steve, Eileen, and Spencer cram in the back. Underestimating the power of this little car, I tap on the gas and the car lurches forward giving us all whiplash. If the key incident wasn't loud enough, Spencer lets out a high-pitched squeal when his head jerks back. The guards must be deep sleepers.

The base comes into view. I slap the brake, and Alice jumps out to push open the chain-link gate. "Weird," she says. "You would think it would be locked. I know this place is not in use anymore, but if there are planes here…Well, I guess our tax dollars can just buy more."

We pull on through to a huge metal building that Alice explains is the hangar. Inside, about ten small planes fill the space. "There." Alice points to one. "It is a Cessna 208. That will do just fine. Let's see if it has fuel." Alice starts checking the plane out, and Steve and Spencer wander off to do some exploring.

I take a moment to hug my sister. "Eileen, I know you can't remember me, but you have no idea how badly I have missed you. When you disappeared, I didn't just lose my sister, I lost my best friend."

"I wish I could remember. It is so weird…it is like when I search my mind for memories, there is just a black gaping hole."

Eileen's face fills with frustration. "It makes me so angry that Denali took so much from me. Who does he think he is? How can he possibly think he has the right to take away my identity?"

"The devil can convince people of some pretty drastic things."

"Ellie," Eileen grabs my hand and squeezes, "I promise that I am going to do everything in my power to remember you. But if I don't, I know that we are sisters. Look at us. We look almost identical, but it's so much more than that. It's hard to explain, but I feel this bond with you that goes beyond memories. I may not remember growing up with you, but I can feel the connection that we have to each other."

"Oh, Eileen, I wish you could remember too, but you are right. We have a bond that no one can take away. I am just so thankful that I have you back."

Steve comes running with Spencer wrapped around his neck. "Alice...Alice!"

"What?" Alice steps off the plane.

"We found some fuel tanks out back. Get the plane going, and we can fuel it up beside the building."

"Great. Good work, you guys." Alice turns back toward the plane. "I just need another minute to finish the safety check. Have you found anything we can put some water in? I think this is about a five-hour flight. I am sure there is no food here since this place has been abandoned for so long."

"No, but we will keep looking." Steve takes off running with Spencer's little hands holding onto his hair.

"Come on, Ellie. Let's look around in here." Eileen starts toward a door in the back.

The room has a damp musky smell. "Look at all of these boxes. I wonder how long this stuff has been in here." Tiny labels are affixed to the corners of the boxes, and I strain to read the faded words. "Eileen, God is amazing. Help me carry some of these boxes to the plane."

"Why? What's in them?"

I wink at her. "MREs. They may not taste great, but they are non-perishable and will give us the strength and nourishment we need."

"Hallelujah...I am so hungry that my stomach is cramping." Eileen grabs a box and cruises toward the plane.

As we approach the plane with the boxes, Steve comes around the corner with jugs of water, and Spencer is behind him dragging a jug with his tail. Steve smiles, "He wants to help. Isn't this little guy great?"

I head back to the storage room because I am pretty sure that I saw a box of medical supplies. Something moves behind me. My body stiffens. Another scurry. I hold my breath and flip around with my heart jumping out of my chest. Spencer's little eyes look up. "Spencer, you scared me to death." He grabs my hand and runs along beside me. I can't help but giggle. "Spencer, I see why Steve loves you so much."

I find the medical supplies while Spencer prowls. "Oooo... eeee...oooo...eeee." Spencer starts bouncing up and down. "Ooooo...eeeee...Oooo...eeeee."

"What is it?" I trudge over to find out what all the monkey sounds are about. Spencer pops up out of a crate, and I am staring down the barrel of a gun. My heart skips about three beats. I bounce my body to the side and grab onto his little wrist aiming the gun at the ground. "Oh, my word. Give me that. You are not supposed to play with guns. What if it is loaded?" I snatch it away from him and check the chamber which thankfully does not have any bullets in it. "That is the second heart attack you have almost given me in the last five minutes." Spencer points to a crate. I look down and the crate is full of guns with boxes of ammunition. "You are right, Spencer. We better take them. After all, these people are releasing a deadly poison to destroy the rest of humanity. I doubt they are going to be shooting marshmallows at us. But I will carry the guns. You take the medical supplies."

When Spencer and I walk out, Alice already has the plane started, and Steve is waving for us to come on.

~

AFTER THE PLANE is fueled up, Alice wheels the plane down the runway. We are all strapped in, even Spencer. Eileen is chowing down on one of those MREs, and three empty ones lay next to her. What can one expect though? She hasn't eaten in two years. That thought blows me away. I lean my head back and close my eyes. I know right now that evil looms all around us, but God has given my sister back to me. That blessing gives me hope in this abyssal darkness.

I feel the plane lift off the runway. All of a sudden, a hard jolt shakes my seat as something ricochets off the side of the plane. The plane jerks hard to the side.

"What was that?" Eileen screams as she covers her head with her hands.

"Hold on, guys, and don't panic," Alice calmly instructs. "We are the target of some flying bullets!"

Alice levels the plane and then maneuvers it low between the mountains using them as a shield. I am astonished at her piloting skills. She is amazing. It is no wonder President Denali wanted her in his army. The question is *Why did he want me?*

"Alright. Everyone can relax. We are all clear," Alice announces as I feel the plane settle into a smooth course.

"I don't think any of us are going to be able to relax until this whole thing is over," I mumble as my insides won't stop shaking. Then I glance over, and Steve's head is bopping side to side. "What are you doing?"

He doesn't answer, but he has some sort of headphones covering his ears. I motion to him, and he lifts one side. "What?" he yells.

"What are you doing?"

"Oh. I found this music thing back at the base. It has this little rectangle thing that pops inside of it, and it plays music. Great music. Some group called *Foreigner.*" He puts the headphones back on and starts bopping his head again.

"I take back what I said." I look at Eileen. "Steve is pretty relaxed."

THE BATTERIES DIE in his music box, so Steve and Spencer fall asleep. Taking advantage of the quiet time, I share over five hours of stories from our childhood with Eileen. She is like a sponge absorbing every detail.

"Guys, make sure your belts are on. There is a wide-open field up ahead. I am going to land there until we come up with some sort of game plan."

I give Steve a shake to wake him up. We get our belts back on, and Alice glides us in for the smoothest landing I have ever experienced in a plane.

We step off to stretch our legs and use the outdoor facilities. Steve and Spencer are the only ones not objecting to using nature as a bathroom. I hike a little way because I prefer to find cover behind a tree. A wide-open field just does not offer enough privacy in broad daylight. A wooded area runs along one side of the field, so I hike in that direction. After I finish with the outdoor bathroom experience, I notice some kind of structure on back through the trees. I crane my neck trying to figure out what it is.

Footsteps crunch through the leaves. I forget about the building and slide behind a giant oak. I hunker close to the trunk and peep around it.

"Ellie."

It's Eileen. "Over here," I wave my arms trying to get her attention through the trees. Alice is trudging along right behind her.

"I guess we girls all had the same idea. No way was I going in the middle of that field," Alice huffs.

"Look." I point through the woods. "I was going to see what that is."

We walk through the trees to an opening where a small, old,

rickety barn stands. Of course, Alice takes off sprinting toward the door. Eileen and I jog behind her. Alice tugs with both hands and the rusty hinges creak as the door opens. We go in leaving the door ajar. Fortunately, the sunlight through the opening gives us enough light to see.

Junk is scattered around, and two large tarps cover some sort of vehicles in the middle. Eileen yanks one of the tarps off revealing an old Kubota tractor. I uncover the other one, and it is love at first sight. A 1970 Volkswagen Beetle convertible is staring back at me. It is baby blue with a tattered and faded tan top. What a unique car. I have never seen one before. I mean I have seen them on television and in movies but never in person. This one could certainly use some TLC, but considering it is moving toward a century in age, that would be expected.

"We just found a mode of transportation to the White House," Alice says as she bounces up and down clapping her hands.

"Really," I say surprised. "I mean the tractor will kind of stand out like a soda machine in a health club, and that Beetle is almost eighty years old."

"Ok. Let's go get Steve and Spencer. We need to get a plan together." Eileen pulls out something that is tucked in her belt. It is the folder Dr. Fleming gave her. "I think we should open these together. I want to know what is in here."

WE FIND Steve and Spencer and bring them back to the barn. I expect him to be in awe of the Beetle, but instead he makes a mad dash for the tractor.

"This is an unbelievable machine. Not only does it have a backhoe, but it has a grapple attachment on the front." A strange excitement rings in Steve's tone. "It is like a giant robot hand but with crazy strength. Isn't hydraulics amazing?"

Spencer climbs up in the seat and grabs the steering wheel.

I laugh. "Weird. Even the monkey picks the tractor over the car."

"Hello." Alice waves. "We came in here to discuss a plan. Remember, we are on a mission to save humanity from some sort of toxic gas."

"And open these folders that Dr. Fleming gave us." Eileen holds her folder up in the air.

"BOOOOOOOM!" We all dive to the ground with our hands sheltering our heads. The whole barn shakes and vibrates making dust rise around us like clouds of smoke. Spencer springs from the tractor seat and crawls under Steve's body.

"What was that?" Alice wails with her hands still covering her head. "It sounded like an explosion."

Steve gets up and eases to the door. "Black smoke is billowing above the trees from the direction of the plane. I think that whoever was shooting at us before just blew up our Cessna."

"So, the question is," I make eye contact with Steve, "are they still looking for us, or do they think they took us out in the plane?"

Steve's gaze passes back and forth from the tractor to the car. "I don't know, but what are the chances that either of these will actually start. There is no telling how long these things have been covered up in here."

Alice has the lid open in the rear of the Beetle. That is the unique feature of those cars. The engine is in the back. "Hey, you guys, let's give it a try. This battery is only six months old. It must be someone's project car."

"Well let's hot wire it and see if it will start." Steve opens the driver's side door and looks under the dash. "Or..." he mumbles, "we could just try this key that is under the floormat." He sticks the key in the ignition and gives it a turn. The engine grumbles to no avail. Steve tries again. It turns over but still doesn't start He takes a deep breath, and I think he is saying a silent prayer. Third time is a charm. The little "bug" is actually purring.

Eileen and I climb in the backseat. Alice slides in the passenger seat with Spencer on her lap.

As Steve shifts the little car into drive, he utters to himself, "There is only a quarter of a tank of gas. Thank goodness, this car doesn't use much."

"An eighty-year-old car just happens to be in a barn with a battery only six months old when our plane explodes, and we desperately need transportation. Ha. Definitely providence... not coincidence." I lift my hands in praise. "God always provides a way."

Chapter Thirty-Three

"Does anybody know where we are or how to get to a main road that actually has signs?" Frustration filters through in Steve's voice. "I have no idea if we are headed for the highway or further into the sticks."

"Look!" Alice points down this narrow gravel driveway to a house that probably should have been torn down years ago. "This place appears to be abandoned. Let's stop here and regroup."

Steve turns the little "bug" down the skinny drive, and the tiny car bounces in and out of holes jumbling us around inside. He pulls the car around back under a couple of huge oak trees. "Hopefully, we can find something around here to cover the car with."

Weeds are grown up all around the old clapboard house. Two steps lead up to the back door. Alice pulls on the screen door which falls off. With no facial expression at all, she turns and hands the screen door to Steve. She turns back to try the old solid wood door, but of course, it is locked.

Steve walks down the back of the house to a window that is about twenty feet from the door. A windowpane is missing, but the window is too high. Cleverly, Steve picks up Spencer, points to the door, and gives the monkey a boost over his head. Spencer grabs hold of the windowsill and swings through the opening. A minute later, the doorknob is twitching, and the sound of Spencer's rattling and scratching lets us know he is trying to open it. Another minute ticks by, and the door swings open.

"Wow." Eileen high fives Spencer. "Are all spider monkeys as smart as you, Spencer?"

He jumps into Eileen's arms like he knows she was complimenting him.

We all proceed in caution through the door into a galley-style kitchen. I have never seen a refrigerator with the freezer on top before, and I don't think I have ever seen that shade of green either. I open the freezer door, and this atrocious smell almost knocks me over. I slam it shut and move on.

"Weird." Alice opens some kitchen drawers. "The place looks like it has been abandoned for a long time, but there is still stuff in the drawers. I mean the stuff is mixed with a lot of dust and dead bugs and mouse droppings, but there is still stuff."

We move from the kitchen into a living room. Against the wall is an old brown couch that is sunk in toward the middle, but it is what is in front of the couch that brings tears to my eyes. A small coffee table that looks like it was probably hand-made sits between the couch and a couple of armchairs, and in the center of the table is a Bible. An inch of dust rests on top, and the leather cover is tattered and torn. Wiping it off, I pick it up and hug it to my chest. The comfort I feel is indescribable because, for the second time today, I know this find is no coincidence. I sit down on the couch and open the Bible. The pages fall open to the book of John, and I use my finger to follow a verse that stands out on the page. I whisper it aloud as I read it.

"Ye are of God, little children, and have overcome them: because greater is he that is in you than he that is in the world. – 1 John 4:4."

Eileen's eyes light up as she hears me reading. "I know that verse, but I can't remember why it feels so significant."

"When we were little, and Mom would tuck us in, she always quoted that verse before she kissed us goodnight." A tear escapes from the corner of my eye and rolls down my face.

Eileen sits down next to me wrapping an arm around my shoulder. Her voice filled with hope, she says, "Maybe this is a sign. If that verse sparked something in my brain, maybe I will eventually start to get real memories back."

"Oh Eileen, I hope so. But, even if you don't, I am thankful God has brought us back together. At least we have been given the chance to make new memories."

Alice, Steve, and Spencer sit in the armchairs across from the couch.

Alice speaks up. "Sorry, guys. But we don't have much time. We really need to get a plan together."

"Why don't we pray first?" I suggest.

"I think that is a great idea." Steve clasps his hands together. "We definitely need guidance. We don't even know how to get back to a main road."

We each take turns saying our part in the prayer. When we finish, Alice offers a thought. "I think we should check out what is in the folders before we do anything else. If something happens, and the folders get destroyed, we will never know what is in them."

"You don't have to tell me twice," Steve says as he pulls out his folder. "I can't wait to find out my real name."

"Ok, then Steve goes first." Alice motions for him to proceed.

He opens the folder and flips through some of the pages. All the color drains from his face, and hard as I try, I can't imagine what could be in those pages that is giving him this look. Steve's facial expression looks like he might cry, throw up, and break something all at the same time.

"Steve." I stand up and cross over to his chair. "What is it?"

"This…this…can't be right," he stutters with a shaky voice. "There is j…j…just no way."

"No way…what?" Alice inquires.

Steve looks up with water-filled eyes. "My name really is Steve."

"Okay, and the problem with that is...?" Alice stares at him in confusion.

"My name is Steve Denali."

Twenty seconds that feel like an eternity of pure and complete awkward silence pass as we just stare at Steve absorbing the words that have just escaped his lips.

Then Alice cracks the silence. "As in President Denali?"

Steve nods. "As in...President Denali's son." Steve turns away so we don't see the pain on his face, or the tears erupt, but his body is quivering. I know he is fighting to hold back the sobs.

"Steve," I rub his back trying to loosen his tense muscles, "you are not your father. However, that does explain why you were moved to building one and given a job when you didn't pass level three. He wouldn't freeze his son."

"But he would erase my memory? What kind of dad does that?"

"Apparently, he thought he could erase your faith in God and make you like him. But you are not him. He might be your earthly dad, but you are a child of God. And that Father has had his hands and arms wrapped around you protecting you because you are part of a greater plan."

Alice jumps in. "You know, Steve, I think maybe you are the key to stopping your father's plan. You had to have disappeared, what...about two years ago? So how has your dad been explaining your disappearance?"

Steve's face reflects mass confusion. "I don't understand. What does that have to do with stopping my dad?"

"Well, someone is bound to recognize you as President Denali's son. Just look for someone that you know and act like you are part of the plan so you can find out where the plane is."

"Uuuum, that would be a great idea, but there is a slight problem. I won't know anybody. Remember, that awesome Father of mine erased my memory."

Alice scratches her head. "Ok, then you will just have to be very observant. Focus on people's faces, especially their eyes. You will notice something in their expression if they recognize you."

"So, you think I can just parade right into the White House?"

I laugh. "It does sound absurd, but Alice is right. You are the President's son. Ordinarily, you really should be living in the White House."

Steve shrugs his shoulders. "Worst case scenario, my father has told them something horrible about me, and they shoot me on the spot."

"That's positive thinking," Eileen chimes in. "But time is running out, so let's address the next problem. How do we get to the White House from here?"

"I don't know, but it's getting dark." Steve walks to the window. "That car will draw less attention at night so let's see if we can find a main road. Then maybe we'll see a road sign."

"We are going to have to find some food somewhere. Our MREs blew up in the plane, and since they erased our old identity, our thumbprint won't work with any of our old credit cards. I guess using our thumbprint would be a dead giveaway of our location anyway." I look around. "Has anyone seen Spencer?"

"That's weird." Steve's eyes start scouring the room. "Where could he have gone... SPENCER...SPENCER!"

We all get up and start searching for Spencer all through the house. I notice a door cracked in the hallway. When I pull it open, I stare down a set of stairs that lead down into complete darkness. Eileen steps up behind me.

"I saw some candles in that kitchen drawer. I will go get them." Eileen trails off to the kitchen and returns with two long, white candles and a book of matches. She hands me the candles to hold, and she strikes a match. It takes a few tries, but she gets the candles lit. I hand one back to her, and we start down the steps with the candles barely lighting the way. When we reach the bottom step, the flicker of the candlelight illuminates a moving outline sitting in the middle of the floor. Eileen and I inch toward the figure coming to a stop when we realize it is Spencer. He is eating something out of a jar.

"Where did you get that?" I take my candle and cast its light around the room. We are in an old cellar with dirt walls, and along one wall are shelves filled with jars. "Look, Eileen, it's homemade canned foods. The lids are sealed so I think it would be safe to eat."

I grab a box from the corner and fill it with some of the jars. I carry the box of jars, and Eileen gets Spencer.

When we reach the top of the stairs, Steve is staring at us. "What is all over Spencer?" He takes Spencer from Eileen. "Is that Strawberry jam?"

Steve can't pry the jar from Spencer's hands, and that crazy monkey has his mouth smushed to the top of the jar licking the jam out.

"Don't worry, Steve. I don't know what is in these, but we brought up some more jars."

WE ATE some of the jars and saved some to bring with us. It turns out, we had jars of peaches, pickles, and jam. Steve ate only the pickles. Alice had some peaches followed by a few pickles. She said she had to have salty after the sweet. I was the opposite. I had pickles and then a few peaches. Eileen is a sweets-only person. She had straight peaches. We decided to save the jam in case we needed a real sugar rush.

We are headed in the right direction now, I think. After eating, we piled back in the car. Spencer called shotgun. Well, he didn't say it, but he got in the front seat and held on. He is a pretty strong little monkey. As a result, Alice, Eileen, and I had to literally squish ourselves together to fit in the backseat. I guess Spencer in the front was part of God's plan though because that hyper little monkey accidentally hit the latch to the glove box which flipped open revealing an old atlas road map.

We find a parking spot along the curb a few blocks down

from the White House on Pennsylvania Avenue. Steve doesn't want any of the security to see him get out of the car. It is a little after midnight, but he thinks the time will work to his advantage.

Steve plans to act like he is in trouble, and he needs to find his father fast. When they don't know where to find him, Steve is going to insist that Air Force One fly him to Camp David until things die down.

We take a moment to ask God to lead the way and work everything out for his purpose. Steve takes a deep breath, steps out of the car, and disappears down the sidewalk. The rest of us are supposed to wait patiently in the car, but Spencer is a little overactive. I think he senses the tension that us girls are radiating.

After about fifteen minutes, the inside of that tiny Volkswagen feels like three people and a monkey crammed inside one of those little plastic Easter eggs. My heart is racing, I am about to vomit, and I need out of this car. On top of that, I think Spencer needs a bathroom break.

We ease from the car. I have some blankets that I brought from the old house, so I grab one from the trunk that is really in front of the car. *I just love this car. It is so weird.* I wrap Spencer in the blanket and carry him like a baby. If the car didn't draw attention, I am certain walking around with a monkey would, especially walking around with a monkey after midnight. Not far from the car, we spot a bench under a tree. Alice and I sit there trying our best to contain Spencer while Eileen nervously paces around in circles.

Suddenly there is some sort of commotion down the street, and the sound of yelling and screaming and pounding feet grows louder as it seems to be getting closer. We dart between two cars to hide ourselves making sure to stay away from the "Bug."

"Stop now! Put your hands in the air… We have orders to hold you here, but we will shoot if you do not stop!"

Steve is running down the street, but before we even have a chance to blink, a giant man jumps on top of him tackling him to the ground. An electrical arc flashes and one of the guys chasing Steve places a stun gun on his belt. In a fraction of a second, Steve is being dragged unconscious back down the street.

Déjà vu. I don't think I can hold it back. Eileen must see it on my face. She caps her hand over my mouth trying to cover any sound that escapes me. Once they are out of sight, Eileen takes her hand away.

"Listen," she lectures me, "if we get caught too, we can't save him or stop Denali. You have to pull yourself together so we can help Steve and find that plane. Now come on. Let's get out of here until we get a plan."

Alice is already climbing in the driver's seat, and of course, Spencer is hanging on to the passenger seat. At this point, all I can think about is Steve, so I just let Spencer have the front and climb in the back as fast as I can. Once Eileen is in, Alice takes off.

"Where are we going?" I have to ask because Alice looks like she has a destination in mind.

"We are going back to the old house, search for anything we can use as weapons, and come up with a plan of action fast. In the meantime, you and Eileen need to open your folders that Dr. Fleming gave you. Something important must be in there, or she would not have given them to you. So, you two have at it. We need all of the facts we can get right now."

"Ok," I utter in confusion. "But I know who our parents are. Remember, you and I still have our memory."

Eileen stares down at the manila folder laying on her lap. "I'll go first," she barely speaks. She opens the folder and starts flipping through the papers. Then her jaw hardens, and she starts flipping back through the pages. Her mouth drops open, and the blood drains from her face.

"Eileen, what's wrong?"

"Is our dad's name Tom Hatcher?"

"Yes. That's right. See there is nothing in there we didn't already know," I reiterate.

Eileen peers over at me with puddles in her eyes. "What was Dad's job before I was kidnapped?"

"Why? What difference does it make?"

"Please, Ellie, just tell me."

"Mmmm..." My mind searches but turns up empty for his exact job title. "He was a legal adviser or something like that for a company in Washington D.C."

"Ellie, there are detailed instructions in here giving my route to and from home, and there is a photo of me." Eileen pulls out one of the sheets. "Then, there is this. A signed contract by Tom Hatcher giving President Denali permission to use me in a research study."

"WHAT?" I grab the piece of paper, and my unblinking eyes fixate on the black ink forming Tom Hatcher's signature. Chills creep up my body, and numbness takes over shielding out the pain as I recognize my daddy's handwriting. How could he sign over his own daughter's life to President Denali? How could he have known where she was this whole time? How could he stand by and watch my mom go through the agony of losing her child? This cannot be real. *Please let this be a bad dream.* I rub the paper with my fingers trying to prove to myself that this is a figment of my imagination, but the texture of the parchment on my skin and the crinkling of the paper don't lie. "This cannot be right."

I jerk my folder open almost dropping its contents. Every cell in my body is trembling. I flip through the papers stopping at a page with my picture and the address of my apartment scribbled underneath in Dad's handwriting. Attached is a letter from my father to President Denali asking him to take me too. "Why on earth would Dad ask President Denali to take me away too? How could he do that?"

"Ellie?" Alice's somber tone flows from the front seat through her down turned lips reflecting in the rearview mirror. "Don't your parents live close to D.C.?"

"Yes, but we don't have time to deal with that right now. We have to find Steve."

"That is the point. We have no idea where they would have taken him, but obviously, your dad is involved in this. Maybe he knows where to find Steve and the plane."

"Even if he does, I don't think it will help us any. My dad literally has not said a word since Eileen was kidnapped. He is mute." Anger at my dad makes my words come out harsh.

"I forgot about that." Alice pauses and taps the steering wheel with her fingers. "I still can't think of any better idea, can you? We have to try to get him to talk."

With her voice unwavering, Eileen grumbles through clenched teeth. "Oh, he will talk. I will make him talk. How dare he take my life away from me?"

"You are right. Dad is the only trail we have right now." I lean forward so Alice can hear me better. "My parents live in Fairfax. The fastest route is I-66 West."

"Ellie, I really think it will be faster if you drive. You know the way. We are only going to waste time if you have to direct me." Alice jerks the wheel pulling the car to the side of the road. The tires screech as she slams on the brakes. In one swift move, Alice opens the door and jumps from the car. Flipping the seat forward, her hand pulls me from the backseat, and she plants herself in my spot. Oblivious to finally being in the driver's seat of my dream car, I push the gas to the floor trying to block out the fact that dad might not talk.

Chapter Thirty-Four

As I turn into the driveway, my chest tightens, and my hands clutch the steering wheel so tight my fingernails dig into my palms. My mom's white Criss-Cross SUV is parked out front. I pull up next to it letting my memory take me away.

My mom wanted that car so bad when it came out. Gas had gone through the roof five years ago finally hitting eight dollars a gallon. Mom said enough was enough. But when she went down to the dealership, the payment was more than we could afford. Instead of being disappointed, she became driven with determination and started saving. She penny-pinched and worked overtime until she had enough money to put down so the payment would be low enough. With excitement in her voice, Mom would tell us all about how the Criss-Cross was versatile. It could run on this new sustainable fuel or electricity. This new fuel was made from water, hydrogen, and carbon dioxide and cost half the price of gasoline. The first time she filled it up at the new hydro fuel station a few miles from our house, Mom's face beamed with pride.

I shift the car into park and turn my eyes toward the sky. *Lord, please help me. I am so scared. How am I going to explain all of this to my poor mother? I just don't think she can handle any more. If she finds out that Dad was involved in Eileen's disappearance...* "Hey, Eileen..." I use my shirt to dab at my eyes, "I know you have been through so much, and it is not fair for me to ask this...but...never mind."

"What is it, Ellie?"

I turn and look at my little sister. "Look, it is just that Mom...she uhhh...well, you are her baby, and when you disappeared, she..."

Eileen puts her hand on my shoulder. "Ellie don't worry. I will act like I remember her."

I nod and push the car door open. Pausing beside the car, Alice picks Spencer up and carries him. "How does your mom feel about monkeys?"

"I highly doubt that she will even notice the monkey," I say as I try to envision my mother's reaction when she sees her daughter that has been missing for two years. Suddenly that thought fades, and Steve's face fills my mind. I miss him so bad it hurts, and I am so scared of what they might be doing to him.

Alice puts her arm around my shoulders. "It's going to be okay. 'Many are the plans in a person's heart, but it is the Lord's purpose that prevails.' Proverbs 19:21. So you see, it doesn't matter what Denali is planning, God's got this."

"Oh, Alice, I am so grateful for you."

"The feeling is mutual. I believe God put us in the same place at the same time for a reason. Come on. We have to get your dad to talk so we can find Steve."

We walk around the house to the back door, and as we pass the window, Mom is in the kitchen, working as usual. It seems that woman never takes a break. I tap lightly on the screen door, and Mom's head pops up.

"Hey, Mom. It's me, Ellie."

Mom drops the plate in her hands and glass shatters across the floor. She doesn't seem to notice or care. In half a second, Mom is at the door choking out her words. "Ellie, where have you been?" She reaches to embrace me when her eyes catch sight of Eileen standing next to me. "Eileen," she squeals. Mom grabs us both in a huge hug. Through tears of joy, she shouts, "Thank you, Lord. Thank you for bringing my babies back."

"Mom, I know you have a lot of questions, but right now, we have an emergency." I gaze into her tear-filled eyes. "I promise that we will explain everything later, but we need to see Dad.

I know Mom so desperately needs to keep her arms around us, but as she steps back, I can tell from the expression on her face that God is speaking to her.

"Tom! Hey, Tom! Come in here!" Mom yells into the living room. "Hurry!"

Dad appears in the doorway. One look at us, and his face turns white, morbidly white. "No. No. He...he...he...prom... ised," he mutters with a weak, raspy voice.

My skin burns as the anger rises inside of me. These are the first words my dad has even tried to speak since Eileen disappeared. "What do you mean, Dad? Who promised?"

"He promised if I would help him and cooperate, he would put you girls somewhere safe and not let you die."

Eileen moves directly in front of him and looks straight into his eyes. "Who, Dad? Who promised?"

"President Denali."

Mom's face fills with fury. "Tom Hatcher, what are you talking about? What have you done?"

Dad shakes his head in slow motion and crumples to his knees. His face is so pale and shriveled, and even though he is far from skinny, he seems so frail and fragile. I take in the sight of my father and realize that even though I have seen him, I haven't truly looked at him in over two years. Dad lifts his hands and covers his beard stubbled face. My dad has delicate hands from years of office work. Really, I think mowing the lawn was the most backbreaking work that I ever saw my dad do. Somehow, he was always fit though, but not anymore. Two years of sitting in a chair staring at a blank television screen has taken its toll. Now he is like a giant marshmallow. His skin is bright white from never seeing the sun, and his body is puffy from only sitting and eating. Even his hair has turned completely white in the last two years.

Eileen gets down next to Dad and places her hand on his trembling back. "Daddy, I need you to be strong. Please. We have to try to stop Denali."

"No...no...you can't stop him," Dad whimpers through his hands.

"Daddy, we have to try." Eileen's begs, "I need you to tell us everything you know. If you don't, everyone is going to die probably in the next twenty-four hours."

Dad pulls his hands from his face, and he peers at Eileen, then me, then Mom. "How could I have ever thought he would really protect you girls? What have I done?"

"Dad," I squat down next to him, "leave the past behind. You have the power to help us right now. I believe God has put you in this position to help save his people. Please tell us everything you know."

Dad wipes his pain-filled eyes with the back of his hand. "Okay, okay." He nods and sniffles. "Here it goes from the beginning." Dad clears his throat and with a hard swallow, he starts to speak. "I was one of Denali's legal advisers. He called me into his office one day about three years ago. Denali told me that he was working on a big project, and he needed my help with it. He reminded me of my oath of confidentiality as his legal adviser. I told him that of course, I was aware that any business I helped him with was kept confidential. Then, Denali proceeded to tell me that he needed to get possession of an old abandoned military bunker inside of Cheyenne Mountain without anyone knowing about it. I asked him if this was some sort of top-secret Department of Defense project, but he said that it was his own personal top-secret project. Denali emphasized that he wanted no one else in the government or elsewhere to know of it. Taken aback by such a strange request, I informed him that it would be hard to get information on a facility of that magnitude, let alone obtain it. President Denali's eyes bore straight into mine, and with an assertive tone, he told me that I would need to be creative and find a way."

Dad stops talking. He crosses his arms hugging himself and just starts rocking back and forth as he sits on the floor. Anxiety inflates inside of me.

"Mr. Hatcher," Alice leans down and wraps a blanket around my dad's shoulders, "I know this is really hard for you, but you have to keep going. We have to know everything, and there isn't much time."

Dad lets out a deep breath. "I knew something was not right, but at that time in my life, I took my job seriously. Besides, who was I to question the President of the United States? So, I told him I would look into it but that he really needed to have a cover story. We were talking about one of the most secure high-tech military facilities that has ever existed in the United States. Someone would notice if it was back in use. If he wanted to keep his real purpose a secret, he just needed to come up with a legitimate reason that he would be using it. If his story was good enough, no one would ever pay attention to what was really going on there. Denali heeded my advice and requested that I meet him back in his office in a week. He said he would have a cover story in place by then."

"So, Dad, at that point, President Denali had not told you anything about his actual plan or what he was going to be using the facility for?" I ask.

"No, not yet. The next week, I met him back in his office. President Denali said that he had gotten the Senate's approval to create a new crime division called Soldiers Against Crime. This new division was going to pinpoint only violent crime because he felt the jurisdiction of departments such as the FBI covered too wide of a range in relation to types of crimes. Like his successful identity theft program had a distinct purpose, this new department would specifically target violence. He continued that he had also nominated himself to be the head of this new department. He explained that he had provided them with an outline detailing how this department would be run.

Each member of this new unit would be carefully chosen by the President himself, and those that were chosen would have to endure intense training. Denali also stated he emphasized to the Senate that this unit would be answering directly and only to him as the head of the SAC. He took pride in assuring me that because of his previous success, the Senate backed him unanimously. President Denali went on to thank me for the advice. At this point, curiosity was getting the best of me, so I finally inquired, 'President if you don't mind me asking, what is the real project you are working on?' I will never forget the way he gazed at me, and quite honestly, the look in his eyes gave me chills. But the words that followed the gaze carried those chills through to my bones."

We are all sitting around Dad absorbing every word with tight lips as he tells the story.

"I don't know how much you girls know about Denali's real plan, but it is terrifying. His words are etched like scars in my head...

"'Tom Hatcher, you are my personal legal adviser so I know I can trust you. After all, our contract clearly holds you to the strictest of confidentiality. And well, if you ever breathe a word of this, people will think you are crazy, and you will most definitely be locked away to work through the problems with your mental state. I will be using the facility to create what I suppose could be called my own personal army. The people that train there will be responsible for repopulating the Earth. I mean, Tom, you see how much I have already done to make the United States a better place. But it is still so far from a perfect society. And you want to know what angers me, Tom? I will tell you what angers me. It is all these people that say they are Christians and followers of God. If this many people are Christians, how is the world in the state that it is in? Really, Tom, how can one claim to be a Christian yet curse, drink, lie, cheat, and steal like it is no big deal? Where is that Christian fruit I hear about? That is why my army will have no knowledge of God. Once I have a trained army that cannot even remember the God they once were so supposedly devoted to, I will destroy the rest of humanity. Then my followers will multiply, refilling the Earth, and we will have a perfect world.'"

Mom gasps throwing both hands over her heart. "Tom Hatcher, why would you keep something so atrocious from me all these years? Please tell me he was pulling some sort of practical joke on you?" Mom looks hurt, mad, and shocked all at the same time.

"It was no joke, Jillian. And, yes, I tried to talk to him. I explained that everybody sins, even Christians. The difference is that Christians are forgiven with their sins washed away by the shed blood of Jesus. True Christians that have been born again and have Christ in their heart don't intentionally live sinful lives. They don't curse and get drunk through the week, and then go to church on Sunday morning. True Christians desire to be like Jesus. I told him there are always people that claim to be something that they aren't. Sure, there are people who say they love God and say they follow him when their actions say otherwise. But there are many true Christians. I explained to him that destroying humanity isn't going to remove God. That made Denali really mad. In a fit of rage, he spouted off that he could not believe I was one of them, and then he slammed his fist down on the desk. Denali glared at me with evil radiating from his eyes and his voice consumed with hate as he ordered,

"'You are going to help me get Cheyenne Mountain ready. There are renovations that will need to be done to get it ready for my special recruits. I have already chosen my first round of trainees. My army will be made up of all young men and women that identify themselves as Christians. Once they are chosen, they will begin training in my renovated facility, and, just to prove how great I am, their knowledge of God will be erased. I have good news for you, Tom. You are in luck. Your

youngest daughter, Eileen, is on my list, which means that her
life will be spared because she will be a member of my army. I
know you are thrilled and will give me your full cooperation
in obtaining her because you will want her life preserved. That
being said, Tom, I suggest you keep your mouth shut tight
about all of this. You will know nothing about the cause of
your daughter's disappearance, that is if you want her to
survive.'

"Eileen, I am so sorry." Dad jerks with every sob. "I didn't
know what else to do. I knew he was telling the truth about
what he was going to do. I wanted you to live. I don't expect you
to ever forgive me, but please know I only went along with him
because I didn't want you to be killed. He told me if I ever
breathed a syllable about what he was doing, he would kill you
anyway. So, the day you disappeared, I just stopped talking alto-
gether, that way I couldn't mess up."

"Dad," Eileen places her hands on the sides of Dad's face and
lifts his head. Glaring straight into his eyes, she says, "Stop
looking at what you have done in the past. If you let the devil
keep you looking back, you can't accomplish the work God has
for you to do. God put you here with the knowledge to stop
Denali's plan. We know that there is a plane going to drop some
type of poisonous gas. What do you know about that?"

"Denali has employed a group of scientists that have
specially formulated this toxic gas. They have determined that
this gas, once it is sprayed from the plane, can enter the
atmosphere, and circle the entire earth in thirty days. The poison
enters the water vapor in the clouds and gets distributed through
precipitation. With the toxin entering the water supply, every
person would be affected. The affected person starts out with
common cold symptoms, but it quickly worsens."

"So…" I think out loud, "this sickness is from a poison. It
cannot be passed from person to person."

"That's right," Dad reassures. "Denali did not want something that could stick around and wipe out his own army. The

toxin would be completely gone in two months. As soon as he wipes out everyone else, and the gas has disappeared, he can then release his army with no risk."

Alice speaks up. "Mr. Hatcher, do you know where the plane is? We are pretty sure Denali is getting ready to drop this gas probably in the next twenty-four hours. That is if we are not already too late."

"I am not really sure." Dad swallows hard as he answers.

"We are guessing he will be using Air Force One since he will be faking his own death in the crash," Alice explains. "Any idea where he could take a plane that big to load the gas?"

A tear escapes my eye. "Daddy, please." I grab his hand. "They took someone really special to me. I have to get to him before it is too late. I have a feeling he is wherever that plane is."

Dad stares at me almost like he is looking into my soul. "Ellie, you know about the letter, don't you?"

"Yes, Daddy. I know you wrote Denali a letter asking him to take me too...but I don't care about that right now. I need to find Steve. Please help."

"Well, in case I don't get another chance to tell you, I want you to know that I only wrote that letter because I knew the gas would kill you too. I wanted you to have a chance to live. I am sorry. Just so you know. And the plane...well, I don't really know for sure, but I do know that Denali had me acquire this huge warehouse for him right outside of Washington. This warehouse is plenty big enough for a plane and has open fields all around it."

"KA-BOOOOM!" A gust of air blasts through the doorway of the kitchen. Eileen and Alice slam up against the cabinets on the far wall. Mom flies backward through the screen door onto the back porch. Dad and I are flat on the floor. A sharp stab digs into my calf as shards of glass and debris pelt down all over us. A nagging buzz fills my eardrums.

Pushing myself up with my elbows, keeping my hands covering my head, I scan the kitchen to see if everyone is alright. *Spencer. Where is Spencer?* Through the smoke, Spencer's body bobbles from side to side as he swings by his tail from the pot rack. Everyone else is crawling across the floor trying to stay below the smoke. The living room has erupted in flames. Well, what is left of the living room is in flames. Dad motions for us to follow him as he crawls on his belly across the kitchen tile to the basement door. Every time I push with my right leg, the pain twists deeper so I pull myself along with my forearms. He reaches up flipping the knob and waves us through.

Chapter Thirty-Five

I hop down the stairs on one leg, holding the rail, but the vibration of each jump is torment. When we get down the stairs, I flip my head around to check my leg. A piece of glass from the living room window is protruding from the muscle.

"Oh, Ellie." Mom pulls off the apron that she is still wearing. She rips off the strings and the pocket from the front. "Squeeze onto the rail. This will be fast." Her hand plucks the glass shard from my leg. Wrapping the fabric from the pocket around the wound, she secures it with the strings. "Come on, honey, we will have to clean it later." She eyes Dad. "See, Tom. One of the kids has been hurt."

"I am sorry, dear, but if we don't get out of here, it is going to be worse." Dad jogs back in front of us and yells, "Everybody, this way, quick!" Against the wall in the corner is a workshop bench with shelves built onto it up the wall. It has been there for as long as I can remember. Dad reaches underneath and wiggles something with his hand. Then he steps back and pulls on the workbench. The whole wall behind it moves revealing a passage. He does not have to say a word. We file through the opening the second it is in sight. Dad comes through and pulls the shelf back into place behind us. We are in abyssal darkness.

Mom erupts, "Thomas Eugene Hatcher, what is this? How long has this tunnel been behind this shelf?" Then she mumbles under her breath through soft sobs, "It has all been one big lie."

Dad says in a tremulous voice. "Grab onto each other and tuck in close behind me. I know this tunnel like the back of my hand."

I put my finger through the belt loop on the back of Dad's pants and clutch Eileen's hand with my other hand. Spencer is riding on my shoulders with his little hands entwined in my hair. Alice takes Eileen's hand and puts her other arm around my mom. We inch along behind Dad. The tunnel seems to slope downhill for a bit, and then it turns right. After that, the elevation starts to rise. It feels like we walk for an eternity, but I think it just seems that way because of the immense darkness and the tiny steps we are taking.

Finally, Dad stops. His hand scratches along the wall, and then there is a screech like he pushes something out of the way. We walk through another opening, and after a bit of clatter, a little click illuminates the room. My eyes follow the light to its source. With a flashlight shaking in his hand, Dad stands there with soot covering his face and his white hair sticking in all directions.

"Tom," Mom's anger booming in her tone, "wouldn't that flashlight have been more useful back at the beginning of this secret tunnel."

"Yes, dear. I see that now. I apologize. I really never thought I would be using this tunnel."

Alice has a trickle of blood running down her forehead.

"Are you okay, Alice?" I ask noticing that she keeps feeling the top of her head with her hands.

"It's just a scratch. No big deal."

Dad shines the light around the room. We are in a small garage or barn or something. He points the light toward the center of the room revealing a dark blue minivan.

Eileen looks at me and then raises a question. "Ummm...Dad...a minivan for a getaway car?"

"It is inconspicuous and the least likely vehicle to be a getaway car which makes it the perfect choice." Dad waves us on. "Come on, everybody. Get in."

Dad climbs in the driver's seat. I open the passenger door, and of course, Spencer dives in and plants himself in the front. Dad gives me a strange look.

"Just don't argue with him," I answer his look. "Everybody, just please hustle into the back."

We all get in as quickly as we can.

"Buckle up," Dad says. He hits a button, and the wall slides to the side, opening just wide enough for the minivan to exit.

"I hope you are headed to that warehouse!" I shout from the back. "I don't know how much time we have to find Steve and stop Denali's plane."

"That is my planned destination. I just hope it's the right place because I don't know where else to go." Dad casts me a glance in the rearview mirror. "So, Ellie...who is Steve?"

"Long story...but to summarize...I met him in the training facility. He helped me, and I would have fallen apart if he had not been there. His memory was erased, but we just found out that he is President Denali's son. We figure that is why Denali gave him a special job in the facility when he failed level three instead of freezing him like the others."

"I remember Steve. President Denali was furious when he found out Steve had become a Christian. He ranted for weeks about how Steve was throwing his life away with the work he was doing in the church." Dad shakes his head. "He really erased his own son's memory? How sick is..." Dad stops his words, and his face glows with realization. Under his breath, I hear him say to himself, "Who am I to judge...who am I... how could I?" Dad clears his throat and asks in a scratchy voice, "Ellie...Eileen...girls, how much do you remember?"

Eileen speaks before I even start to open my mouth. "We are fine, Dad. No need to worry."

"Eileen, I didn't ask if you were fine. I asked how much you remember of your life before going to that training facility."

Eileen giggles. "Dad, I remember plenty. Don't worry."

"Ok. Eileen. What kind of car did you drive?" Dad peeks in the mirror at her and raises his eyebrows to signal he is waiting on her answer. "Or you could tell me the name of your high school?"

Eileen just stares out the window.

"Ummm, Ellie, how about you? What do you remember?"

"Dad, I remember everything? I had my own apartment, and I was going to college. I started out in nursing and switched to criminal justice after Eileen disappeared. Is that enough?"

BAM! Almost like it appears out of thin air, a black SUV rams into us from behind. The van lurches forward with a hard jerk. Our seatbelts catch snapping us back, and Spencer lets out a squeal that could break glass. Dad pushes a button under the dash, and the minivan thrusts forward like a rock in a slingshot.

I grab my chest. "A nitrous oxide system on a minivan, Dad? Really?"

"It worked, didn't it?"

All of a sudden, we veer off the road onto a little dirt path through thick trees and brush. On terrain created for a monster truck, we are in a minivan bouncing around like marbles in a child's push me popper toy. Mom is praying, Eileen has tears streaming down her face, and Spencer is whimpering with his little monkey hands over his eyes. Just when it looks like we are crashing right into a wall of trees, the van moves through the leaves and limbs into a small clearing just big enough for us to open the doors. Dad pushes his door open and steps out. The rest of us follow except for Spencer who still has his hands over his eyes. Dad moves to the front of the van and pulls some tree branches to the side. We are standing with our toes to the edge of a cliff overlooking a huge building.

"That's the warehouse. I don't see any sign of life down there though." Dad's eyes keep scanning the area turning his head to check behind us.

Then, to our surprise, the black SUV that was chasing us drives into the lot of the warehouse. It pulls into one of the spaces and parks. Three men dressed in black get out and stride with determination into the building.

"Well, now we know something is going on here," Dad says. "Let's get a quick plan together. I think your mom and the monkey should wait here in the van. The monkey can't be quiet enough, and your mom has already had enough shock and stress in the last hour to last a lifetime."

"Now, Tom, don't you think you are going to tell me to stay here! You have lied and took my babies from me. You will not tell me what to do. You have lost that right. Do you understand me?"

Wow, I have never heard Mom talk to Dad that way before. I think the anger is her way of not falling apart right now.

"Jillian," Dad says in a weak voice, "I don't blame you for hating me. I hate me. I just have no idea what is waiting for us down there."

"Mom," I grab her hand, "please stay here and take care of Spencer. He can't stay here alone, and I really don't think you should be climbing down the side of a cliff when your blood pressure is obviously through the roof."

Mom leans forward and peers off the side of the cliff. At some point, Spencer must have gotten out of the car because he sidles up next to mom and hugs her leg. Mom lets out a deep breath and looks down at Spencer. "Oh, come here." Mom reaches down and picks him up. "We'll be in the van." She turns taking a step toward the van.

The moment Mom takes a step, a faint whistle with a puff of air whips past me, and Eileen collapses to the ground. Everything blurs except my sister lying there in the dirt and leaves. *No. No. No. I just got her back. This cannot be happening.* My throat tightens. My knees lock. My heart takes off out of control. *I will not have a panic attack right now. Lord, help her. Please let her be ok. Don't take her from me again.*

Chapter Thirty-Six

A rustle in the shrubbery over by the van alerts Dad, and he instantly grabs Mom pushing her behind him. There is nowhere to go, and I would not leave Eileen anyway. As I fall to my knees beside Eileen to check her pulse, Dr. Fleming steps out of the bushes.

My entire body fills with rage. I have never felt such a loss of control before. My legs become springs, and I lunge at her from the ground.

"What have you done? How could you? I thought you were helping us?" My body pounds into her knocking her to the ground. With my weight on top of her, I wrap my hands around her neck. She is trying to speak, but it is the voice inside me that I hear. A little whisper demanding me to stop. A force takes over that won't let me tighten my grip on her throat. I lift my shaking hands, and Dr. Fleming takes them in hers.

"Ellie, I am here to help you. It's okay. I only hit her with a tranquilizer dart."

Alice steps forward. "Dr. Fleming, I don't understand...why..."

Dr. Fleming jumps up. "Look I have a lot to tell you guys

but right now we have to attend to Eileen." Dr. Fleming pulls a needle and a scalpel from a bag.

"Why are you doing this to my sister? You are not touching her with that." I reach out for the stuff.

"Please, Ellie. We don't have much time. How do you think they keep finding you? You, Steve, and Alice all cut out your chips, but you guys forgot Eileen's. I am using a device right now to scramble her signal, but I don't know how long it will last, so we have to cut it out of her."

Alice looks confused. "So why did you hit her with a tranquilizer dart. Couldn't you just have told us?"

"I was afraid that as soon as you heard me rustling through the trees, all of you would run. I didn't have time to chase you." Dr. Fleming moves quickly toward Eileen. "Besides, we would have to sedate her anyway to cut the chip out. There is no way that she would just let us do it."

I understand but... "Dr. Fleming, how did you know Eileen is petrified of needles?"

Dr. Fleming half smiles. "Are you kidding? Eileen is the whole reason they had to start sedating the trainees to put the chip in."

"I can picture it now." I shake my head. "I guess erasing her memory wouldn't have erased her innate phobias. Hurry up, Dr. Fleming, we have to save Steve." Just as I finish my sentence, Dr. Fleming stands up putting the scalpel and the chip in a bag. "Oh...well, I guess it goes a little faster when you have the right medical supplies. How long until she wakes up?"

"What I gave her isn't strong at all...by my calculations, about three more minutes."

The wind sweeps through the trees, but with all our nerves on edge, we freeze with fear that the movement of the leaves is something more. It is amazing how long three minutes can seem when you are in hurry. But just as Dr. Fleming predicted, in approximately three minutes, Eileen starts grunting and squirming.

"Wh...what happened? My head hurts." Eileen rubs the back

of her head where Dr. Fleming cut the chip out. "Dr. Fleming, what are you doing here?"

I grab Eileen's hand. "Eileen, Dr. Fleming realized that you still had the microchip locator. That is how President Denali's peeps keep finding us. She sedated you and took it out. Now, we have to get moving down to that warehouse before it is too late." Eileen sits up, and I look at my sister's weak face. I really don't know how her body is even functioning. "Look, Eileen, I think you should stay here with Mom and Spencer. You need to let this sedation wear off, and your body must be really weak. You did just get revived after being cryogenically frozen. The fact that you are even able to move right now is beyond comprehension. You are a walking miracle, you know."

"No way. We go in there together." Her hand still in mine, she rises to her feet. "God brought us back together. He meant for both of us to do this."

As much as I want to argue with her, I know in my heart she is right. "Let's go then."

"Yeah, we have to hurry and save your man...and the world." Eileen smiles.

I squint my eyes at her. "I don't..."

"Oh please. We don't have time for you to deny it. I saw the way you looked at him as soon as I got thawed out."

I open my mouth to spit out my comeback, but a bunch of clapping catches my attention. I glance over, and Spencer has Mom playing pat-a-cake. "Mom...what...?"

Mom shrugs her shoulders. "Don't ask me. He started it, but it is a lot of fun. You guys should do it too."

Dad clears his throat to get our attention. "Girls, down this bank is the only way. I will go first. Stay close together and help each other balance." Dad takes a step. "Wait!" He turns back around. "Girls we need to pray." He closes his eyes and lifts his hands to the sky. "Lord, I don't know if you still hear me after the mess that I have made, but my girls need you. My wife needs you. Lord, guide us. Help us to find Ellie's friend and stop Denali from hurting your children if that is your plan. Give us strength, Lord. And, Lord, thank you. Thank you for bringing my girls back. Amen."

Dad steps down off the edge and one by one we follow. I go last, or at least I think I am going last, but Dr. Fleming steps off after me.

"Dr. Fleming, I am so sorry about earlier." My shoulders stoop under the weight of my conscience. "I am so ashamed."

"Ellie, don't you worry about that. I would have done the same thing. The situation looked bad. I mean your sister was lying on the ground, and I was holding the weapon."

"It doesn't matter. I lost control and attacked you. Please forgive me."

Dr. Fleming pats my shoulder. "Forgiven and forgotten."

As we carefully maneuver down the steep embankment, I notice tears in Dr. Fleming's eyes.

"Dr. Fleming, you don't have to go with us. You have already done so much to help."

"No," her voice trembles, "I have to."

"Ok, but you are obviously scared. Well, we are all scared, but I can see the tears of apprehension in your eyes."

"Ellie, I am not afraid to go in there. I am afraid of not being prepared before I do…just in case."

"What do you mean?" I cast her a confused glance.

"Ellie, I am not saved. I mean it is even worse than that. I knew Denali wanted the world to be without God. I knew Denali's plan and did nothing to stop it." Dr. Fleming sniffles. "I was working for him and helping him. I am no better than Denali."

"Dr. Fleming, do you believe in God?"

"Yes. Just look at everything that has happened. It is no coincidence that so many people lost their memory of everything else but still knew God."

"Do you believe that he sent his only son Jesus to die on the cross for your sins?"

She nods.

"Then you need to pray. Ask for his forgiveness. Tell God

that you are ready to live for him and ask him to come into your heart. Do it now...you never know what the next minute might hold."

"You're right. I need to do this now. I can't go any further without being sure that I have God with me." Another tear rolls down her cheek. "Go on ahead. I will catch up. I promise."

"Are you positive you don't want me to pray with you?"

"Thanks," she says, "but I need to do this on my own. I have a lot to ask forgiveness for."

I embrace her in a hug then let go and keep moving down the bank with the others. When we are almost at the bottom, Dad stops. Sweat is gushing down his face, and his shirt has perspiration rings.

"Let's stop here...huuuuuh...a...huuuh...minute." Dad sputters his words between panting breaths. "We...huuuuh...need...a...huuuuh...plan."

"Dad," I slip past Alice and put my arm around him, "are you okay?"

"Fine, honey...huuuuh."

"I think you should sit for a minute." I point to some rocks forming a ledge on the side of the bank. I hold onto him as we walk over, and he leans back against the ledge.

"Thanks, Ellie. I am okay now. My sedentary lifestyle for the last couple of years has obviously taken its toll on me." Dad cracks a little smile. "You were always the strategizer. Do you have any thoughts on our grand entrance to this place?"

I smile back. "Kind of hard to make a plan when I have no idea even where the door is." I peer through the thick brush toward the warehouse. "I am sure there has to be security cameras too that will announce our presence."

"Of course, there are cameras...Ellie, I don't want to be pessimistic, but I have my doubts about this. We don't even have any weapons."

"No, we don't have guns or grenades or any of the stuff they have." I lift Dad's chin up with my fingers. "We have God! God that parted the Red Sea. God that let David defeat a giant. God that brought Shadrach, Meshach, and Abednego out of a fiery furnace unburned. God that shut the mouths of the lions and kept Daniel safe. God that loves us so much that he let his son die on the cross so that we could live with him forever in Heaven."

"All of this does have to be part of God's plan." Dad laughs.

"I know it is...but why do you say that?"

"Just look at the posse he has put together to go into this battle. This has to be the work of God. He uses the weak to show his strength. And we have an old man, an old woman, a monkey, a girl that has to be sedated for her to get stuck with a needle, a girl with OCD, a doctor lady, and, well, I don't know enough about Alice to analyze her. But, if she is part of this group, maybe that says it all."

"Come on, Dad, we better get this posse moving. God did not put this army together to sit around."

"Right on. Ellie, I am glad you take after your mom and not me. Your mom has always been a brave woman. Look at all she has been through without me there to help her. You are a strong woman just like her. I am so proud of you. I hope you know that." Dad stands up. "So, what's the plan?"

We peek through the leaves of the bushes and let our eyes scan the building. We are at a diagonal from the corner of the warehouse, so we have a clear view of two sides of the building. A giant roll-type door is on one side. The other side is the one facing the big parking lot where the black SUV is parked.

The rumble of an engine startles me. It sounds like it is headed right for us. Just as I turn my head to look for the source of the noise, something huge flies off the top of the bank to our right headed toward the other corner of the building. As this huge shadow sails overhead, a tiny streak shoots off it right into the top of a tree. The giant mass erupts in flames as it crashes at the bottom of the cliff. Dr. Fleming's voice faintly filters from a distance as she is shushing my mother who is whimpering. I don't know whether to watch the explosion or turn to see why my mother has climbed down the bank. I choose to turn for just a second.

"What are you doing down here?"

Mom is shaking. "I couldn't stop him. I was so nervous that I had to go to the bathroom. When I got back to him, it was too late. He wouldn't get out."

"You have got to be kidding me!" Dad's voice bleeds disbelief. "That monkey just drove our minivan off of the cliff!"

Just as I twist back around, Spencer comes swinging through the trees toward us. Now I realize that he was the tiny streak we saw. He must have jumped out.

Alice speaks up, "Guys I think we can use this, but we have to move now."

I look back toward the lot and about ten men including the three that were in the SUV come bolting out of the building toward the flames.

"Spencer gave us a distraction. Let's move through the trees quickly and run in from the side of the building with the giant roll door." Alice slips past us and takes the lead. "I bet that is where the plane is."

We all step as quickly and carefully as we can. Dad is now carrying Spencer. I am not quite sure how or when that happened. Dr. Fleming is in the back helping my mother along. There is no word to describe our group other than "WOW." Easing up as close to Alice as I can get, I ask in an undertone, "What about cameras?"

"Dr. Fleming is using that scrambler device thing of hers. We are hoping it will work long enough to get us inside."

We get to the side of the building with the giant door and out of sight of the group gathered around our burning van. We step out of the protection of the trees taking bold strides of faith toward the big door. Anxiety pounds in my chest, and my body tingles with every beat that pushes blood through my arteries. *What if we are wrong? What if Steve isn't here? What if the plane isn't here? What if we are too late? What if…? What if…? What if…? I can't think like this. I can do all things through Christ who strengthens me. I can do all things through Christ who strengthens me. I can do all things through Christ who strengthens me. I can do all things through Christ who strengthens me. I can do all things through Christ who strengthens me. I can do all things through Christ who strengthens me. I can do all things through Christ who strengthens me. I can do all things through Christ who strengthens me. That's it. Replace the bad OCD thoughts with good ones.*

"Hey, Ellie, what if we actually pull this off and save the world?" Eileen's words pull me from the conversation in my head.

I smile because I know her words are actually God's voice shutting down the devil's whispers. I look at her filled with new strength. "You know what, Eileen? With God, there are no what ifs...He has already won the battle." Even though I speak the words to Eileen, I am really saying them as a reminder to myself not to worry.

We get to the side of the building and crouch beside the big door roll door that is closed. Our eyes all connect with the certainty that we are all thinking the same thing. *Now what?*

The burning van is not going to hold their attention much longer, and even if we could open the giant door, we don't know how many people are behind it. I look up and down the side of the building. *Ok, God. What do you want us to do?*

Chapter Thirty-Seven

Spencer jumps off Dad's shoulders and scampers along the side of the building. Dad gawks at us, shrugs his shoulders, and turns to follow Spencer. I shake my head and motion for everyone to follow. The fate of the world's population is at stake, and we are playing follow the leader with a monkey. Spencer gets to the back corner of the building and barely peeks around. Well, he is a really smart monkey. The coast must be clear because he takes off around the corner. We all stay close together and try to move with stealth.

I slip around the corner and immediately lose my breath. There sits Air Force One. Knowing that we have found the plane is actually a relief, but the appearance of the plane stops me in my tracks. Alice is right. On the side of the plane is President Denali's face. Well, it is not an image of his whole face, just the top half. That upper part of his face covers the entire side of the plane using two of the windows as his eyes. The window eyes look like Denali is stalking me, but the concept is so ridiculous that I have to hold back a laugh. *How could I find any humor in this moment? I think this stress is causing me to crack.*

I trudge on with our little army taking in the area as I go. An air strip extends from the back lot out into a huge field that seems to go on forever.

My gut tells me that we should be rushing over to check out the plane, but Spencer starts climbing a ladder attached to the side of the building extending to the roof. *Great! Mom and Dad can't climb up that, and we can't leave them down here.* How is it that moms can read your mind?

Mom slides past me. "I know what you are thinking, and I have you know that I am fully capable of climbing this ladder. You just need to worry about your dad. He is the one that has been doing nothing but sitting for the last two years." She takes off up the ladder after Spencer moving at such a crazy fast speed that she is actually closing the gap between them.

Alarm is plastered all over Alice's face, and she starts trekking up behind Mom. I can tell she is worried about what is at the top with Spencer and Mom in the front. Eileen moves next, and I motion for Dr. Fleming to go ahead of me.

"Dad, you go next, and I will follow you up."

He smiles at me. "No, ma'am. It's ladies first."

"Please, Dad. We don't have much time, and I can give you a push if you get tired."

He frowns, and then grabs hold of the ladder. After he gets up a few rungs, I begin to climb behind him. The ladder seems a little wobbly, but I try not to think about it. As I look up, Spencer is nearing the top. The ladder pops and creaks, and the higher we get, the more it pops and creaks.

"Ellie," Dad calls down to me, "I hear something."

"I know. This ladder doesn't sound very sturdy."

"Not the ladder. It is kind of a roaring mechanical sound."

"Oh no. This is not good." Another giant roll door is rising on the back of the building.

"Don't panic, Ellie. Just keep climbing," Dad tries to calm my anxiety.

A sudden vibration flows down through the metal ladder

jarring my hands, and then a quick jerk snaps through my body almost making my feet slip off. My eyes widen in shock and fear at the sight. The top of the ladder has broken loose from the side of the building, and Spencer is hanging in the air. Suddenly, the sound of a motor pulls my head down where a huge tanker truck is coming out of the door. *This is bad! This is really bad!*

And we know that in all things God works for the good of those who love him, who have been called according to his purpose. Romans 8:28. Thank you for reminding me, God!

The ladder starts bending in the middle. Everything seems to be playing out in very slow motion. I don't know how my mother isn't screaming because aside from Spencer, Mom is the highest up the ladder. The top of the ladder is tilting toward the plane, and at the same time, the tanker is driving toward the plane. Dad is screaming for Mom to hold on tight. She yells back something about her being stronger than he thinks thanks to his butt imprint on the couch for the last two years. Spencer's little dangling body is headed right for the top of the plane. As the falling ladder descends, the driver of the truck must be dumbstruck when he sees a monkey coming down from the sky because the truck crashes right into the wing of the plane. The hood of the truck crumples, and smoke billows from the engine. Spencer lands on top of the plane, and Mom somehow touches down right on the roof of the tanker. The driver leaps from the truck, and just as he plants his feet on the ground, Mom loses her balance, falls off the truck, and plows down on top of the man. They crash to the ground, and the man reaches for the gun on his belt. The rest of us are suspended in the air about twenty feet from the ground. Alice, Eileen, and Dr. Fleming are moving as fast as they can using the ladder like monkey bars, which seems ironic when I think of how we got on the ladder to start with. Dad sees the gun, and he lets go. Maybe it's the adrenaline rush, but surprisingly, he makes a cat-like landing.

The man is struggling to get his gun with Mom still on top of him. He shoves her hard with his left arm as he pulls the gun from its holster with his right hand. Dad's face is red with rage, and he tackles the man, pinning the arm with the gun to the ground. But Dad's strength can only hold the man for a few seconds.

Alice, Dr. Fleming, and Eileen make it to the top of the tank on the trailer of the truck and are trying to climb to the ground. The man torques his body enough to push Dad off and roll over on top of him. At the sight of Dad at the mercy of the man, I drop to the ground. Mom picks up a piece of metal debris from the damaged wing of the plane and brings it down on the man's head, but she is two seconds too late. The gun goes off, and Dad falls to the side with his arms pulled tight to his chest.

Mom grabs the gun from the unconscious man and runs to Dad. "Tom!" Tears are gushing down her face. "Help me, girls. We have to find a way to get him to the hospital."

Eileen and I collapse down above Dad's head. Dr. Fleming and Alice are in the background mumbling something about tying up the truck driver.

Dad gently takes Mom's hand. "Jillian, it's okay. It is my time. I just want you to know how truly sorry I am for every-thing. I was a coward for not standing up to Denali to start with and a jerk for abandoning you when you needed me most."

"Tom…you just saved my life." Mom wipes her eyes. "See, I need you. You can't leave me now."

"Jillian, you are the strongest woman I have ever met. You will be okay. Besides, you have really been without me for the last two years."

"Tom, I am a nurse. This is not that bad. We just need to get you to the hospital." Mom looks over at me and Eileen.

"Dad, Mom is right. We are taking you to the hospital. You are going to be alright." I rub the top of Dad's head. "Please, Daddy."

Dad rolls his eyes back and forth between me and Eileen. "Girls, please, please forgive me. I don't want to die without your forgiveness. I only wanted you girls to survive. I never meant any harm to come to you. I love you. From the bottom of my heart, I love you, girls."

Eileen's tears are dripping from her eyes. I can't imagine how she must be feeling since she really can't remember Mom and Dad. "Daddy, it's ok. There is nothing to forgive. You did what you had to do to protect us. Don't you remember the story of Joseph? His brothers may have sold him as a slave, but it was part of God's plan. Joseph ended up saving his family from the famine. God used the brothers to put Joseph where he needed him to be. We were in that facility because God wanted us to be there." Eileen clears her throat and wipes Daddy's tears with her hand. "I love you, Daddy!"

Still rubbing his head, my eyes peer down into his. At this moment, I wish my memory had been erased. This is my daddy. He taught me to ride a bike and to drive a car. When I was scared, he would check under my bed for monsters and sit with me until I fell asleep. "Daddy, don't leave me. I understand why you did what you did. You couldn't fight Denali alone. This is Denali's mess, not yours. I still need you. Who will give me away if I ever get married? My kids will need a grandfather." The tears pour, and my heart feels like it is being cut from my chest with a dull knife. "I love you, Daddy!"

Alice is mumbling behind me. I think her and Dr. Fleming are keeping a look out, but what are we going to do anyway if someone else comes? "Dr. Fleming," Alice asks, "can't you help him? Aren't you a doctor?"

I had forgotten about that. I turn around and plead, "Please Dr. Fleming, do something."

"Ellie, I'm sorry. I can't."

"You haven't even tried. How can you say that?" I can't hide the anger in my voice.

"Ellie, you don't understand. I would if I could." Dr. Fleming falls to her knees. "I found my papers before I left the compound. I am not a doctor. I've never even been to college."

I turn back to my dad. "Please, Daddy, let's get you to the hospital."

With half-closed eyelids, Dad rolls his eyes up at me, then Eileen, then Mom. His voice is so weak, it barely comes out a whisper. "You guys need to hurry up. You need to go save the world. Just never forget how much I love you." Dad closes his eyes, and we all know.

Chapter Thirty-Eight

I know we need to go, but I can't. My body is paralyzed with grief, and I can't seem to force my body into moving. At the moment, I can't even remember what we are supposed to be doing. A strange silence surrounds me. Maybe I have just shut completely down, and I am blocking the existence of the rest of the world. Right now, nothing seems real. I refuse to accept that this is real. My daddy cannot be gone.

Someone is shaking me. Why won't they stop shaking me?

"Ellie, please, you have to wake up. Come on."

I must have dreamed all of this. That's it. None of this was real.

"Ellie, you passed out. Come on. Someone's coming. We have to move."

Eileen. That's Eileen. Have to move... "What?"

"Ellie, get up." Eileen is pulling on my arm.

I shake off the cobwebs and sit up. It was real. My dad is there lying on the ground. The tornado of thoughts swirls through my head...Steve...the plane...not much time. Then a voice is saying something.

A man's voice. "Frank, have you got the plane...what...what on earth? What happened... Frank?" The footsteps pound faster like he is running toward us. Then the steps stop with a heavy thump.

Dr. Fleming is motioning about something. As my vision clears, I focus on the man lying on the ground. "What did you do?" I say in shock.

Dr. Fleming holds up a little orange gun. "Tranquilizer. We need to hurry. In case you forgot, it only lasts about five minutes. Alice, are there any more ratchet straps in that truck?"

The truck driver is flipped on his side next to the door of the truck with a ratchet strap wrapped around and around his whole body like the stripes on a candy cane pinning his arms at his sides and binding his legs together. I don't think I have ever seen anyone tied up quite like that before. Alice and Dr. Fleming have taken off one of his shoes and stuffed his sock in his mouth.

Alice pulls another ratchet strap from the truck and rushes over to Dr. Fleming. They start wrapping the strap around the tranquilized man the same way. Spencer jerks the other shoe and sock off the first guy and tosses the sock to Alice. She stuffs it in the second guy's mouth. My gag reflex kicks in, and I try to push the thought of how disgusting that is out of my mind.

Eileen guides Mom over to us. Mom's red and swollen face now holds a blank icy stare. I don't know how she is holding it in. She has been through so much that I guess she has learned to bottle it up. Alice points between the plane and the building as if asking which way that we should go.

I point to the tank on the truck and mouth the words without sound, "That must be the poison." I look back and forth between the plane and the warehouse. "The plane can't go anywhere now so let's check the building first."

Spencer runs back, kisses my dad's head, and scampers to catch up. We creep to the side of the building. The huge door is open where the truck came out. Dr. Fleming has her tranquilizer gun, Alice has a gun that she took off the second guy, and Mom still has the gun that she took from the truck driver. I wish I had a weapon, but at least we aren't empty handed now.

As we edge up beside the door, muffled conversation filters through the opening.

I can barely make out a deep male voice. "Alright, Frank and Atturo should have the plane ready by now. Martin and Liam, you guys get Junior to the plane. Everybody else get your gas masks, and let's go."

Footsteps move in various directions. We flatten ourselves up against the side of the building because there is nowhere else to go. I can't tell how many footfalls are headed our way because my heartbeat is too loud. Suddenly another man's voice starts yelling, "Hold up. We have a problem. That van is empty which means they are here somewhere. New plan. Everybody spread out until we find them. The boss says to dispose of them. Martin, you go check on Frank and Atturo."

Ok. Think. That means only one is headed this way right now. I glance over because I am furthest from the door. *Oh no.* Mom is the one standing by the door. She has the gun, but she… *Has my mom ever touched a gun before?* No time left to think, Martin, walks out of the door. I had not even seen Spencer climb up, but he is perched on top of the door frame. Spencer jumps on Martin's head and covers his eyes. Mom springs forward and whacks Martin right in the side of his head with the handle of the gun. The man collapses to the ground. Spencer high fives Mom and I stand paralyzed and speechless by what just took place.

Dr. Fleming's mouth stands agape, and she looks at Mom and says, "Although very effective, you know that is not how a gun works, right?"

Mom squints her eyes. "Dr. Fleming, every life is precious. God made every one of us. Taking someone's life is a last resort. He wasn't exactly threatening our lives yet, now, was he?"

"Mrs. Hatcher, you are a wise lady!" Dr. Fleming smiles. "Now what?"

"Thank you, Dr. Fleming. It feels nice to be appreciated." Mom points toward Denali's stalking window eyes. "We have no time. Everybody, run and find a way to get on that plane."

I don't get it, but Mom must have a plan. We take off running to the far side of the plane. A set of metal stairs have been pushed up to the door. Alice clanks up the metal steps first, and the door is already twisted open. The rest of us sprint up the steps and follow Alice through the door of the plane. As soon as all of us are inside, Mom seals the door closed. I look around astonished at how big this plane is. It is a Boeing 797Z, so I am not sure exactly what I expected. I have only seen the inside of commercial passenger planes aside from our small single-engine plane that Alice flew. This thing is laid out like a mansion.

"Okay Mom, what is the plan now?" I am in high hopes that she really does have a plan. She is my mom. Moms are supposed to have the answers, right?

"Just sit down and pray!" Mom starts toward the cockpit.

I open my mouth to tell her that Alice knows how to fly a plane, but Alice elbows me.

"Shhh," Alice says barely audible as she leans her head toward my ear. "Your mom needs to stay busy."

"Umm. Mrs. Hatcher, where are you going?" Dr. Fleming seems worried. "You know this plane won't fly."

"Dr. Fleming. I am aware of that, but we also have to save the world and a certain young man that has quite significant meaning to my daughter. She has just lost her father, and I am not going to let her lose the man she loves too." Mom takes another step. "Oh, I am sure we will probably be fired upon pretty soon, but this is Air Force One so I would think it would be built to deflect bullets."

I am taken aback by her words. The realization spurs my deepest fears. I could lose him, and she is right. I do love him. My hands are trembling. My body is tingling. My heart is aching. *Lord, please help. Please keep Steve safe. I am so scared. Please show us what to do. Lead us Lord. Amen. Whenever I am afraid, I will trust in You. Psalm 56:3.* The words echo in my mind. I know God is reminding me that he is here with me. I have to stop panicking and give Him complete control. I close my eyes and breathe in. The plane starts to move. How does she know anything about operating a plane? It doesn't matter. God is in control.

Mom turns the nose of the plane straight toward the door of the warehouse. Two men are standing in the doorway waving and pointing at the wrecked truck, and they appear to be yelling. As soon as they see the plane move, they pull out automatic rifles and unleash what feels like an eternity of blasts. We cover our heads in reflex as the bullets pummel the plane pounding like a hailstorm on a metal roof. More men rush out firing on us, but Mom keeps driving the plane straight at them centering the nose of the plane with the door.

Once they realize the bullets are not penetrating the plane, and mom is not stopping, they scurry in all directions diving out of the way. The nose of the plane plows through the doorway and the side of the building. The wings implant in the walls of the building, and flames erupt shooting up from beneath the aircraft.

Dr. Fleming starts jerking gas masks from the cubbies above the seats and tossing one to each of us. Her voice rising with the chaos, she yells, "Move, people. Time is of the essence."

My eyes lock on the cockpit door waiting for Mom to come out. But she isn't. Why isn't she coming through the door? *This can't be happy...*

Thankfully, before I finish my thought, the cockpit door flies open. Mom has on her gas mask and looks like an elderly Martian. *Thank you, Lord,* I say in my mind as we rush for the door.

Mom keeps chanting Psalm 23:4 in a loud rhythm like a war cry.

> *"Yea, though I walk through the valley of the*
> *shadow of death, I will fear no evil; For you are*
> *with me..."*

We use the broken wing as a slide. The metal is twisted and sloped at an angle toward the ground. One by one we sit down on the bent wing and glide down to the tip. At the tip of the wing, we each take a four-foot plunge to the concrete floor.

The smoke from the plane is so thick that it shrouds us from the men until we all reach the ground. Alice still has a gun, so she leads the way and steps out of the smoke first. Without looking back, she waves with urgency for us to follow.

I move from the cover of the smoke into the openness of the huge warehouse. Rows and rows of military vehicles and tanker trucks are lined up across the warehouse floor. A hallway lies straight ahead. I am guessing it may lead to offices, so I take off in hopes that everyone else will follow. The pitter-patter of Spencer's scamper sounds on the concrete behind me, so I know that at least he is following me. The hallway turns out to be a vending area linking to another huge room of the warehouse. This huge room has six huge clear vats filled with some sort of liquid that I am sure must be more of the poison.

Eileen touches my arm, and I read her lips. "Which way should we go?"

A clanking noise gives us a startle, and our heads turn in unison to check out the sound. A steel door on the left is barely cracked open. Alice extends her arms with both hands gripping her gun and cautiously moves toward the door. Dr. Fleming has her tranquilizer gun in ready position, and Mom follows at the back with her gun.

Alice removes one hand from the gun and reaches to push on the door. Just as her fingers make contact with the metal door, a cough echoes from down the hall. We turn and retreat to the vending area pressing ourselves against the wall between the Coke and Pepsi machines. After a coughing fit, a man appears in front of the candy machine on the opposite wall. With his back to us, he starts digging in his pockets for change. He is an older man, balding with a gray combover hairstyle, and he is carrying a bit too much weight in his mid-section. Thankfully, the man is entirely too focused on finding the right change for his snack to notice us…that is until Spencer lets out a big sneeze.

The man whips his head around, and Mom brazenly catches his attention covering the rest of us.

"Oh. Excuse me. I am so sorry." Mom says with such sincerity. "Hey, maybe you could help me. I was told this place was hiring so I came down to fill out an application, but I can't find anyone in any of these offices. Could you direct me to the human resources department?"

"Ma'am," the man says politely, "you should not be here. This place is not in operation right now. You could get hurt in here wandering around. Let me help you back to the exit."

Mom's hand flies up, and she places it on her heart. "Oh my. How embarrassing. I don't want to burden you. I can show myself out. I really do appreciate you being so kind and helping out a damsel in distress. You are such a gentleman. And a handsome one at that. You have a good day now."

The man's eyes light up after Mom's compliments, and he appears to be blushing. "Well now, Ma'am. You are no trouble at all. It would be my pleasure to at least walk a lovely lady like you to the exit."

I can't stand the thought that Mom is getting out of my sight, but I know she is buying time for us to check out the room. I don't want to waste the sacrifice that she is making. I dart for the door with Alice on my heels. I push the door open as Alice points the gun into the room sweeping from side to side just like on those television cop shows. The room is dark, but the light shining through the open door falls on a figure in the back corner of the room. The figure starts wiggling and grunting.

"Steve." I run to him and thank God that he is alive all at the same time. Steve is propped against the wall with his wrists bound behind his back around a metal pipe running up the wall. His ankles are bound together with bungee cords, and his mouth is covered in a huge piece of duct tape running from ear to ear.

Eileen works to loosen the bungees on his ankles while Dr. Fleming tries to figure out how to get his arms loose from the pipe. Alice is standing guard with her gun, and Spencer seems to be helping her.

Eileen finally gets the knot out of the bungees, and Steve's legs are free. I get the corner of the duct tape and tug, trying to be as gentle as I can. As it peels away from his mouth, I can tell it hurts because his face turns red, and his jaw stiffens. With water-filled eyes, he looks at me. I mean he really looks at me. His eyes burn into mine as if he has no awareness of anyone else in the room.

"Ellie," he says with a hoarse voice, "I was so scared that I was never going to see you again. You are all I have been able to think about."

I gaze back into his eyes and nod. "I know. You haven't left my mind. I was so afraid that I wouldn't be able to find you." It is like time freezes, and we just stare into each other's soul for a minute.

A loud clatter breaks our trance, pulling us back into the tiny room. Dr. Fleming has popped the brackets off that holds the pipe to the wall, and they bounce and clank off the concrete floor. Dr. Fleming stands and starts moving the pipe to the side. She tilts the pipe sideways and lifts it releasing Steve's arms from the pipe. His arms are still secured behind his back, but at least he can move away from the wall.

I reach for his wrists to figure out how to get his arms free when gunshots vibrate through the building. No one will say it, but we are all thinking it. Well, except Steve who has no idea what has taken place or, for that matter, that my mom is even here. Spencer grabs my leg, and when I tilt my head down, his bottom lip is stuck out and quivering. I swallow hard pushing down my worst fears and focus on Steve's wrists that are bound with twine. I know we need to move fast. Dr. Fleming pulls out a pocketknife and cuts him loose.

"Thank you." Steve stretches his arms and then moves them in circles. "Okay, I guess we need to find that plane which I am pretty sure I was intended to be on when it crashes."

My mind flashes back to the man ordering Martin and Liam to get "Junior" to the plane. Now I get it. He was talking about Steve since he is Denali's son.

"No worries. The plane is already incapacitated." Alice puts her hand on the doorknob and keeps her gun ready in the other. "The problem is there are a lot of tanks filled with the toxin, and this place is full of Denali's goons. It won't be long until they have another plane."

A noise hisses on the other side of the door. Alice brings her finger to her lips signaling everyone to be quiet.

"Ellie, Eileen...where are you guys?"

The sound of the faint whisper tosses the heavy anchor from my heart and lifts it to the clouds.

Alice creaks the door open, and there stands my mom holding her gun. She slips through the door, and Alice closes it after her.

"Mom, thank goodness you are alright? What were those gunshots? Did you have to shoot someone?" I throw my arms around her.

Steve's eyes nearly pop out of his head. "Your mother is here too?... I mean, hello, Mrs. Hatcher. I'm Steve. It is so nice to meet you."

Mom throws her arms around him squeezing him tight. "Oh, thank heavens! Steve, praise God you are safe."

I shake my head. "This is not really the best time for introductions. Mom, the gunshots?"

Mom releases Steve and turns back to face me. "Oh, well, you know that gentleman that was showing me to the door...it turns out that we know each other. Sort of. It is really a long story, but his name is Dukakis. See a few years ago, your dad made me go to some frilly highfalutin Christmas party so he could impress his clients. Well while I was trying to find a non-alcoholic beverage at this party, I met this woman named Betty. Well, Betty worked at the White House..."

"Mom, we don't have much time. Who is Dukakis, and who shot who just now?"

"Oh, Dukakis is Dennis Denali's brother. But come to find out, he got wind that Dennis was covering up something really bad in this warehouse so he came here pretending that Dennis sent him to help so he could figure out what was really going on in this place. When he bumped into me at the vending machines, he was worried I would get hurt in here. That's why he was so nice to walk me to the door. We had almost made it to the exit when one of them goons jumped out, but before he got his gun lifted, Dukakis shot him. I realized then that he was a good guy." Mom takes a deep breath, but I don't speak up fast enough. She starts with the rest of the story. "So, Dukakis took my hand and pulled me into this little office. He asked me what I was really doing in this warehouse because he knew I was not here for a job application. I decided at this point, what could it hurt to tell him everything? As I told him the story, we discovered that we knew each other. He apparently used to know your dad pretty well, that is, before your dad took a vow of silence. Anyway, Dukakis was torn up when I told him what happened."

"Uuuum. What happened?" Steve questions as his head twists back and forth waiting for one of us to tell him.

I turn to Steve with my voice barely audible. "Dad came with us. Actually, he is the one that knew to come here." My voice starts to crack. "One of Denali's men... Dad didn't make it."

Steve's arms curl around me pulling me into his body as he speaks to my mom. "Excuse me, Mrs. Hatcher," Steve clears his throat, "but where is this Dukakis guy now?"

"He is out there by the vending machines. He is trying to buy a Reese's Cup, but the machine took his money. He says he has low blood sugar and needs that candy bar pretty bad."

Steve has a concerned expression and urgency reflects in his tone. "Let's get out of here."

Alice turns the knob. "That's weird."

"What's weird?" I ask reading the alarm on her face.

"The door is jammed or locked or something. It won't open." She starts pushing and shaking the door, but it doesn't budge.

Spencer starts tugging on my arm making his little monkey noises and pointing. "What?" *Uh oh.* Smoke is pouring out of the vents in the ceiling and under the door.

Mom's face reddens with anger. "I do believe that Dukakis is a liar. I have been hoodooed. Wait. No. This cannot have anything to do with Dukakis. Why would he shoot that man to protect me if he is bad too?"

Steve looks around. "Well, right now we don't know anything for sure except that we have to find a way out of here and fast. Dr. Fleming, what did you use to get that pipe loose?"

Dr. Fleming pulls out something that resembles a pocketknife. "It's one of those multi-tool things like a Swiss army knife. What are you going to do?"

"I am going to take the hinges loose and see if we can wiggle the door out." He kneels with the tool by the door and focuses on the bottom hinge.

The smoke already has this small room cloudy. Alice starts coughing and squats down to the floor to get a breath. I notice the gas mask pushed up on top of her head.

"The gas masks. I forgot we have them." I pull mine from the top of my head.

Still coughing, Alice pulls hers down.

"Here, Mom put this on." I slip the mask over her face.

Just as Steve pops the first hinge, the door flies open. Dukakis is standing there with a gun in one hand and a Reese's cup in the other. "Jillian, do you know how many doors I had to open to find you, and I have full hands. Hurry up and come on. Those morons have set the building on fire." Dukakis turns takes a bite of his candy and starts down the hall with all of us behind him. "The sprinklers are on so maybe that will help. The fire doesn't seem to have spread to this area. It is just full of smoke."

"Sir, here, take my mask. This smoke is really thick." Eileen rips her mask off and extends it to Dukakis.

"No Eileen, your body is still recovering. Put that back on," Dr. Fleming orders as she tears away her own mask. "He can take mine."

As the realization flows through my mind, a giant neon sign illuminates in my brain. We are the morons that started the fire. Fire would be the reason we have the gas masks to start with.

Dukakis leads with Mom right on his heels. Steve and I stay close behind Eileen and Dr. Fleming with Spencer and Alice bringing up the back. We weave through the part of the warehouse with the huge vats that probably contain more toxins. I am pretty sure that it would not be a good idea for those vats to catch fire. The poison would be released in the smoke. Hopefully, those sprinklers will keep them wet enough not to burn.

When we get close to the exit, the wail of sirens approaching fills me with hope. "Dukakis," I yell, "we have to tell the firemen about the toxin. They need to keep those vats soaked so they don't burn."

"You all are not going anywhere." The barrel of a gun breaks through the smoke followed by a man that I am sure is a descendent of the Anakim. Towering above us at nearly seven feet, the man has a natural aim that is level with the top of our heads.

He shifts the gun, pointing it at each of us. "Hmmm… which one of our little saints should I sacrifice first?" He moves the gun again, this time pressing the barrel against each of our heads.

With locked knees and clenched fists, I stiffen every muscle in my body as if that would deflect a bullet. The cold metal tube pushes into my forehead, and I squeeze my eyelids tight. He doesn't pull the trigger. He lifts it continuing his game rotating down the line. The gun presses against Steve's temple. "Maybe junior here should go first."

The man moves his hand to shift the weapon again, but the view from his soaring position causes him to overlook a small detail. As the gun passes between Steve and Alice, Spencer, who is beneath the smoke walking between them, leaps upward. The angry monkey knocks the man's arm straight up. In a smooth motion, Steve grabs Alice's hand that still holds a gun straight down at her side, lifts her arm, and pulls the trigger. The giant drops his gun as he thrusts his arms down to cover the bullet hole in his stomach. His body doubles over, and he tumbles to the floor.

WE BURST out of the door as the fire trucks are pulling into the lot. Dr. Fleming and I sprint toward the trucks hoping that they will take our warning seriously.

One of the firemen instructs us to get out of the way, but when we keep waving and yelling, he rushes over. "Ladies," he questions, "are there people still in the building?"

"Possibly," Dr. Fleming starts pointing at the portion of the building with the vats, "but you guys can't let that side catch fire. It is full of toxic chemicals. Please there is no time to explain. Just tell your men it is imperative that those chemicals don't burn."

I interject. "There is also a tanker out back filled with the chemical too. You have to send a truck back there to check."

He turns and runs back to the truck at full speed while screaming into his phone.

Dr. Fleming and I trot back over with everyone else. Dukakis is on a call spouting out the details to the authorities while he paces back and forth gesturing with his hand as he talks. Alice and Eileen are sitting on the pavement with their eyes fixed on the building. Mom is holding Spencer, and he appears to be crying. Out of the corner of my eye, I notice that Steve is staring at me. He walks over and puts his sheltering arms around me pulling me close.

With his arms still around me, Steve kisses my forehead. "You know, Ellie, it's weird how you don't realize how you feel about someone until you think you may never get to see them again."

I look up at him. He has the deepest brown eyes that carry me away from the horrors of the day. "I know exactly what you mean."

"I never want to have that fear again." Steve strokes my hair from my face and tucks it behind my ear.

I smile at him. "Me either."

Before another word can escape, he leans down and gently

brushes his lips against mine. As my lips push against his, I have no doubt that this is the man of my dreams.

Dr. Fleming clears her throat. "Ummm, guys, I really hate to interrupt, but I need to tell you something."

Steve and I turn and face her. Her jaws are clenched, and she is wringing her hands together.

"Dr. Fleming," Steve says, "I have been curious how you joined the group. You seemed determined to stay at the complex when we left."

Dr. Fleming lets out a strained giggle. "Well, I was. Then, I stumbled upon my own folder. Once the shock of its contents wore off, I knew that I couldn't sit back behind the scenes hiding out inside of a mountain. I had to take action to help you guys."

Steve looks surprised. "You didn't know about your past?"

"No. I just thought I did. Apparently, my memory was erased just like yours. However, you are a Christian, and you have Jesus living inside of you. When your memory was wiped out, Jesus was still in your heart. When Denali took my memory away, I had nothing. I wasn't a Christian."

Steve tilts his head like he is processing her words. "You say you were not a Christian as if that status has changed."

"Yes, just a few hours ago actually, and I have you to thank for opening my eyes. I found a notebook on your desk in the complex that had a whole bunch of Bible verses written in it. Since there are no Bibles in the compound, I knew you must have remembered all those verses and wrote them down. I was absolutely astonished that with your memory wiped of everything else, even your earthly identity, you could still remember those verses. I knew right then how powerful God is."

"So, you have given your life to God now?" Steve's happiness echoes in his voice.

"Yes. I prayed right over there on that cliff as we headed down to find you. I realize now that Denali can't erase your faith in God because once you invite Him in, He is actually living inside you."

"Oh, Dr. Fleming, I am so happy for you." The most genuine smile spreads over Steve's face.

"Thank you. I understand what that peace that passes understanding feels like now." Dr. Fleming coughs and clears her throat. "So, anyway, I need to tell you what I found in my folder." Dr. Fleming closes her eyes as she continues to speak. "First, I am not a real doctor. I am nothing even close to a real doctor. Not only do I not have a medical degree, but I also do not have a high school diploma." She looks away in embarrassment. "I am a high school dropout. My father apparently had a dream of me becoming a doctor, so once my memory got removed at the training facility, he created my new identity to match the image of the daughter that he always wanted."

Steve and I both stare at her in ultimate confusion.

"Steve, I am your sister. Dennis Denali is my father too. The only difference is his little plan succeeded with me. He made me into the Godless creature he wanted. You, on the other hand, blew his plan out of the water because you forgot Denali but kept your eyes on your Heavenly Father."

Dukakis charges over. "I just got off the phone with the Department of Justice. They are sending agents to the underground complex in Colorado, and some are on their way here now."

"I hope they are able to save all of those people in the cryo lab." I still cannot get the image of aisle after aisle of those frozen bodies suspended in tubes, out of my head.

Dukakis rubs his eyes and then looks at Steve and Dr. Fleming. "So, I haven't had a chance to ask, but I have been wondering how you two got mixed up in all of this. The last account I had, Steve, your dad said he had to send you overseas to some special hospital. Dennis said you got Lyme disease hiking or something. And Teresa, he said you were going to medical school in Switzerland."

"Teresa." I smile at Dr. Fleming. "You know, you look like a Teresa."

Steve sticks out his hand to Dukakis. "Dukakis, it is nice to meet you. I forgot that you recognize us, but the problem is we don't know you at all. Teresa and I were subjects in the complex, and our awesome dad took our memories away from us"

"I cannot believe my brother is capable of all of this. I know he is power hungry but trying to create his own personal army of followers and killing people."

"Yeah," I say, "it is all pretty twisted."

"To top it off, to hurt his own kids like this. Dennis was real upset when you became a Christian, Steve. Well, I guess upset is a little mild. He was livid. Then when Teresa said she was a Christian too, he did seem to go over the edge. But then one day, he just brightened up and never mentioned it again. I thought he had just accepted it, but that must have been when he started hatching this horrid plan."

Teresa's face takes on a blank expression. "Dukakis, did you just say that I was a Christian too?"

"Yeah, well, you claimed to be, but I think you just declared yourself a Christian because you saw how upset it made your dad when Steve accepted Jesus. You were tired of your dad planning your life for you, and I think you were willing to do anything that would get under his skin. You tended to have a bit of a rebellious streak."

"So, why don't you think I was really saved?"

Dukakis explains, "Well, Teresa, when Steve got saved, he was always reading his Bible, helping other people, and pretty much talked about Jesus all of the time. But you never changed. There wasn't any 'fruit' as they say."

Teresa gives a nod. "In that case, it all makes sense."

"What makes sense? Nothing about this mess makes sense," Dukakis mumbles.

"What I mean is that it makes sense why Denali couldn't erase Steve's faith in God, but I had no recollection of God or Christianity at all." Teresa covers her face with her hands. "I am sorry. I just can't refer to that man as Dad. He manipulated me and turned me against God. On top of that, he convinced me that all Christians were bad and ruining the world. He even made me feel that I had earned a top position on his team and gave me a job as a doctor in the facility. I became as evil as him."

Concern covers Dukakis's face. "Teresa, what that man did to you is horrible, and you cannot blame yourself. As far as your personal relationship with God, I hope you get that fixed. All you have to do is ask God to forgive you. Jesus has already paid the price and suffered for all our sins. And surely you see God's work and true power in all of this. I mean just look at this crew that saved the day. For crying out loud, there is a monkey in the group."

"Don't worry, Uncle Dukakis," Teresa says winking, "I already took care of it. God has given me a second chance, and I am not wasting it."

"Uncle Dukakis." Steve looks away a for a second. "Umm...I feel a little awkward having to ask this, but...you know...never mind, I can talk to you about it later."

Dukakis's forehead crinkles. "What is it, Steve?"

"Well, you know I don't remember anything. So, where is my mom?"

Teresa's face grows blank. She doesn't speak. She just stares and listens.

"Oh. You wouldn't remember." Dukakis's lips stretch into a straight line, and the veins in his neck start to twitch. "Well, I guess it was about five years before Dennis became president. You were probably about fourteen or fifteen. Steve, your mom was in a bad car accident. A car came around a curve on the wrong side of the road. She swerved and went through the guard rail. Her SUV rolled down an embankment. It hit a tree and caught fire." Dukakis put his hand on Steve's shoulder. "Son, I am sorry. I can't imagine what you are going through."

"What was her name?" Teresa blurts out.

Dukakis turns and places his arm around Teresa. "Cynthia. Your mom's name was Cynthia."

Teresa's eyes shimmer with moisture and a tear rolls down her cheek.

Steve has his head turned away from the group. When he

turns back around, his eyes are blinking away the tears. He steps over, Dukakis moves aside, and Steve pulls his sister into a hug. "Teresa, we are family. We may not have our parents, but we have each other."

Dukakis chimes in. "You two always have your Uncle Dukakis too."

Out of the corner of my eye, a fireman crossing the parking lot toward where Mom, Eileen, and Alice are standing, catches my attention. Mom is still holding Spencer, but she has her arm around Eileen. Streams of tears, some bitter and some sweet, collide in rivers. Mom has lost her husband and found her daughter. Hopefully, Mom's mind will stay occupied filling Eileen with all the memories she is missing.

Steve nudges my arm, and we go over to see what the fireman has to say. It is the same one that we warned about the vats of poison.

"Excuse me, I just wanted to thank you for the warnings about the toxins. The fire is under control, and apparently, you were right because this place is crawling with officers and government agencies investigating. The Department of Homeland Security has the building completely locked down now." The fireman wipes some of the soot from his forehead. "Anyway, we also found the tanker truck. There were three guys back there. Two were tied up. I don't know if you all had anything to do with that, but the police are escorting the ambulance with those two to the hospital. The third guy has already been taken in the ambulance."

"The one not tied up is our dad. He was killed protecting my mom." I choke up as that statement passes from my mouth. I still can't absorb that he is really gone. "Do you know where the ambulance is taking his body?" Instantly I feel bad for my words because Mom starts sobbing. Eileen embraces her, and they sink down onto the pavement.

The fireman looks at Mom and then moves his eyes back to me. "I am a little confused. The man I am talking about had been shot and had lost a lot of blood, but he was still alive.

However, he was unconscious when we found him. I am pretty sure they were taking him to George Washington University Hospital."

Mom leaps from the ground. "We have to get there fast." She takes a step and then stops. "Spencer drove the van off of the cliff. We don't have a car. How are we going to get to him? He needs me."

Another man in a dark blue suit strides up and flashes a badge. "Excuse me. My name is Arthur Jones. I am with the Department of Homeland Security. I am going to need to get a statement from each of you, but right now we need to evacuate this entire area until we know what type of chemicals we are dealing with. Has anyone taken your contact information yet?"

The fireman interjects. "Sir, these people need to get to the hospital right now. The man that was transported with the gunshot wound was their dad and that lady's husband."

"I see. I am so sorry. You guys get to the hospital, and I will meet you there in a bit. If he wakes up, I am going to need to speak to him as well."

Dukakis springs forward. "Come on. I will get you all to the hospital."

We all sprint after Dukakis.

The fireman yells, "Follow me. I will clear the way with the fire truck."

Dukakis leads us to a full-size silver van with racing stripes down the center of the hood. On the side of the van are the words 'RUN WITH ENDURANCE.' We get in, and of course, Spencer gets shot gun. Dukakis floors it as he looks over at Spencer. "What's up with the monkey getting the front seat?"

"Apparently that is where he likes to ride, and it is not worth arguing with him." Alice blurts from the seat behind Dukakis.

Dukakis whips the van in behind the fire truck that is already exiting the parking lot with its lights flashing and the siren blasting.

Teresa is in the very back seat, but she can't contain her

curiosity. Almost screaming so she can be heard, she asks, "Uncle Dukakis, what is up with the racing stripes on a van?"

"Oh, this is my work vehicle."

"Well, what is it that you do?" Teresa keeps on.

"I am a pastor. I use this van to pick up some of the elderly members of the church that aren't able to drive anymore. The 'RUN WITH ENDURANCE' is a reference to Hebrews 12:1."

"Wow!" Eileen exclaims. "You and your brother are polar opposites."

"Well, in case you didn't catch on, Dennis did not have me on the 'save' list. I was on his 'poison and let die' with everyone else list."

Dukakis squeals his tires as he almost makes the turn into the hospital on two wheels, and then we about fly out of our seats as he screeches to an abrupt halt in front of the emergency room entrance. "I will let you guys out here and go park the van."

Steve jumps out first and helps my mom out. Eileen, Alice, and I follow them through the entrance. Teresa stays in the van with Dukakis since Spencer can't go in the hospital.

Mom approaches the desk in a frenzy. "My husband was brought in here. His name is Tom Hatcher."

The lady at the desk proceeds with no urgency. "Okay. Let me have a look." She speaks as slowly as she types into her computer. I am shocked that the clerk is typing with only her index fingers.

"Ma'am," Mom tries to hold back her frustration and be polite, "could you please hurry?"

"Doing my best." The lady drags out her words. "Yes, he was brought in with a gunshot wound. The doctor is with him now so you all will have to wait in the lobby. I will enter a message that Mr. Hatcher's family is waiting, that way the doctor will know to come and talk to you as soon as he is finished."

I thank the clerk for her help, and Steve leads Mom into the lobby. He points to some open seats. Mom doesn't sit down though. Instead, she crumples to her knees kneeling in front of them.

She closes her eyes tightly and clasps her hands together with her elbows on the seat of the chair. "Lord," she utters, "I have so much to thank you for. You have brought my girls back to me. You have led us through this battle today. And, Lord, you let Tom speak again. I know I have been angry with him over this mess, but I know I probably would not have handled the situation any differently than he has. Lord, forgive me for being so angry and judgmental. I still need him. Lord, please don't take him from me." Mom lifts her hands toward the ceiling. "I praise you no matter what. But if it be your will God, let me have another chance with Tom. I love you, Lord. Amen." Mom stands up and turns collapsing into the hard, plastic chair.

I sit down next to her and pull her head onto my shoulder. Mom's shivering body vibrates beneath my hand. "I love you, Mom. I know that I haven't been there for you, and I am so sorry."

Mom lifts her head, and her soft eyes focus on me. "Ellie, you were dealing with losing a sister. More than that, she wasn't just your sister, she was your best friend. I am the mom. I am supposed to be there to protect and help you girls, not the other way around. So, don't you dare feel bad. You were doing your best to cope. It meant so much to me that you were working so hard to find her."

"I wish I had your strength, Mom. You amaze me at how you have kept it all together with everything you have been through." I sniffle and try to swallow the lump in my throat. "You know, I used to dream of becoming a nurse just like you. As a little girl, I watched in awe at the difference you were making in so many lives. When you would talk about your day at work, love would radiate from your voice, and I could tell that you sincerely cared about each and every one of your patients. You would even pray for them at dinner. You taught me what it truly means to show the love of Jesus. I remember Dad bringing me and Eileen down to the hospital one night to bring you something to eat. Dr. Jim told me what a special mom I had. He bragged about how you never let a patient leave the hospital without making sure they had the chance to know Jesus. Dr. Jim said you had a special gift because the gospel would just naturally pour right out of your mouth, and people would devour it right up."

"Oh, Ellie, I am not as strong as you think. I just ask God to get me through one minute at a time. Thanks for sharing that story. I had no idea you paid that much attention to me when you were little. The sad thing is I have been a nurse that long, and I didn't check your dad's vitals." A long sigh escapes from Mom's lips. "Why would I not have done that? Why would I not check for a heartbeat? Hmm. Some nurse I am. If we had gotten him to the hospital then, you know he would have been fine."

"Mom, don't you beat yourself up. He is your husband, and you thought he had passed. You weren't thinking from a nurse's perspective. We all thought the way his voice faded, and his eyes closed that he had left us. And we did not exactly have a lot of time for an examination. There were people with guns." I grab her hand and squeeze. "After all, if we had left for the hospital then, you wouldn't have driven the plane into the building, and the fire department wouldn't have shown up. That poison could have been floating in the air this very minute."

"I know all of that is true, but I can't get past the fact that I did not check him out better. I have been a nurse for thirty-five years, and if that isn't a good enough reason, I have been married to your father for thirty years. I know that he has zero tolerance for pain. For Pete's sake, he acts like he is dying if he gets the sniffles." Mom's lip starts to quiver and her face scrunches. "I just don't know what I would do without him. He has to make it." She puts her face on my shoulder and bawls.

After a few minutes pass, a gray-haired man with a surgical mask pulled down to his chin and wearing blue scrubs steps out into the waiting room. "Hatcher family," he announces scanning the room.

Mom stands and waves, "We are right here. How is my husband? Please tell me he is going to be alright."

The man points to a private room off the waiting room. "Let's step in here."

We follow him into a tiny office with a small desk and several chairs. My stomach heaves into my throat with fear as I sit down. *Why did he call us into this private room?*

He leans back on the small desk and pulls a pair of spectacles from his coat pocket. He slips them on and then folds his arms across his chest. "I am Dr. Kramer. I am assuming you must be Mrs. Hatcher." He peers down through his glasses at Mom.

"Yes, I am Jillian Hatcher. Is he okay?"

The doctor smiles. "Yes, he is going to be fine."

Mom leaps to her feet and throws her arms around the doctor's neck. "Thank you."

The doctor's body stiffens at mom's sudden burst of affection. He gently removes her arms and keeps talking. "No need to thank me, ma'am. I had nothing to do with this miracle. This is actually the most bizarre case I have ever seen. Mr. Hatcher's condition appeared much worse than it actually was. He was unconscious when he was brought in. He had been shot in the chest, and from the looks of his shirt, had lost a lot of blood. However, the wound turned out to be only superficial. The bleeding was from small vessels located just beneath the skin."

"I am a little confused." I scoot to the edge of my chair. "If he was shot directly in the chest, how was the wound only superficial?"

"Well," his mouth spreads into a toothy smile, "that is the bizarre part. Mr. Hatcher had this little money clip card case in the pocket of his shirt. The metal case deflected the bullet." The doctor holds up this small, dented case. "Obviously, as I stated, I have never seen anything like this, so I did a search on the numbers inside this case. This metal case contains a layer of diamine which is actually made up of two layers of graphene. Diamine is bulletproof. However, what are the chances that a bullet would have hit in the precise location of this little three-

and-a-half-inch by two-and-a-half-inch case? The superficial wounds Mr. Hatcher received are probably from the deflection of the bullet. It must have grazed across the top of his skin."

I don't believe it. My skin tingles as I recognize the little case. "May I see it?" I ask extending my hand.

"Of course." The doctor places it in my fingers. "I am sure you guys will want to hold on to this little gem as a reminder of this miracle."

I gaze in a trance at the little case in my hand and slowly rub my thumb over the indention made by the bullet. I remember like it was yesterday. I was sixteen and had driven Eileen and myself to the mall to do our Christmas shopping. We were walking along laughing hysterically because Eileen had stood in a line full of small children for thirty minutes waiting to talk to Santa. Eileen's laugh switched to a squeal when we walked past this vendor in the center. She ran over pointing to this metal credit card case with a money clip in the glass display. It was painted with a white horse rearing up with clouds filling the background. I knew exactly what she was thinking because Dad would always tell us when we were little to keep an eye out for Jesus. He said Jesus would be coming back through the clouds riding on a white horse. We bought it as a Christmas gift from both of us.

I flip it over in my hand, and there on the back is the engraving, "To the Greatest Dad Ever. Love, Eileen and Ellie." I pry open the dented case and slip out its contents. Gasping, my hand flies to my mouth. Instead of credit cards or money, two wallet size photos lay in my palm. Daddy was carrying baby pictures of Eileen and me in his shirt pocket near his heart. I clasp the case to my chest and erupt in a fit of tears. I can't hold back. I don't want to hold back. I can't believe Dad was still carrying this thing, and that he was using it to hold pictures of us. And God used it to save his life.

Forgetting anyone else is in the room, I get down on my knees and thank God for giving me more time with my daddy. When I open my eyes, everyone else is down there with me, even

Dr. Kramer, because there is no disputing that this was a miracle of God.

We have all been given a second chance. Job 14:7 says, "For there is hope for a tree if it is cut down, that it will sprout again, and that its tender shoots will not cease." Every one of us has been given the opportunity to sprout again, and I promise to give this second chance my all.

Epilogue

One year later...

My dad and I stand on the sidewalk outside the little white church. "Are you ready?" he asks.

"More than ready." I can't stop smiling. "I never thought I could feel this way about anyone."

Dad laughs. "Then you are ready. He is a good man, Ellie. Steve and Teresa have been through a lot with their dad, but they have embraced God as their true father. It still must have been hard for them to testify against Dennis and see him get handed the death penalty. Consequently, it is sort of ironic that Dennis is the one that fought to have the death penalty brought back."

"Steve and Teresa have never gotten their memory back so they can't really remember him as a father." Thoughts of that compound flow through my head. "Thankfully, the government quickly put together a team of experts in cryonics that was able to save most of those people that were frozen, but over a hundred people still lost their lives. It's hard to believe that it has been a year, and those scientists of Denali's that put those people in those tubes are still awaiting trial. Homeland Security hasn't even closed the investigation yet. They are trying to determine exactly who was directly involved. Apparently, Dr. Eckert, Dr. Blakely, Ingrid, and Felipe all claim that they had no knowledge of President Denali's real plan. They say they really thought it was a training facility for the Soldiers Against Crime. I just wish Steve and Teresa could let go of their guilt because they are not responsible for their dad's actions."

"Time will heal them, and they will eventually realize that this is not their burden to carry. On the other hand, I will always have those lives on my conscience. I know I have asked God to forgive me, but I can't get past the 'what if' that eats at me. Those people might not have died. Eileen might remember her childhood."

"Daddy, God will use all of this for good. I don't think you could have gone up against Denali on your own. I am just so thankful that they gave you immunity for testifying against him. I can't imagine you not being here to give me away. Besides, you have to look for the silver lining. If I had not been taken to that facility, I would not have met Steve. Everything worked out according to God's plan."

"Ellie, when did you become so smart?" Dad lifts one side of his mouth into a lopsided grin.

"I think I get it from Mom." I snicker gently punching his shoulder. "Just kidding. But you know what else? That facility really helped my OCD. I had to face a lot of fears that I had avoided. I can go into public restrooms now. Shaking hands is still a work in progress, but it grosses me out much less than it used to."

The distant sound of the piano from inside the church pulls us from our conversation.

"I guess we better get going. Your future husband awaits." Dad leans in and kisses my forehead. "Now let's go."

I pinch the sides of my dress lifting it as I climb up the steps. My heart flutters as Dad pulls the door open.

As I place my hand around Dad's arm, he lifts my chin with

his other hand. "Ellie, you are the most beautiful bride that I have ever seen. I love you, baby girl."

We step inside, and every pew in the little church is packed. Daddy walks me down the aisle to the beat of the wedding march. When we move past the front row, Alice grabs my hand and gives it a squeeze. I smile at her, and then notice her other hand is clutching Gerald's. They really make a great couple. Gerald Jameson is Bob's real name, and it just so happens that he now owns his own gourmet restaurant. He had just graduated from culinary school when he received his letter from President Denali.

Steve stands at the altar of the church dressed in a white tuxedo with a black bow tie. When Dad and I reach the altar, Dukakis starts to speak.

"Who gives this woman to be wed?"

Dad answers, "Her mother and I." Dad hugs me with tears in the corners of his eyes and gently moves my hand to Steve's arm.

Steve and I say our vows. Once Steve gets him to stop bouncing up and down, his best man, Spencer, hands over my ring. Eileen, my maid of honor, gives me Steve's ring. We place them on each other's hands, and Dukakis officially pronounces us husband and wife.

After Steve kisses his bride, we turn and face our guests as Mr. and Mrs. Denali. *How bizarre.* Our names are the same as the man that almost took our lives from us. My fingers caress Steve's hand as he clutches mine, and I am taken back to our first meeting when I opened my eyes and saw him staring down at me. And then I remember the day those men dragged Steve away, and my heart ripped open at the thought that I may never see him again. But the harder the mountain is to climb, the better the view. And this is absolutely the happiest day of my life.

Steve and I walk down the steps outside the church using our hands to shield our faces as our family and friends pound us with birdseed. Parked by the curb is the little Volkswagen "Bug" decked out in shaving cream, toilet paper, and tin cans. I am pretty sure Alice and Teresa had something to do with that. Steve opens the passenger door for me to get in, and Spencer jumps in taking his usual position.

Laughing, I pick him up. "Oh, no you don't. Not this time little guy!"

"Steve." A lady calls out from behind us.

Steve and I both turn toward the sound of the voice.

Steve stares at her with a blank face, but I know immediately who she is.

"Wow. I know who you are. I saw you in the tube."

Steve's face lights up as he remembers. "Yes. You were the woman in the first lab with the animals, the one where we found Spencer."

Dukakis steps out of the crowd, holding a Snickers bar with Teresa by his side. Dukakis's face turns ashen as his head fixes on the woman. His eyes bulge out from his head, and his candy bar thumps as it hits the pavement. "Talk about running into a ghost. Cynthia, is that you?"

A look at: Letters to Bentrock

J.B. Cyprus

A brilliant and satirical look at today's spiritual warfare—told through letters written by a Senior Tempter to a new, Junior Tempter under his tutelage.

The Evil One has updated and modernized his lies and temptations, but his objective is the same: steer one more soul onto the broad road that leads to his home Below.

Follow along as Senior Demon Deumus teaches fledgling tempter Bentrock how to steer his prey, a Texas prison inmate, toward the wide gate that leads to destruction. One would think that securing the damnation of this "bunch of criminals, thugs, and addicts" would be an easy task, but, as Deumus notes, it is not. "If they start to consider themselves - now naked and in a cage - the terrible, awful, incontrovertible truth occurs to even the hardest heart: I was made for more than this."

Readers will find themselves immersed in this realistic look at how tempters cynically leverage the modern culture and our human weaknesses to pursue their prey, both in prison and in the "free world". Fortunately for our inmate, he is not alone in this fight. None of us are.

In the tradition of C.S. Lewis' classic work The Screwtape Letters, Lucifer's tempters pursue a new generation of "Prey" inside a Texas Prison.

AVAILABLE NOW

Acknowledgments

I would like to thank my husband and children for believing in me when I didn't believe in myself. I am so blessed to have such a wonderful family.

Thanks to all my family and friends for supporting me in my writing.

Thank you to my mother, Carolyn Bryant, and my niece, Tawny Jenkins, for sacrificing their time to proofread. Thank you, to my dear friend, Denise French, who texts me words of encouragement daily.

And most of all, I thank God because I could do nothing without Him.

About the Author

F. D. Adkins is a Christian fiction author and freelance writer. Her hope is to pass along the comfort that comes from having a personal relationship with Jesus while offering her readers a brief escape from life's struggles through an action-packed story full of suspense, twists, turns, love, and a few laughs. In other words, her passion is sharing her faith through fiction.

She has been married to the man of her dreams and her best friend for 23 years. She loves spending time with her family, reading, writing, and always enjoys a good cup of coffee. She also has a soft spot in her heart for all animals especially dogs.

She lives in South Carolina with her husband, Steve, their two teenage children, Landon and Layna, and their dog, Lucy. She posts stories of faith and devotions weekly on her blog.